Academy Mystery Novellas

Volume 5
Women Write Murder

Academy Mystery Novellas

Volume 5

Women Write Murder

Edited by
Martin H. Greenberg & Edward D. Hoch

ACADEMY

CHICAGO

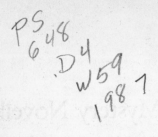

PS
648
.D4
W59
1987

Published in 1987 by

Academy Chicago Publishers
425 N. Michigan Avenue
Chicago, Illinois 60611

Library of Congress Cataloging-in-Publication Data

Women write murder.

  (Academy mystery novellas; v. 5)
  1. Detective and mystery stories, American. 2. American fiction—Women authors. 3. Detective and mystery
stories, English. 4. English fiction—Women authors.
I. Greenberg, Martin Harry. II. Hoch, Edward D.,
1930–   . III. Series.
PS648.D4W64 1987   813'.0872'089287   87-19448
ISBN 0-89733-267-9 (pbk.)

Academy Mystery Novellas are collections of long stories chosen on the basis of two criteria—(1) their excellence as mystery/suspense fiction and (2) their relative obscurity. This second criteria is due solely to the special limitations of the short novel/novella length—too short to be published alone as a novel but too long to be easily anthologized or collected, since they tend to take up too much space in a typical volume.

The series features long fiction by some of the best-known names in the crime fiction field, including such masters as Cornell Woolrich, Ed McBain, Georges Simenon, Donald E. Westlake, and many others. Each volume is organized around a type of crime story (locked-room, police procedural) or theme (type of detective, humor).

We are proud to bring these excellent works of fiction to your attention, and hope that you will enjoy reading them as much as we enjoyed the process of selecting them for you.

Martin H. Greenberg
Edward D. Hoch

Contents

Life is a Brutal Affair
  Helen McCloy 1

Thornapple
  Ruth Rendell 65

The Frightened Millionaire
  Craig Rice 107

Murder Goes to Market
  Mignon G. Eberhart 163

LIFE IS A BRUTAL AFFAIR
by Helen McCloy

Helen McCloy was born in New York City in 1904, and now resides in Boston. Her twenty-eight mystery novels began with Dance of Death *(1938), the first adventure of psychiatrist detective Dr. Basil Willing, who appears in nearly half her books and many of her short stories. Married for a time to mystery writer Brett Halliday, she is active in the Mystery Writers of America and served as its first woman president in 1950.*

There is no series detective present in "Life Is a Brutal Affair." It could best be described as a tale of romantic suspense, but that term does little to convey the mounting tension as Frank Bly returns fifteen years later to the town where someone had tried to kill him—and thought they'd succeeded. It is one of Helen McCloy's very best works.

"Life Is a Brutal Affair" was first published in the September 1949 issue of the American Magazine *under the title "Better Off Dead." It appeared under its present title in* Classic Stories of Crime and Detection *(1976), edited by Jacques Barzun & Wendell Hertig Taylor.*

His name could not betray him. They had known him as Frank Bly. He was Stephen Longworth now. Would anyone in Yarborough remember his face? After fifteen years?

He turned to look into the beveled pier glass that came with this apartment at the Waldorf. His hair was flecked with steel-gray now, at thirty-two. At seventeen, when he was last in Yarborough, his hair had been brown, his face plump, his skin tanned by that long summer on the water. His mouth then was a boy's, loose-lipped, plastic as clay. This was another face, lean and pale, with a man's hard mouth. The eyes were still a lively hazel, set wide under slanting brows. Yet they had changed most of all. They had lost a boy's trust in others and doubt in self.

It was years since Bly had thought of going back to Yarborough. By the time he had enough money he was no longer interested. Or thought he wasn't, until he saw her picture in the paper this morning.

An old picture from the files? Or was Tessie really the same after all these years? No photograph ever did her justice. There was nothing pretty about the shape of her features or the shadows they cast, and that was all a camera could catch. Her enchantment lay in life itself which is motion—her swift step, her light breathing, the grace of her hands, the movement of intelligence in her eyes, the various inflections of her voice—and what else? Coloring? Say, rather a sort of bloom or sheen that lay upon her. Instinctively she avoided all soiling of body and spirit. Or so he had thought until that night when he wondered if she could be the one who tried to kill him.

Again Bly looked at the newspaper picture. A smudge of printer's ink on pulpy newspaper. Tessie, who should have been painted on ivory with a brush of gauze. He reread the caption: *Mrs Llewellyn Vanbrugh of Yarborough*. But Tessie's married name had been Mrs Geoffrey Vanbrugh. Llewellyn was her own maiden name. With a thrill of shock he realized what the change meant. She was divorced.

What a fine, wavering hairline held the boundary between love and hate! Did he hate her now, as he hated the others? Was he going back simply to punish all four of them? Or to discover the truth about Tessie? How had she explained to the world Frank Bly's sudden absence that next morning? Was he just another unsolved case of disappearance? An open file, gathering dust in the Missing Persons Bureau of Yarborough Police Department?

He wouldn't stop at a hotel. He would do in Yarborough as he did in London or Rome, Marrakech or Peking—rent a comfortably furnished house and enter into the life of the place at his leisure.

He glanced at his watch. Dillon, clerk in the law firm that handled his affairs, should be at his desk by now. Bly put through a call:

"Dillon? . . . Longworth speaking. I want you to get hold of a real-estate agent in Yarborough, Pennsylvania, and find me a furnished house for the winter. . . . Nothing big; just ten or fifteen rooms and an acre or so, on the east bank of the river outside the town. . . . No, I've never been there—I've just heard about it."

He frowned as he put down the telephone. Almost a slip, that. Frank Bly must remember that Stephen Longworth had never been in Yarborough.

There wouldn't be any of the usual pitfalls involved in the use of a false name. The initials "S.L." were on all his belongings and it was habit to answer when anyone said "Steve" or "Mr Longworth." He even signed contracts as Stephen Longworth. All New York knew him under that name, including police and reporters. Outside Yarborough there was no one alive today who had known him as Frank Bly except a few oil prospectors in faraway Persia and his former chief in the OSS.

It was not his incognito alone that gave him confidence. In the last fifteen years he had learned to take care of himself. He smiled a little, remembering the starving Arab who tried to stab him in Mosul, the frightened little crook who tried to hold him up in Chicago, the Malay sailor who ran amuck in Bangkok.

He crossed the living-room to one of Marie Laurencin's wan, delicate portraits and swung the picture back on hinges, revealing a wall safe. Inside, in a shallow drawer, lay two guns—the revolver he had carried prospecting in Persia, the automatic he had used overseas during the war. A revolver is accurate and therefore merciful, but it is too big to be concealed. An automatic is inaccurate and therefore merciless, but it can be concealed in the hip pocket of an ordinary suit or even in the palm of the hand. To a crook this advantage outweighs the risk involved—an automatic may jam.

Bly was neither cop nor crook. Merely a potential murder victim. He could use either, in self-defense.

It was characteristic of the man that he chose the automatic. He had taken risks all his life. And he was not merciful to enemies.

After Bly's train left Philadelphia he looked up from his book. He wouldn't have been surprised to see some Yarborough faces. They were always running up to New York for a day or so of shopping. Covertly he studied the younger women. Had Tessie's daughter, little Nan, grown up to be like this or that? How old had she been that summer—five or six? She would be at least twenty now.

The woman in the seat beside him was middle-aged, short and stout with plump, small-boned hands squeezed into tight gloves. Aside from that she was dressed with elegance, all in black except for the brown of her mink scarf and the dark green of her *coq* feather turban. Though the smooth cheeks had a stuffed look, the black eyes sparkled with vitality.

Her eye caught his and she spoke pleasantly. "I beg your pardon, but is the next stop Yarborough?"

"Yes, it's the only stop between Philadelphia and Wilmington."

"Thank you. I should know because I live there. But

I so rarely go to New York by train that I've forgotten. You know Yarborough?"

"Only by hearsay." He smiled. "A typical small town."

"A small city," she corrected him gently. "There's a difference."

He laughed. "What difference? There may be more money in Yarborough than in a small town, but I've been told it's just as provincial."

"Who told you?"

Some perverse imp tempted him. Why not launch his campaign here and now with a piece of calculated audacity? It was quite possible the gist of this conversation might be repeated to Tessie or to one of her friends. Yarborough was a place where gossip traveled faster than sound.

Bly answered, "A fellow I met in Cairo during the war. Some years before that he had worked in Yarborough as a boatman for some people named Vanbush or Vanbrugh. His name was Frank Bly."

She must have blanched, for suddenly her lipstick looked artificial, a smear of red grease caking slack lips. Her eyes were shocked, incredulous. She spoke in a whisper: "But that's impossible!"

"What do you mean?" He was as bewildered as she.

"You can't have met Frank Bly during the war. Not the Frank Bly who used to be the Vanbrughs' boatman."

"Why not?"

She swallowed and her full throat quivered. "Because—fifteen years ago Frank Bly was—murdered."

Later that afternoon, after Bly had been driven out to the modern house which was to be his temporary home in Yarborough, he kept returning to that remark. He scarcely listened as the real-estate agent, Mrs Quinn, pointed out the splendid view of the river. He was wondering if he should have questioned that woman on the train. At the moment it had seemed prudent strategy to murmur, "Oh, really? Then I must have mistaken the name. It couldn't have been Frank Bly I knew in Cairo."

But even now he could not quite repress a shiver. It had been too much like reading your own obituary in the morning paper. Or dreaming that you are in a grave-yard, stumbling over a tombstone marked with your own name.

Should he go to the police or the *Yarborough Chron-icle* to get details of "the Bly Case," as it was probably called? No, there would be photographs. Police and newspapermen are trained to recognize faces from pho-tographs. Aside from them, his incognito was safer than he had expected. The layman, who sincerely believed Frank Bly was dead, would be almost incapable psycho-logically of recognizing him in a living man, Stephen Longworth.

"— and the cedar closet is upstairs at the end of the hall, and—"

Smiling, Bly interrupted Mrs Quinn: "Wasn't there a murder in this neighborhood years ago?"

"Not in this house!" Her face looked like a bulldog's if a bulldog were ever heavily rouged and powdered.

"But there was a murder near here?"

"I suppose you mean that boatman of the Van-brughs'. The house is a good half-mile down the road."

Bly forced the casual note into his voice. "Who was the murderer?"

"He was never caught."

"No question of accident? Or suicide?"

"N-No." Mrs Quinn hesitated. "There were blows he couldn't have inflicted himself. And the police said nothing in the river could have made wounds that shape.

His body was in the water five weeks before it was found."

Bly felt that shiver of horror again. It might so easily have been his own body. "Who identified the dead man?"

"The Vanbrughs, I suppose. They were the only people around here who really knew the man. I never saw him. I do hope this old story doesn't worry you, Mr Longworth. After all, it happened years ago. Probably when you were a child. That gray hair doesn't deceive me!"

She prattled on until he managed to get rid of her.

Alone, he lingered on the terrace as twilight silvered sky and water. How often he had gone to sleep in his bunk at the Vanbrughs' boathouse with this same sound in his ears—the ceaseless splash and ripple of the river's swift current. Whose murdered body had been dragged out of that current fifteen years ago? And why was it identified as Frank Bly?

He had been such an ordinary boy, his father the postmaster in a small Pennsylvania town, his mother the daughter of a bank cashier in the same town. There he had lived all his life until both parents died. After that first winter alone, working days and taking courses at night, he had drifted south to Yarborough, hoping for a summer job in the peach orchards, and finding a better job as boatman. Not the sort of boy who gets himself murdered. Yet someone had tried to kill him, and later another victim had been buried under his name.

The first meeting after his return to Yarborough came sooner than he had hoped. It was at a Field Club dance for the Community Chest. Bly stood in the archway to the ballroom watching the dancers, particularly a tall girl in flaring white taffeta. Mrs Quinn sidled up to Bly. "Charming, isn't she? Her name is Nancy Vanbrugh."

Little Nan. He had forgotten that her eyes were tawny, the color of brown sherry by firelight. He had forgotten that her hair was a more golden brown. He did remember the thick, golden lashes and the heavy eyelids that gave her such a sleepy look.

They were dancing when she said, "I hear you've been in Persia, Mr Longworth?"

How impersonal! What would she do if he said, "Nan, don't you remember? I'm Frank, the boy at the boathouse. You once said you were going to marry me when you grew up."

Instead he answered, "I was there for three years."

"I'd like to hear more about it."

"You shall."

A boy her own age cut in. She smiled at Bly over her shoulder as she drifted away.

He got his hat and gloves and drove home, deeply disturbed. He hadn't thought much about Nan in the last few years. He had no reason to suspect her as he suspected the others. No child of five could have struck those blows. What would happen to Nan when he did discover the one who had struck him, unseen, in the darkness? Vanbrugh was her father; Tessie, her mother.

Two days later, walking through the woods, he was caught in a cloudburst. He had turned back toward the house, when he met Nan, riding a big-boned roan. Leather and tweed and whipcord protected her body, but her fair hair was dark with rain, plastered to her head.

"It's only a step to my house, Miss Vanbrugh. My housekeeper will give you hot tea and rum."

"I'd love that." She smiled. "Most people call me Nan."

They sat on a bearskin rug in front of a roaring fire while the housekeeper brought hot buttered biscuits and strawberry jam with the tea and rum. Outside, rain lashed against the window.

Nan laughed. "Wonderful! It never rained enough in Arizona to make you appreciate the sunshine. It was like a painted face that never changes color."

"You were there a long time?"

"Ten years. Boarding school. Eight to eighteen. Then college. I haven't been home much. Just holidays."

"If you'd been my daughter I wouldn't have sent you away."

"There were reasons. My parents were divorced. And now I want to hear all about Cairo."

"Cairo?" He hadn't mentioned Cairo to anyone except the woman on the train.

"Someone said you'd been there, too."

"Who?"

"I'm afraid I don't recall." Her eyes slid away from his toward the fire.

He looked at her somberly. She was the one weak place in the Vanbrugh armor. From her he might wring all sorts of artless admissions. Only, he didn't want to. Suddenly he realized she was the weak place in his armor, too. He wouldn't mind hurting the others. But he couldn't hurt them now without hurting Nan.

That night after dinner he lingered on the terrace while the moon rose, turning the riverbank into a badly developed photograph of itself.

There had been no moon that other night fifteen years ago. For a long time he had had nightmares about that horror. Now, deliberately, he forced himself to relive it in the waking state.

There had been no intimation of evil, then, before darkness fell. Bly had only to close his eyes now and he could still see Tessie Vanbrugh as she had looked that afternoon on the sunlit terrace when the packing-case arrived. Her hair was a light brown, straight and long, parted in the middle, coiled on her neck. It had the texture and glitter of the finest silk. Excitement had brought a faint pink into her cheeks, delicate as an apple blossom, but the skin at temple and throat was white, laced with violet veins. She had linked arms with her guest, Denise de Beaupré, a small, quiet girl from France, dark and sweet as a black cherry.

"Be careful, Frank!" Tessie's voice sang like a taut wire when his ax struck at the heavy timber. "There's an inlaid cabinet inside. It's more than valuable. Unique."

When he wrenched the last plank away he saw pads and rolls of old newspaper stuffed with excelsior lashed to the cabinet with twine, to cushion it against the inside of the case when it was moved. His penknife hacked at the twine. He heard Denise catch her breath. It was almost a cry of pain. "Oh—"

"I'll be careful, Miss de Beaupré," he tried to reassure her. But when the last of the padding had fallen away he couldn't help wondering what all the fuss was about.

It was just an oblong chest, standing on four sturdy carved legs held together with a stretcher. The drop-leaf front was a solid slab of dark wood inlaid with paler wood in a pattern of flowers. To Frank they were dull as dead flowers, dried and pressed between the leaves of a book, and they had the same look of flat, faded fragility.

It was then that Geoffrey Vanbrugh came out on the terrace with his neighbor, Dick Strawn. Vanbrugh was the larger man with the deeper voice, almost a handsome man, with his warm, brown eyes and the small beard that he wore because he was an artist and liked to be different from other men. His eyes glowed as he saw the cabinet.

"Denise, are you sure you want to sell? After all, it was your father's and it's perfect."

Denise smiled. "You forget I'm a French teacher with nothing but my salary. I'd much rather have the money."

"Then that's settled." Vanbrugh took Tessie's hand. "Your birthday present, dear."

The apple blossom turned to rose. "Oh, Geoff! I had no idea you were going to buy it!"

Vanbrugh turned to Bly. "Let's move it into the living-room, Frank. It's pretty heavy and we must be careful."

"A music cabinet!" Tessie was ecstatic. "For all that sheet music we've been keeping on top of the piano."

"I'll get it." Denise hurried to the piano at the far end of the long room.

Tessie knelt before the cabinet, pulled down the drop leaf. "What's this?" She was looking at a flat parcel of newspaper.

Vanbrugh unwrapped it. "The key. Hand-wrought iron. The packers must have wrapped it in paper to keep it from scratching the wood."

"I don't want a huge key like that sticking out and catching my dress every time I pass the cabinet!" said Tessie. "I shall leave it just where it is, in the paper, so it won't scratch anything." She pushed the parcel to the back of the shelf, and began piling record albums in front of it.

Bly went back to the terrace. Strawn was sitting on the coping. Bly began to pile the loose boards and old newspapers inside the shell of the packing-case. "Is that cabinet really valuable, Mr Strawn?"

"Yes, Frank."

"You're sure?"

"It's my business to be sure. You know I'm an art dealer."

"I didn't know. Say, these old newspapers are French."

"You'd expect French packers to use French newspapers for packing, wouldn't you?"

"But these are dated ten years ago!"

"Naturally. The cabinet has been in storage in Paris ever since Miss de Beaupré's father died in 1926."

"Will it be all right if I take the packing-case down to the boathouse? I promised little Nan I'd make her a doll's house, and this is just the thing for it."

"I'm sure nobody wants the case."

"All right if I take the papers, too? I studied French last winter at night school."

"Of course."

Vanbrugh came out on the terrace. "Better tune up the cabin cruiser, Frank. We're going on the river."

As Bly turned away he heard Vanbrugh say, "What are you waiting out here for, Dick? Your commission?"

Strawn laughed. "Partly. I don't like to talk money in front of women. Did I tell you Denise wanted half in cash? So she can start a checking account and draw on it immediately without waiting for a check to clear."

"Yes."

It was nearly dark when they brought the cruiser back to the boathouse, where Bly had spent the rest of the afternoon working on Nan's dollhouse. Strawn and Vanbrugh came out of the men's locker-room looking worried. Vanbrugh spoke to Bly: "Please come up to my study as soon as the boat is shipshape."

In the study Vanbrugh did most of the talking. He was quiet and pleasant about the whole thing. So was Strawn. It was Bly who became shaken and shrill.

"Mr Strawn tells me he left five thousand dollars in cash in the men's locker-room this afternoon, Frank. Fifty new one-hundred-dollar bills, fresh from the bank. He couldn't take it with him on the river because he was wearing his bathing-suit. Just now, when he went into the locker-room, the money was gone."

"But, Mr Vanbrugh, I don't know anything about it! I didn't know there was money in that room. I haven't been there since yesterday."

Vanbrugh's friendly brown eyes were more troubled than angry. "I'd much rather you told me the truth, Frank. You know I wouldn't prosecute."

"Neither would I," put in Strawn. "I just want the money back. I'm not a rich man and five thousand— well, it's five thousand!"

"Maybe a tramp—" faltered Bly.

"How could a tramp get into the boathouse this afternoon without you hearing him? You were there all the time."

"I took the money out of my wallet and wrapped it in paper so nobody would suspect what it was," added Strawn. "Colored paper from an old candy box, lilac and silver."

Vanbrugh went on more vehemently: "You know, Frank, you were practically a tramp yourself when you wandered into Yarborough."

Strawn intervened. "Don't be hard on the boy, Geoff. I was a fool to leave such a sum in an unlocked place. I was just throwing temptation in his way."

"All right." Vanbrugh dropped his voice. "See here, Frank; if you'll give back the money and clear out tonight I won't say anything about it to anyone. Neither will Mr Strawn. But if you don't do that I shall have to call the police."

"But how can I if I haven't got the money?"

There was a heavy silence. Strawn stood leaning against a bookcase, studying lines in the palm of his hand. Vanbrugh sat behind his desk, gaze level, accusing, sure of Bly's guilt, waiting for him to break down.

He broke, but not the way Vanbrugh expected. "What am I going to do?" he sobbed. "I didn't take the money! I didn't know anything about it!" He crouched over a chair, shoulders heaving.

Strawn laid a hand on the back of Vanbrugh's chair and leaned down, speaking so softly Bly couldn't hear what he said. Vanbrugh rose and left Strawn, put a kindly hand on Bly's shoulder. "Sorry, Frank. Afraid I lost my temper. Take a night to sleep on this, and if the money's back in the locker-room tomorrow morning we won't say anything more about it." The firm hand gave Bly's shoulder a little apologetic shake.

"Thanks." Bly struggled to his feet and made for the French window, almost running. "See you in the morning." He stumbled out the window and hurried down the path through the woods to the boathouse. They had both been damned decent, he thought. Most would have called the police the moment they discovered the money gone, without warning the man they suspected. But they were all such decent people—the Vanbrughs and Strawn and Denise de Beaupré—the very nicest people Bly had ever known.

He did not look back when he heard footsteps behind him. He knew it was one of the four, for no one else used that path. There wasn't another house within miles of the Vanbrughs' home and Strawn's bungalow in those days. The Vanbrughs kept only one servant, an old cook. Bly would have recognized her step by the creak of her shoes. Strawn had no servant. And it wouldn't be Nan. She was always in bed by six.

Bly didn't look back because he wanted to be alone to think things out for himself. If he could get to his bunk in the boathouse and snap off the lights, not one of the four would disturb his apparent sleep. They were considerate in all the obvious ways. If they failed in the less obvious ways that was just because they could not think of him as one of themselves.

Perhaps he wouldn't have cared if he had not fallen under the spell of Tessie Vanbrugh's beauty. It was pain to wonder if, under all her careful kindness, she thought him a stupid, loutish boy who would never be anything but a boatman. Couldn't she see that this summer was an economic accident? Something that had nothing to do with the real Frank Bly?

He stopped at the edge of the pier. He no longer heard footsteps behind him. No one was following him. It must have been the echo of his own footsteps. He could stand here and smoke a cigarette before he turned into the boathouse.

Two miles across the water he could see the lights shimmering along the opposite shore. The current was running fiercely, slapping the piles of the pier. The wind was brisk. He cupped the match flame in his hands and bent his head to it.

That saved his life. The first, smashing blow glanced off his head instead of crushing his skull. The jar threw him off balance. With man's ancient, arboreal instinct both hands went out, clawing wildly for the branch that wasn't there. His feet slipped. There was a great splash, and then the shock of cold water. He came up to the surface with a shuddering gasp. He couldn't see. Something sticky gummed his eyelids, trickled down to his lips. From its taste and consistency he knew it was blood.

Arms threshing wildly, his one hand caught a pile of the pier, and clung. He got the other hand on the same pile, braced his knees against it, and inched his way up. At last his hand could grope for the edge of the pier above. He found it and gripped, panting. Another blow crashed, and he heard the bones of his fingers snap. Dazed, he thought, *This is murder.*

He couldn't see above the edge of the pier. He couldn't hang on. One hand was crippled; the other, slipping. A second, fainter splash, and the cold water revived him a little.

He was a good swimmer. He gave himself to the river, hardly making a sound that could be heard above the rushing water, just paddling enough to keep himself moving, head below the surface. The current was taking him. He had a chance of reaching the opposite shore a mile farther downstream. A fighting chance. If he kept his nerve—

He waited a long time before he let the water break over his face and looked back at the shore he had left. He could see the Vanbrugh house on top of the hill, lights shining from every window. Hill and trees, boathouse and pier were all one mass of darkness against the faintly luminous sky.

He could not see a human figure. He could not see anything moving. But sound carries far across water, and it was silent out there in midstream, where the river met no obstacles. Now he heard a faraway sound—footsteps ringing hollow on the planks of the pier, dwindling as they receded up the path through the woods toward the house.

It was one of them. One of those four decent, considerate people whom he had trusted, the nicest people he had ever known. Their charm, their sensitive gentleness was on the surface—illusion. The secret reality was ugly, desperate, violent. In some way he didn't understand he had drawn that violence upon himself. Somehow, his very existence must threaten one of them without his knowing it. But which one? And how?

It would be his word against theirs. He had no evidence. He hadn't seen who had struck those two blows. Even if he had, who would believe him? In Yarborough they were all known and respected, and he was not. They had money. He had nothing but the shirt and jeans and sneakers he was wearing and a few dollars in his wallet at the boathouse. Police would be impressed by their testimony. A countercharge of attempted murder without supporting evidence would seem like a foolish boy's wild effort to revenge himself.

So he couldn't go back now. But—His young jaw hardened. Some day he would go back. Some day.

On the terrace a soft footfall slithered over flagstones, and jerked him back to the present. The housekeeper was a shadow among shadows, gaunt in black. "Mr Longworth, the telephone. Mrs Vanbrugh."

As he crossed the living-room, his knees turned to water. Tessie—

The wonderful, clear, light voice was the same: "Mr Longworth? I called to thank you for taking such good care of my little girl this afternoon. We should be so happy if you would dine with us tomorrow. I hope this isn't too short notice?"

A voice like pigeons' cooing. A shimmer in the tone like the iridescence of pigeons' plumage.

His own voice sounded harsh by contrast. "Not at all. I shall be delighted."

Back on the terrace, he looked again at the lights along the other shore.

Some day—

This was it.

The Vanbrugh living-room seemed smaller than he remembered it. Everywhere he saw evidence of economic erosion: the neat darn in the faded chintz slip cover, the

bald spot in the Mohammedan prayer rug, silver un-
evenly polished. Fortune had stood still here while time
moved on.

Tessie or Nan had done all that could be done to
make the room festive for this evening. Long-stemmed
red roses in a great bowl of cut crystal. A brisk wood fire
on the hearth that brought a blush to the yellowed white
woodwork. But these touches were falsely gay, rouge on
an old, worn face.

The inlaid cabinet was still standing where Bly and
Vanbrugh had placed it that last morning fifteen years
ago. Bly glanced at it almost resentfully, with an obscure
feeling that somehow it had been the starting point of
all the trouble.

A man in well-worn tweeds was dozing in a wing
chair before the hearth. His hair was brown, but his small
beard was a badger mixture of brown and gray. He rose.
"I didn't hear you come in. I'm waiting for Tessie. I'm her
former husband, Geoffrey Vanbrugh."

"And I'm Stephen Longworth." Bly searched the
warm brown eyes for a flicker of recognition. There was
none.

From the stair outside came the sound of a footfall.
How well Bly remembered that light, swift foot that
seemed to fall upon his heart in the old days. He turned
toward the portieres. He thought wildly that this was
another guest. Not Tessie. Then the ravaged face smiled,
and he saw Tessie's ghost among the ruins of her beauty.

She was wasted and hoary as one of the Fates, a
haggard old woman in a dress filmy and gray as smoke,
which brought out the leaden tones in her parched skin
and dull hair. The bloom, the sheen, the glow, so long
remembered, were gone with the sunshine of that last
summer. All that remained was the buoyant step, the
lilting voice, the lightly drawn breath that now seemed

to animate a dying woman. Had time alone done all this to Tessie?

"Why, Geoff!" She gave Vanbrugh both hands, but there was pain in her eyes. "I had no idea you were here!"

"I was leaving Key West for New York when I got your telegram. I came here instead." He was looking at her with the same eager light in his eyes. Bly thought, *He still loves her.*

"If you're giving a party tonight—" he began.

"You'll join us!" she interrupted. "Not a party. Just the Strawns and Mr Longworth."

The Strawns. So Dick Strawn had married some other woman. Had he ever cared for Tessie? After all, there was no evidence he had, except Bly's own jealous imagination.

The doorbell rang. Bly saw Strawn through the portieres, in the hall, handing hat and gloves to the maid. His hair was a little thinner, his figure a little thicker, but he still wore that look of world-weary resignation. He came into the room with the woman Bly had met on the train.

Hatless now, her hair was satiny black stitched sparingly with silver. Black lace draped cunningly hid the absence of waistline. Jewels brought out the vital spark in her dark eyes. She tottered across the waxed floor on plump feet squeezed into tiny black slippers.

Tessie was saying, "Mr Longworth, Mrs Strawn."

"We've met before. On the train, wasn't it?" There was a ring in her voice like the clashing of swords. "You startled me by saying you had met Frank Bly in Cairo. I was so relieved when you admitted you might have mistaken the name. I'm like Madame du Deffand: I don't believe in ghosts, but I'm afraid of them."

Strawn kissed Tessie's withered hand. "My dear. . . . Hello Geoff; what a pleasant surprise! . . .

Mr Longworth . . ." Either Strawn believed he was meeting a stranger for the first time or he was a better actor than Bly had ever suspected.

Nan came into the room with a whisper of taffeta. "Why, Father!" She ran to kiss Vanbrugh. "Mother, you didn't tell me he was coming!"

"I didn't know it, myself." Tessie looked gratefully at the maid, who chose that moment to announce dinner.

Afterward, in the living-room again, Tessie sat in the wing chair pouring coffee. Vanbrugh was on the sofa facing the fire, Mrs Strawn on his left, Nan on his right. Strawn sat on a hassock close to Tessie. Bly stood with one hand on the mantelpiece looking down into the fire. He couldn't wait much longer. Conversation was flagging and soon the party would break up. How could he bring the talk back to the only subject that interested him without drawing attention to his interest by changing the subject?

It was Strawn who gave him the opportunity.

"All sleeping pills are dangerous. A good murder mystery does the trick better."

"I agree." Bly was careful to keep his voice casual, his curiosity idle, as he went on: "And, speaking of murder, I wonder who really did kill Frank Bly?"

There was a startled hush. He might have dropped a lighted match or upset a glass of brandy. His moment had come at last. This was the turning point.

Vanbrugh spoke slowly: "Fifteen years is a long time. We'll never know."

Bly kept his voice level. He must speak like Stephen Longworth, a stranger casually interested, tactless enough to force the subject on people who had been close to it. "I've gathered that the murderer was never caught. That whets my curiosity. Just who was this Frank Bly? And what actually happened to him? Some of you were witnesses, weren't you?"

"I doubt if we remember details now," said Tessie carefully. "Freud would say we'd forgotten because we didn't want to remember. It was unpleasant. Especially for Nan."

"Oh. . . ." Stephen Longworth must show belated embarrassment at this point while Frank Bly watched every face. "I'm sorry. If any of you would rather not discuss it—?" The note of challenge implied a different wording: *If any of you are afraid to discuss it.*

Strawn was quick to scotch the unspoken suspicion. "Why shouldn't we? Nan is grown up now. It doesn't bother you any longer, does it, my dear?"

"Oh, no." But the face Nan turned toward Bly was wan. "I was ill afterward. They had a psychiatrist. And then they sent me away to boarding school and college. I used to have nightmares. But I've outgrown that."

Tessie made a little gesture of dismay. "Why can't we just forget?"

"I wonder if he forgets?" There was awe in Nan's voice.

Bly looked at her sharply. Could she have seen or heard something when she was only five? Something never revealed? That would explain the psychiatrist and the nightmares.

"He? Who?" demanded Mrs Strawn.

"The murderer, whoever he was. Imagine living for fifteen years with—that."

Strawn smiled sardonically. "It has happened, Nan."

"You're horrid and cynical, Dick," Nan said. "Sometimes I really don't see how you put up with him, Denise!"

"Denise?" faltered Bly.

"Mrs Strawn," explained Nan.

"I was born a Frenchwoman, Mr Longworth. Denise de Beaupré. I first came to Yarborough as a French teacher at one of the schools here."

"Oh." He had been so sure these four would not recognize him. Yet, illogically, it had not occurred to him that he might fail to recognize one of them. Denise had been so different then. Slender and dark, quiet and sweet, the one who smiled and watched and listened while the other three talked.

Now he had a flash of intuition that events were moving too fast to be quite spontaneous. It could not be chance that all the principal actors in the old drama were brought together again so soon after he reached Yarborough. Which one of them had planned this dinner tonight? Denise, who was so startled at his casual mention of Frank Bly on the train? Nan, who had ridden toward his house yesterday, perhaps hoping to meet him? Tessie, who had recently telegraphed Vanbrugh, possibly asking him to return? Or Strawn, who had kept himself in the background?

It was to Strawn that Bly turned now. "You haven't answered my question. Who was Frank Bly? An old friend?"

"Well, Geoff." Strawn looked at Vanbrugh quizzically. "You hired him."

Vanbrugh turned a musing glance on the fire. "I first met Frank Bly one rainy evening in June in a wayside diner. He was on the seat beside me, and he pitched forward in a dead faint. He was starving. I offered him a job for the summer looking after the cabin cruiser I had then, and he jumped at it."

"You should have handed him a ten-dollar bill and wished him luck," remarked Strawn.

"If only you had!" Denise spoke bitterly. "Think what we would have been spared!"

"But I should have lain awake nights wondering what happened to him after the ten-dollar bill was gone," objected Vanbrugh. "So, instead, I brought him home that night in my car."

"I remember." Tessie sighed. "I came to the front door when I heard Geoff's car. The boy was still hungry. I took him into the kitchen and gave him bread and ham."

"And a can of beans." Frank Bly had let the words slip. Now Stephen Longworth added swiftly, "Isn't that standard for starving men—a can of beans?"

"Possibly." Tessie seemed to dislike the flippant tone. "I don't recall giving him beans."

"I took him down to the boathouse with blankets and towels." went on Vanbrugh. "There was a sort of guesthouse on the upper floor. A big room with three bunks, a shower, and a kitchenette. I paid him seventy-five a month. He saved nearly all of it."

"You were soft, both of you," said Strawn. "And see what happened? Just what you might have expected. You got into the worst trouble of your lives through Frank Bly. Good heavens, Tessie, have you forgotten? Geoff was nearly arrested for his murder! And we still don't know what really happened. What did we know about Bly? Nothing—except what he chose to tell us. All that stuff about losing his parents and trying to earn enough money to go to college may have been a pack of lies. He may have been what we call a juvenile delinquent nowadays, a hopeless drifter, an unemployable with a criminal record. When you took that wretched boy into your home you took mystery and violence into your lives."

"Now, Dick!" Denise rebuked him gently. "Whatever happened was not Frank Bly's fault. After all, he was the one who suffered most. He was killed."

"People who get murdered always do something to

provoke it," retorted Strawn. "If not something vicious, then something imprudent."

Words almost welled to Bly's lips: *But I didn't do anything to provoke it—anything!*

Strawn was turning to him for support. "You agree, Longworth?"

Bly smiled wryly. "Do murder victims think so?"

Strawn laughed. "No one knows what they think, once they become victims!"

Bly stifled an impulse to respond, *I'm the one man in the world who does know—a murder victim investigating his own murder.* Instead, he spoke as Longworth: "Where was Bly killed?"

Vanbrugh answered, "On the pier, outside our boathouse."

"And when?"

Strawn answered this time. "We don't know the hour, but it must have been the night after the money disappeared."

Tessie had gasped aloud. Denise's eyes had narrowed. But it was Nan who looked from Strawn to her father in surprise and cried out, "The money?"

Vanbrugh was taken aback. "Dick, I've never told anyone else about that. Not even Tessie or Nan."

Strawn looked at Bly. "That was a slip of the tongue, Longworth. The business about the money has been a secret between Vanbrugh and me all these years. But since I did mention it, I see no harm in explaining now. It can't hurt anyone after so long. The truth is that Frank Bly was a thief."

"I don't believe it!" Tessie's voice fluttered, the sound of wings when a bird spies a cat stalking its nest. "And I'd rather talk about something else."

Denise spoke crisply: "I agree. After all, there's nothing any of us can do or say now that will bring Frank Bly back to life!"

"No, Denise; no, Tessie." Strawn looked from one woman to the other. "Now we've started this, we're going to finish it. Otherwise, Mr Longworth may think we're afraid of the truth. . . . Longworth, you see that inlaid cabinet at the other end of the room?"

"I've been admiring it all evening."

"Shortly before Frank Bly was murdered, Denise learned that I was an art dealer as well as the Vanbrughs' only neighbor. She was their house guest at the time. She showed me a photograph of the cabinet. It was in storage then, in a Paris warehouse with the rest of her family furniture, and she wanted to sell it. Acting as her agent, I sold it to Vanbrugh for ten thousand dollars."

"More than I could afford, even then," put in Vanbrugh. "But—well, look at it, Longworth, and you'll understand why I had to have it. It's a true sixteenth century inlay, the kind that preceded marquetry. The kind that looks like embroidery instead of painting. When it was first made, the inlaid ivory and fruitwood were stained in vivid Christmas colors—red, green, and white—and it must have been as blithe as Botticelli's *Primavera*. Though the colors have faded, even now you can see the lyrical Renaissance gaiety of the springy lines."

"The cabinet arrived here by barge from Philadelphia," Strawn went on, "one Saturday afternoon, a few hours before Bly disappeared."

"How well I recall that day!" put in Denise. "I was so embarrassed, because the packing-case was addressed to 'Mrs. Richard Strawn.' When I wrote my father's lawyer asking him to send me the cabinet, I mentioned that I had just become engaged to Dick. Somehow, he got the idea that we were already married."

"As if it mattered!" Strawn looked at her fondly, then

turned back to Bly. "To seal the bargain, Vanbrugh had drawn half the amount in cash from his bank that morning."

"I needed that cash." Denise smiled reminiscently. "I wanted to open charge accounts in several dress shops so I could start buying my trousseau. For that you need a bank's reference. And I didn't want to wait even the short time it takes to clear a deposited check."

Strawn continued, "As soon as Vanbrugh verified Denise's claim that the cabinet was in good condition, he handed the money to me as Denise's agent. The day was hot. Tessie suggested a cruise and swim in the river. I couldn't take the money with me; we were all in bathing-suits. And the bank was closed Saturday afternoon. So I left the money in the men's locker-room at the boat-house, wrapped in some colored paper I found there. You can guess the rest, Longworth. When we came back from our cruise that package of money was gone."

Denise was aghast. "Why didn't you ever tell me?"

"Or me?" Tessie looked at Vanbrugh tragically.

"My dear, we were trying to spare you both a rather unpleasant shock," said Vanbrugh. "We talked it over with Bly in my study privately."

"How naïve we were!" Denise smiled ruefully at Tessie. "Do you remember sitting in this room together with cocktails and wondering why the men didn't come out of the study?"

"Yes and I recall hearing voices, though I couldn't catch the words."

"They were still at it when you went upstairs to kiss Nan good night," added Denise. "I stood at the window watching the clouds over the river. I could see the upper floor of the boathouse above the trees, and I noticed there were no lights. I wondered where Frank Bly was, but it didn't occur to me he was in the study."

"Of course, Bly was the obvious suspect." said Strawn. "When we went out on the river he stayed behind at the boathouse. But we wanted to give him a chance to make restitution before we called the police."

"It was ghastly." Vanbrugh signed. "I'll never forget it."

You'll never forget it! Bly smiled grimly, and said aloud, "I suppose this Bly denied everything?"

"Of course." Vanbrugh drew a long breath.

"Then you both assumed his guilt without any evidence at all, just because he was the most likely person!" Nan was shocked.

"Nan, who else could it have been?" protested Vanbrugh. "Every one of us had an interest in the orderly completion of the transaction, except Bly. Dick wanted his commission, your mother and I wanted the cabinet, and Denise wanted the money. There was no one else but Agatha, our cook, and you know that motherly old soul wouldn't be tempted by money. She had all the comforts she wanted. She had no vices and no vicious relatives to prey on her. So we gave Bly until morning to return the money. He left the study by a French window, lifting his hand and saying, 'See you tomorrow.' Standing by my desk, I could see him through the window as he walked across the lawn and took the path through the woods to the boathouse. I never saw him again. He simply walked out of our lives, and his last words were a lie: 'See you tomorrow.' "

Strawn nodded. "I said, 'I need a drink. Any liquor in the dining-room?' You said, 'Yes. I'll join you in a minute.' But you were a long time coming. I was on my third drink when you drifted in."

"I needed time to think," explained Vanbrugh.

To think? Bly's smile curved skeptically. So it really could have been any one of them. Each had been alone when Bly heard the footsteps behind him on the path. Vanbrugh, ostensibly in the study; Strawn, ostensibly in the dining-room; Denise, ostensibly in this living-room. And Tessie? Had anyone ever thought to ask Nan just when her mother came to kiss her good night that evening or how long her mother had stayed?

"I remember that next morning," resumed Vanbrugh. "A sunny day with a sky blue and white as a Della Robbia plaque. I went down to the boathouse early, hoping Bly had put the money back in the locker-room. It wasn't there, and neither was Bly. He had left everything, even his own wallet and money. The earth on the pathway was still moist from the night's rain, but there were no footprints. It was inexplicable and frightening, like a horror story."

"Seemed obvious to me," amended Strawn. "He had gone before the rain and taken our money with him."

Bly looked at Strawn thoughtfully. "So you reported the theft to the police then?"

Vanbrugh answered for Strawn: "No, we didn't."

"Why not?"

"Tessie believed the boy had drowned during the storm, because she didn't know about the missing money. When I saw how hysterical she was about his death I knew she couldn't stand his arrest for larceny."

"So?" Bly prompted them.

Strawn laughed. "What would you expect of anyone as quixotic as Geoff? He sold some life insurance and gave me four thousand to pay Denise. The least I could do was waive my commission."

Denise made a comic face. "Then, Geoff, I owe you four thousand."

"Nonsense!" responded Vanbrugh. "I got the cabinet, and it's worth more today than all I paid for it."

"Who found Bly's body?" demanded Bly.

A small voice spoke from the sofa: "I did."

Bly was astonished. "Nan! You?"

Tessie leaned forward, pain in her eyes again. "Nan, dear, I'm sure Mr Longworth will excuse you."

"He needn't." Nan tossed her shining hair. "It's all so long ago it doesn't upset me now. I was five and a half, going on six. Mother and Father and Denise had gone to a luncheon party Dick was giving at his bungalow down the road, to introduce Denise to his family. Agatha was in the kitchen and I was supposed to play within sight of her window. I soon realized she wasn't paying much attention to me. I slipped down the path to the boathouse.

"It was autumn, hot as summer but drier. All the leaves had turned scarlet or yellow, lovely transparent colors that took the sun like stained glass. I felt wonderfully free in the sunlit stillness. I took off my shoes and stockings and sat on the pier dangling my feet in the cold water. Then I saw a water spider trying to climb the pile under the pier. I got a stick and leaned over to tickle the insect, and then I saw it—him.

"He was face down, floating in the water under the pier. He was wearing a white shirt and blue jeans and sneakers. I poked at him with the stick. And then"—Nan caught her breath—"I knew he was dead.

"I was screaming when I ran into the kitchen still barefoot. Poor old Agatha thought I had hurt myself."

Tessie shuddered. "Nan was still sobbing when we got home. I remember her words to this day: '*Frank—under the boathouse—he's dead.*'"

"The body was in bad shape," said Vanbrugh. "But it seemed about Bly's weight and height and coloring. And he had been missing for five weeks, just about the time the body had been dead. So there could hardly be any doubt about the identification."

"Was the missing money in his pockets?" asked Bly.

"No." Vanbrugh admitted it uneasily.

Bly persisted, "Did you tell the police about the money then?"

Strawn shook his head. "It seemed wiser to volunteer as little information as possible. Nan was violently ill, the money was gone, and Frank was dead. Geoff didn't want Tessie to know he'd been a thief. I didn't see how the police could recover the money, for it must have fallen into the water. And then, that theft might have given the police the wrong idea. A quarrel over money that ended in a fist fight, one killing blow, and a body pushed into the water so it would pass for a drowning accident weeks later. That might have been the police case. As it was, they couldn't make a case against any of us. Total absence of motive will create a doubt in the mind of any jury, and the police know that."

"The whole thing will always be a complete mystery," concluded Vanbrugh. "Who took the money? And why? Who killed Frank? And why? There's no evidence, no clue, no motive, nothing. Just the money gone and the boy dead, by the hand of some unknown man or woman."

"Woman?" Bly repeated. "Could a woman have inflicted the wounds?"

"Oh, yes." It was Denise who answered. "The police doctor said they looked like hammer blows. It's the weight of a hammer that does the work. Not the force of the arm that wields it. Anyone could have murdered Frank Bly, even a child."

Strawn spoke slowly: "If he was murdered."

Tessie gasped. "What do you mean? Suicide?"

Strawn's heavy lids veiled his glance, then he looked up, eyes slyly mocking. "Mind if I tell, Geoff?"

"I suppose not. But why?"

Strawn looked at Bly. "I'm going to tell you something I've never told anyone else except Geoff. I don't believe Frank Bly is dead."

Bly knew his self-control must crack in another moment. Had Strawn recognized him, after all?

But Strawn's glance did not rest on Bly. It wandered from face to face and came to rest on Vanbrugh. "Because, four years later, that money was returned to me—anonymously."

Nan cried out, "Oh, Dick, that can't be! Even if Frank were alive he wouldn't return the money unless he took it!"

"Isn't is extremely possible he did take it?" retorted Strawn.

Bly recovered his voice. "How was the money returned?"

"By mail in fifty bills of one hundred dollars each," answered Strawn promptly. "I hadn't kept the numbers of the missing bills. I couldn't tell if these were identical, but the amount was significant. It came to my office in a plain, white envelope postmarked New York. Not even registered. Then I knew that Frank Bly was alive, that we two must have made a mistake in identifying the body as his. For no one else in the world knew about the missing money except Bly and Geoff and myself.

"I tried other theories. None of them worked. Would Bly's murderer take the money from Bly and then return it to me? No murderer would risk having the money traced back to him. Bly must have run away with the money as we first believed. Who the other man was, who murdered him and why is a puzzle, something we'll never know. But I'm sure Bly went away as far as possible from the scene of his theft, so far that he, himself, didn't know he was listed as dead in the police records of Yarborough."

"Dick, no!" Nan's clenched knuckles were white on her knees. "Frank Bly wouldn't steal."

"My dear child, you were five years old when you knew him. How could you judge his character then?"

Bly changed the subject. "What became of the money then?"

"What do you suppose?" Strawn was bland. "I gave four thousand to Geoff and kept the rest as my commission on the original transaction."

"And you two never told us." Denise glanced at her husband curiously. "I had no idea you were capable of such—reticence."

Tessie was looking at Vanbrugh. "It proves once more that people can live together for years without ever really knowing each other." Her tone was gentle, but Vanbrugh turned aside abruptly as if she had wounded his feelings.

Strawn defended himself stoutly. "There was nothing to tell. Just another mystery: "Who was the dead man? Who killed him and why? And what did become of Frank Bly?"

Denise leaned back in her corner of the sofa, with the calculated art of a Parisian. She was smiling now, teeth even and white against the red lips. She spoke to Bly, her voice soft, faintly derisive: "Isn't it time you told us? Haven't you played with us long enough? What did become of you, Mr. Bly?"

Vanbrugh cried out, "Denise! What on earth—?"

Tessie spoke in a whisper: "Bly?"

Nan closed her lips tightly.

Strawn was looking hard at the stranger. "I've suspected it for the last fifteen minutes. That's why I decided to tell about the return of the money. I didn't want you to think that we were suppressing any of the facts, Bly."

It was a relief to Bly. He stood silent, his back to the fire, facing their intent eyes, watching them as the stunning realization came to one after another.

"I am Frank Bly," he said quietly. "And I am very much alive."

Vanbrugh nodded slowly. "By heaven, you *could* be Bly at thrity-two, though the gray hair is confusing."

Tessie said, "I was so sure you were dead. Otherwise I would have known you."

Bly addressed Denise. "How did you guess? Or have you known all along?"

She was still smiling, enjoying her little triumph. "I suppose it was because I met you by chance on the train, without being told beforehand who you were supposed to be. The others met you only after a rather elaborate build-up about an entirely different personality—Stephen Longworth. Believing is seeing. They believed you were Longworth so they didn't see you as Bly. And of course the physical change is great. On the train at first you looked vaguely, confusingly familiar to me. As we talked I tried to visualize your face without gray hair at the temples, but I couldn't. Then you, yourself, gave me the association I needed. You dropped a sly hint that Frank Bly was still alive, and fifteen years dropped away from you. That's why I was so startled then. Until that moment I had honestly believed Frank Bly was dead. Even then I wasn't absolutely sure."

"So you planned this dinner tonight to make sure?"

"With Tessie's help, yes. I told her about our talk on the train, but I didn't mention my suspicion that you were Bly to anyone. Not even to my husband."

"I had no idea you were capable of such reticence." Strawn echoed her own words, with a smile.

Denise went on: "I soon discovered you were known as Stephen Longworth in Yarborough. That puzzled me. Isn't it illegal to pass under a false name?"

Bly shook his head. "Not a false name. A pen name. Stephen Longworth signs publishers' contracts and endorses their royalty checks. He is a real person. Perhaps more real than Frank Bly."

Strawn's ugly, intelligent face had settled into a stolid mold. "Longworth—or Bly—would it be indelicate to ask you if you did take that money?"

"Most indelicate. You say yourself it was returned."

"By you?"

"I haven't admitted that I took it. Why should I return it if I hadn't?"

"Then"—Strawn's voice rang out with sudden vehemence—"just why have you come back?"

Slowly Bly looked from one tense face to another. "You really want to know? Most probably it's because one of you four nice people tried to murder me fifteen years ago, and I want to find out which one of you it was."

Strawn said, "Preposterous! You're accusing us?"

Vanbrugh said, "Really, Bly. How could someone attack you without your seeing who it was?"

"I was struck from behind, in the dark. Next thing I knew I was in the water. I couldn't see above the pier. When I got into midstream it was too dark to see anyone on the pier. Whoever it was tried to beat me back when I tried to climb out. My fingers were smashed. There are the scars." He held out his right hand. "That was why I ran away. I barely escaped with my life and I was afraid to go back. You were hostile. You had charged me with theft. How could I expect to make a countercharge of attempted murder stick without evidence, without money to pay a lawyer?"

"But, Frank"—Vanbrugh was trying to sound reasonable—"even if you were attacked, why are you so sure it was one of us?"

"Who else could it have been? Who else used that path through the woods?"

They had no answer to this.

Bly went on in a level, dispassionate tone: "Now I have come back, I find that someone else actually was killed in that same place, about that same time. A man who was my height and weight, dressed like me. I don't know who he was. I don't know if he was killed because he was mistaken for me. Or if I was attacked because I was mistaken for him. Or whether someone had a motive for killing both of us, even though we were strangers to each other. I don't know if you made an honest mistake when you identified his body as mine, or if his identity was so incriminating to one of you that it had to be concealed at all costs.

"It's even possible that one of you deliberately drove me away with an accusation of theft and an attempt at violence so that his body could be buried later under my name. But one of you must know the answers to all these questions. Because nothing you've said explains why one of you tried to murder me. And that I intend to find out."

Bly walked out of the room. No one spoke in the living-room. He let himself out the front door and walked down the drive.

At the sound of a car, he looked back. The Strawns were going home already. Vanbrugh stood in the lighted doorway, watching.

Bly left the drive and started down the path through the woods to the boathouse.

The path looked as if it had not been used for years. Branches interlaced overhead, shutting out the stars. He felt his way through dead leaves that rustled at every step. After a while he heard the rustling of feet in the leaves behind him.

Again? He smiled tightly, waited, breathless. There was no further sound. Nerves? Memories? He went on and turned a corner. The boathouse should have blocked his view, but there was the river placid and silvery in the starlight. All that remained of the boathouse was a pile of charred timber. The pier still extended over the water, but several planks had rotted away.

A twig snapped. He spun around on his heel. Nan stood on the path, a wraith in shimmering white. "Frank! I'm so glad you're alive!" She ran forward, soundless on pine needles. So that was why he had heard footfalls only on the upper part of the path tonight and that other night, fifteen years ago.

"Do you remember saying you were going to marry me when you grew up?"

Her laugh wavered. "Children are silly!"

"It wasn't silly. It was charming. You're the only one who has bothered to say you're glad I'm alive. Thank you, Nan."

She was standing close, eyes wide and bright. He bent his head and kissed her gently. For a moment her lips responded, warm and firm. Then she drew back, with a little catch in her breath. "You—you were in love with Mother long ago, weren't you?"

"Was I?" He shook his head doubtfully. "A lonely boy's daydream, Nan. I never told your mother or anyone else." His gaze shifted to the burned boathouse. "When did that happen?"

"A few days afterward. They said it was a short circuit." Again her eyes slid away from his. "I must go back. It's late."

"I'll go with you."

"No, please. I'd rather go alone."

Bly walked along the riverbank to his own home. The house was dark, but on the terrace one of the French windows was standing open. He stopped just outside the window.

Only the faintest light reached the room from the sky outside. It passed over a dark cloak, it edged a feathery crest of pale hair and lay gently along a clean jaw line.

He whispered, "Tessie."

She turned with fluid grace. "Why are you waiting outside?"

"I saw someone in the room. I didn't know who it was at first."

He pressed a switch. The lamp cast a softly shaded radiance, but now he could see the worn, hollow face. The cloak was not really dark. It was violet velvet held at her throat by an amethyst clasp. Even her smile was old, tired, wise, resigned.

She said, "I can't believe this. I must look at you."

"I've changed."

"So have I. You know why I'm here?"

"No." To be alone with Tessie, to have her seek him out, ask his help, once his idea of pure heaven. And now, who said the middle years of life are always a parody of the youthful dreams? Arabs had a bitter proverb: *Beware the curse of an answered prayer.*

"You must know you once had the power to enchant me," he said. "Perhaps you thought you could use that power once more."

She rose. The cloak fell from her shoulders, lying in crushed folds about her feet, so flowery a color that he almost expected it to give off the fragrance of crushed violets. "That wasn't kind. You are mocking me." The smoky dress swirled about her ankles as she moved to face the wide, unframed mirror over the mantlepiece. "Look in the mirror! Could that old woman ever charm any man again?"

"Mrs Vanbrugh—"

"You called me Tessie a moment ago."

"You haven't really changed. Your spirit is the same."

"Valiantly spoken, Frank, and falsely."

"Tessie." The name slipped out again. "You have one thing on your side when you talk to me—memory. You and Geoffrey Vanbrugh were good to me when I had no other friends. In a way I loved you both. That may be why I became so bitter afterward when I was sure one of you had tried to kill me."

She leaned toward him impulsively. "But you were not killed. And now you're a success. What have you to gain by raking over the cinders of an old crime?"

"Perhaps I hope I can prove that I was mistaken, that you and Vanbrugh and the Strawns really are the kindly, pleasant, normal people you seem to be. Now we're alone, why don't you tell me what really happened and why? I might be satisfied with that."

"Oh, Frank!" It was a cry of anguish. "Can't you guess why I came here tonight? To ask you to go away and—forget. If you don't you'll hurt someone I love."

"Nan?"

"Of course not. She was a child then. I mean Geoff."

Bly weighed his next words. "I can't see how anything I do now can hurt Vanbrugh—unless he is the murderer."

Her voice dropped, softly as a dead leaf falls, so light the air can almost support it. "That's it, Frank. He is."

"Vanbrugh? Are you sure?"

"Quite sure." She shivered and hugged her knees as if she were cold, a schoolgirl gesture oddly appealing in one who looked so old and frail.

Tessie was speaking in a low, rapid voice: "It was the night after you disappeared. Denise and I didn't know about the accusation of theft. I thought you had drowned in the river. Denise thought you had got into some scrape that made you ashamed to come back. That night Denise and Nan and Agatha all went to bed early, and Geoff had gone out to dinner to see some man in Yarborough about a portrait commission. I was alone in the living-room, playing the piano and watching the moonlight on the river, when I saw a light in the boathouse.

"Then I thought Denise was right. I thought you were in such trouble you were afraid to come back openly, so you had come back secretly at night to get your money and books and clothes. But if you were in trouble I wanted to help. I thought of a gambling debt or a drunken party, nothing worse.

"I put on a dark cloak—this same cloak; Lyons velvet wears for years—and I went down to the boathouse. It was like a dream even then. Now it's vague as the memory of a dream. It was a lovely night, a fresh breeze on the water and the rippling sound of little waves. I wasn't wearing anything that would rustle. I don't believe I made a sound on the path."

"You always had the lightest step in the world, the most softly drawn breath," murmured Bly.

"I was wearing a dress something like this that floated around me, and I had that feeling of drifting or flying that you have in some dreams. And it had all the inconsequence of a dream, for when I walked into the lock-erroom I came face to face with a stranger."

"Tramp or burglar?"

"Oh, no, not a criminal type. An educated man. Sub-tle and clever and—evil. I never knew his name. I hardly saw his face. The light I'd seen was his flashlight. He turned it on me while he stood in darkness. He was about your height. I thought he was you until he spoke. I said, 'Frank, you're back!' He echoed me: 'Frank?' Then he said, 'Oh, the boatman. Were you fond of him?' His tone was nasty. I said, 'I shall telephone the police that someone has broken into our boathouse.' I was too angry to be frightened. But he didn't seem afraid of the police. He laughed and said, 'I'd like to talk to the police myself!'

"The boathouse extension was disconnected after you left. I ran up the path and lost my way in the woods. It must have been fifteen minutes or more before I reached the house. I was taking off my cloak in the hall when Geoff came in. I knew something dreadful had hap-pened. His eyes were—What word can I use? Tortured. Yet I knew the pain was not physical. The dream was turning into a nightmare. I was snatching at reality when I said, 'Geoff, there's a man in our boathouse, a stranger.'

"Geoff dismissed that in two bald sentences: 'Tessie, there is no man in the boathouse now. Forget that you saw him!' Then he went on in a dull, dead voice, speaking words I shall never forget: 'Tessie, if anyone should ever ask you where I was this evening, you are to make just one answer. You are to say that I was here with you all the time.'

"I was lucky. No one ever asked me where Geoff had been that evening. For when the body was found every-one assumed that it was your body, and you were sup-posed to have been killed when you disappeared." Tessie's arms dropped from her knees and hung loosely at her sides, as if she were exhausted.

"Was this why you divorced Vanbrugh? Even though he is Nan's father?"

"I divorced Geoff because he is Nan's father." Her breast moved as if she were sighing, but he could not hear that gentle breath. "Can you imagine what it was like? Living with a man you know to be a murderer and never a word about it spoken between you? That's Geoff's way. He never spoke of unpleasant things. He's sensitive and reserved. An artist. I knew that if I did ask him he would deny the whole thing. He would think that the less I knew about that horror, the easier it would be for me to bear it. But I couldn't let Nan grow up with— that. When I asked Geoff for a divorce he never asked me why. He knew. He might not have given up Nan so easily if it hadn't been for the doctor who said she must be sent away to boarding school."

"Yet you let Nan see him from time to time?"

"I wasn't afraid of Geoff. I knew he wasn't vicious or maniacal—dangerous to Nan or me. I'm sure he killed on impulse under tremendous provocation. It was only not knowing anything and having to live with mystery and terror, day after day. I wanted to but I couldn't. A few weeks ago, when I heard there was a stranger in town asking questions about Frank Bly, I telegraphed Geoff to stay away. Instead, he came here as soon as he could. His idea of protecting me."

"Does Nan know?"

"Of course not."

Bly looked at her almost with awe. "Do you realize what you've been telling me? If Vanbrugh did kill this man, he is also the man who tried to kill me. He may have mistaken me for this other man in the dark. That would make the second, successful attack premeditated."

"Oh, no! Geoff isn't capable of calculated violence." Tessie frowned. "Perhaps this stranger attacked you?"

"A comfortable solution." Bly's voice was arid. "Put it all on a stranger who is dead and cannot speak for himself! But why?"

"I don't know." The last word was long-drawn as a moan. "Frank, I don't want to know. I'm so afraid." She looked at him now, and he recalled the word she had used for Vanbrugh's—*tortured*. "It may be something that will hurt me, and I've had enough of being hurt. Truly, I have. I suppose it's no use." She glanced toward the mirror with the saddest smile he had ever seen. "Would it have made a difference if I had still been the Tessie Vanbrugh you used to know?"

Bly surprised himself. "Don't Tessie! You know that I shall go away now and forget everything."

"You'll go?" Joy leaped into her eyes. "Soon? Now; tonight?"

"Tonight if that will make you happier. There's a late train to New York. But let me take you home first."

"Oh, no! Someone might hear us, and I'm supposed to be asleep in my own room. Alone, I can be very quiet."

"As you wish." He took one of her hands, brushed it with his lips. It was like tasting ashes.

Then she was gone, and Bly was alone in a bleak world with a bitter flavor in his mouth, the aftertaste of dead youth.

Upstairs, he threw a few necessities into an overnight bag, with the automatic he no longer cared about, then changed into his oldest, most comfortable tweeds. In the lower hall he caught a glimpse of his own grim face in the mirror as he put on his hat. He looked down at the right hand, flexing the fingers that had healed long ago. Had Geoff done that?

Suddenly he couldn't believe it. Not Geoff, the man who had fed him in the roadside diner and taken him home. But then who?

With a shrug he picked up his bag.

A strange voice spoke from the living-room: "In a hurry?"

Bly turned to face the arch. "Who are you?"

The man who ambled toward him was on the wrong side of fifty, shrunken and tough as old leather. His clothes were a little too prosperous, almost flashy. His stolid manner was overdone.

"I'm Archibald D. Gesell. The door was unlatched." He held out a gold badge enameled with the words: *Yarborough Police Commission*.

Bly collected his wits. "Very well, Mr. Commissioner. I can't imagine what you want of me, but—"

"No idea why I'm here?"

"None whatever." Bly tried to smile amiably as he said, "You tell me."

Gesell contemplated the toe of one boot. "Man was murdered tonight. Man you know and saw tonight. And you were sure hellbent on making yourself scarce mighty quick."

"Who was the man?"

Gesell looked up. "Geoffrey Vanbrugh."

Tessie, Tessie, why do I always end by doubting you? It was you who said, "You'll go soon? Now; tonight?" Did you know then that Vanbrugh was dead, that my sudden departure for New York must focus suspicion on me? And when you were spinning that fine tale about Geoff, delicate and intricate as everything else about you, did you know that poor Geoff could never dispute a word you told me, because he was no longer alive? Haggard and gray and old as you look, you still have magic and mystery. You can still weave the old, bewitching dance around me with your eyes and hands and voice, so I believe anything you say, do anything you ask of me.

Bly looked at Gesell. "Didn't Freud say that men go through life making the same mistake again and again?"

"I don't get you."

"Never mind, Mr. Commissioner. I'm at your disposal."

Gesell looked down the room toward the dining-room. "Okay, boys; come on in. Mind if we go through that bag of yours, Mr Longworth?"

"Not at all." As heavy footfalls clattered across the floor, Bly remembered too late the automatic in the suitcase.

The sky turned from pale gray to a paler blue, bathed in the pearl light that comes just before dawn. Then it was a fiery rose-red. And still Gesell's monotone went on:

Why had Bly walked to and from the Vanbrugh's home instead of taking his car? Why hadn't he gone to bed when he got home? Why was he carring an automatic? Could his housekeeper substantiate his claim that he had been alone reading in the living-room for several hours, then decided on impulse to catch the late train to New York? Was he quite sure that he had not had any visitors?

"No. No visitors." Bly lit his twentieth cigarette. "I walked to and from the Vanbrughs' just because I like to walk. I sat up late reading because I like to read. Now will you tell me how Vanbrugh died? And when?"

"We're asking the questions, Mr Longworth. What's your business?"

"I write."

"For newspapers or magazines?"

"Neither. I write books about foreign countries."

"What was the name of your last book?"

Inwardly Bly cursed the modern publisher's fancy for eccentric titles with promotion possibilities. "*In Thought Again*. Asia. Matthew Arnold's poem. Asia bowing in deep disdain and plunging in thought again. That's the name of my book."

"I see." Obviously he didn't see. "You write under your own name, Mr Longworth?"

Tessie and Nan, Denise and Strawn—have you already told the police that I am Frank Bly? Their records show that Geoffrey Vanbrugh was a witness in the unsolved murder of Frank Bly. If I'm identified as Bly they'll dig out the whole story.

Bly took a deep breath. "All my books are signed Stephen Longworth."

Gesell might not be bookish, but he was sharp. "And that is your own name?"

A detective spoke up: "That's how he signed the lease for this house. I saw it, because my sister works in the real-estate office."

"Okay." Gesell rose. "You're not to leave Yarborough until we give the word."

The door slammed.

Bly let out his breath and went to the telephone. Like an automaton he went through the familiar motions of smoking with one hand and dialing with the other. A distant bell throbbed. A gruff voice said, "Mrs Vanbrugh's residence. Who's calling?"

His conscious mind was far away, his oldest reflexes in control as he answered, "Frank Bly."

He slammed the telephone into its cradle, breaking the connection. They couldn't trace a dial call, but that gruff voice had certainly been the voice of a policeman stationed in the home of the murdered man to screen all visitors and telephone calls. Gesell wouldn't believe in a voice from the dead. Gesell would start looking for a stranger in the neighborhood who might be Bly under another name. If Stephen Longworth was going to act at all, he would have to act fast. At any moment now he might lose all freedom of movement. Holding him as a material witness, they would call it.

He dialed Strawn's number, and Strawn, himself, answered.

"Longworth speaking. I must talk to you, but not over the telephone."

"Could you come here? The police have left us. I don't believe they'll be back today."

"I'll be there in ten minutes."

Bly remembered Strawn's house as a simple bungalow, weather-beaten shingles in a tangle of underbrush. Now two wings had been added, and the whole was freshly painted white with wine-red shutters. Even the brush had been cleared away to make a terraced garden descending to the river by easy stages.

A maid showed Bly into a great living-room, the original bungalow with all partitions removed. Denise reclined on a chaise lounge near one of the garden windows, her ample figure disguised by a loose, cream-colored housecoat, her small, plump feet shod in cherry-colored satin that matched her lipstick. Strawn looked as limp and wilted as the white shirt and dinner jacket he had been wearing ever since last night. Between them stood a small table with a breakfast tray and an extra cup for Bly.

"Thanks." He drank the coffee gratefully. "What happened?"

Strawn groaned. "We left just after you did. We got home as our clock was striking two. Denise went to bed. I stayed downstairs to drink a whisky and soda. I was finishing it at a quarter of three when the police came."

"And Vanbrugh?"

"He stood in the doorway as we drove off. Apparently he didn't go back into the house. He sat on the terrace a while—there were cigarette butts—and then wandered down to the site of the old boathouse. It was Nan who noticed the light still on in the living-room windows at two-thirty. From her bedroom windows she could see the light reflected on the grass outside. She went downstairs. The living-room was empty. Then she realized that she hadn't heard her father come in, so she went down to the river."

Nan, Nan, will you never learn caution?

"He wasn't in the water," said Strawn bluntly. "He was lying on the old pier, the back of his head crushed. He couldn't have done it himself. And it wasn't the fall. He had fallen forward. Nan called the police. Tessie was fast asleep when they reached the house."

Fast asleep? I doubt it, Tessie. If you were in bed at all you were wide-eyed, staring at darkness, longing for sleep. But thank heavens you got back in time before the police arrived.

"It's the second time Nan has found a body." Denise frowned. "If she hadn't been so little the first time—"

"Well?" Bly spoke sharply.

"Oh, I don't know, but there have been child murderers. Who can tell what goes on in the mind of a child? It can't understand right and wrong."

Bly controlled his first flash of anger. But it lent force to his voice as he turned upon Strawn. "You hear that? Even Nan is going to be suspected now! Isn't it time you told the whole truth?"

"Bly, it's not my secret," protested Strawn. "I can't."

"No?" Bly's tone was ominous. "Either you tell me now or I tell the police you're hiding something. I want the whole story now."

Strawn looked utterly defeated, eyes dull, mouth slack. "Can't you guess the truth?"

"I don't want to guess. I want facts."

Strawn winced. But he went on in a lifeless voice: "That man whose body was identified as yours. It was Tessie who killed him."

No, Tessie, I don't believe it! You might beguile a man, bewitch him and trick him, but you wouldn't kill, would you?

Bly's voice was expressionless. "Why do you think so?"

"It goes back to the night after you disappeared. Geoff came here late and woke me. He told me to throw on some clothes. He needed help. He led me down to the boathouse pier and—well, the body was there. Dead. I said, 'Geoff, did you kill him?' Geoff answered, 'Of course not. I heard a cry as I was getting out of my car. I came here and found him, lying just as you see him now.' I was sleepy, perhaps impatient. I said, 'So what? Do you call the police while I wait here?' Geoff shook his head. 'No, Dick, we can't do that. Not after what he said just before he died.'

"That woke me up. I said, 'He was alive?' Geoff replied, 'He was dying. He died as I knelt beside him. Legally, the words of a dying man are evidence, not hearsay, even at second hand. Death is supposed to dig the truth out of people.'

"I knew then that it was going to be something pretty terrible. I said, 'For the love of heaven, Geoff, what did he say?'

"Geoff answered in that dreadfully quiet voice people use for the really bad things of life: 'He said that Tessie killed him.'

"It was a shock, even to me. Think what it must have been for Geoff, her husband. You know Tessie. You know how impossible it is to associate her with ugliness. I had sense enough to ask, 'He said it in those words?'

"Geoff shook his head. 'Not in just those words. He was gasping for breath and it came out brokenly: *"I have pain . . . at the head. . . . Your wife she is vicious, a murderess . . . she killed me."* ' " Strawn buried his face in his hands.

"So you and Vanbrugh pushed the body into the water hoping it would be carried out to sea? Or at least far down the river?"

Strawn nodded without uncovering his face.

"You were a good friend to Vanbrugh. And to Tessie."

Again Strawn nodded.

Denise was lighting a cigarette in an ivory holder mounted in gold. Her eyes were skeptical but tolerant, intensely Gallic. "That friendship!" She shrugged.

"Who was he?" demanded Bly.

"I have no idea. I never saw him before."

"Why did you and Vanbrugh identify him later as Frank Bly?"

"Nan gave us the idea. Mistaking the body for yours when she found it face down in the water. Tessie had no motive for murdering you, a boy she had befriended and mothered. She must have had some motive for murdering this other man. His identity would have revealed that motive and led the police back to Tessie. We thought it was safe because we thought you were dead anyway. Drowned. Otherwise, you wouldn't have left your own money in the boathouse. You'd either have taken it with you or come back for it."

Strawn dropped his hands and looked up. "Now perhaps you can imagine how we felt four years later when I received that five thousand dollars anonymously. It couldn't be anything but conscience money from you.

It proved that you were alive, that there was one man in the world who would know instantly, if he ever returned to Yarborough, that the dead body buried as Bly was not Bly. One man who would be sure to believe that Geoff and I had killed the other man, since we had identified him falsely. Who but a murderer would have a motive for false identification?

"I told Geoff he ought to tell Tessie you were still alive. But he wouldn't. He said they had never discussed the dead man at all. He even managed to smile as he said, 'What did you expect, Dick? A man can't go to his wife and say, "Well, dear, I've just learned you murdered someone last night. Anyone I know?"' "

"Geoff couldn't accuse Tessie to her face of murder. She would have denied it. She's a romantic. She cannot face unpleasant realities. She would probably lie to herself about it and believe her own lie. Telling herself that she didn't really mean to kill him, only to stun him. That he staggered back when she struck with the hammer, so he really killed himself.

"I asked then if Tessie had never said a word to him. Reluctantly he answered, 'Only once. That night I found the man dying she was in the hall when I finally got back to the house. She said something about seeing a strange man at the boathouse. Pretty plain, wasn't it? She was trying to find out if I had seen or heard anything. Almost a confession. I said there was no man there now. I said she should forget she had seen one. Then I realized something. She had been alone. She had no alibi and it must be worrying her. I saw a way to reassure her. For I had been alone, too, until I wakened you. So I was free to tell her that if anyone ever asked her where I had been that evening she was to say that she and I had been together all the time. That was practically telling her I knew, wasn't it? If she had wanted to confide in me I gave her the opportunity. But she didn't.' "

Strawn paused, and then said, "That's just the way Geoff told it to me."

"And I never knew! All these years!" Denise crushed her cigarette stub furiously. "Oh, Dick, you were not fair to me."

"I wanted to spare you," he insisted. "Just as Geoff wanted to spare Tessie."

Bly was grinning sardonically. "So I was right. You and Tessie and Vanbrugh were all holding some things back last night."

"But it was you who exploded the bombshell," returned Strawn. "Your story of the attack on you fifteen years ago. Geoff was deeply disturbed and I was the only one who knew why. He couldn't believe that Tessie would have done such a thing. If she hadn't, why, then, perhaps she hadn't killed the other man either and the whole thing was a ghastly misunderstanding between them. On the other hand, if she had tried to kill twice, she must really be dangerous and he had done a wicked thing to protect her for so long."

"*Vicious . . . a murderess . . .*" Denise repeated the words of the dying man as if she could not quite believe them. "She was all that and worse if she killed Geoff last night."

"But why would Tessie kill Geoff?" demanded Stawn.

Denise sighed. "She didn't know Geoff had confided in you, Dick. She thought Geoff was the only man in the world who knew she was guilty. And she was afraid he might break down now and admit it under the new pressure from Mr Longworth—I mean, Bly. So, in a way, Mr Bly is responsible for Geoff's death."

"Am I?" Bly walked over to the window. On the river a white-sailed boat was tacking against the wind, buoyant as a bird, accenting by contrast the wormlike progress of a long line of loaded barges.

"That cabinet of yours, Mrs Strawn," said Bly. "It was brought to Yarborough by barge, wasn't it?"

"Yes, what of it?" Denise was daintily surprised.

"Those barges made me think of it again. Somehow, the cabinet from France seems to have been the starting point of all this business. Money changed hands because of it and then disappeared. The same evening I was accused of the theft and nearly killed at the boathouse. One day later another man, a stranger, was actually killed in the very place where I had been attacked, and then, five weeks later when his body was found, he was buried under my name. And finally the boathouse burned down. The pattern is queer because the connecting links are missing."

Denise turned to Bly with a brilliant smile. "Just why did you send the money back four years later?"

Bly returned the smile. "You forget, Mrs Strawn, I have never admitted that it was I who took the money or that it was I who returned it."

Strawn was irritated. "Why don't you admit it now? Shouldn't you tell the police? If the whole story comes out you can clear up that one point for them. And you must have taken it or you wouldn't have sent it back."

"I admit nothing."

"Why not? No one will prosecute now you've returned it."

"But people would think less well of me, wouldn't they?"

"I don't know that they would. A boy of seventeen, without family or friends or a penny of his own. A man who went straight afterward, made a success of his life, and returned the money. Lots of people have darker secrets than that!"

"Have they?" Bly seemed to be turning this over in

his mind. Again he looked at Denise. "How valuable is that cabinet today?"

"It can't be valued in money. There are only a few examples of sixteenth century inlay left in the world to-day. The most famous, one quite like this, is in a museum in New York."

"How did your father acquire such a museum piece?"

"That's an amusing story. He bought it for two hundred francs from a peasant in Brittany who was using it as a rabbit hutch. The peasant didn't know the value of inlay. My father did."

"So there you are."

It was Nan's voice. She was standing just inside the French window, hatless, her hair wind-blown.

"Nan!" Bly took a step toward her.

"If you hadn't come back, if you had let the dead past bury its dead, he might be alive." There was no reproach in her voice. It was dull and flat, tearless as her eyes.

"My dear child!" Denise rose and put an arm around the girl's shoulders. "Let me ring for fresh coffee. I'm sure you haven't had breakfast."

Listlessly Nan moved away from the embrace. "I don't want coffee or anything else." She turned to Bly again. "Why did you play that trick on the police?"

"Trick?"

"That telephone call. Saying Frank Bly and then cutting the connection."

"It was a slip of the tongue."

"A policeman answered the telephone. Gesell questioned Mother again. Mostly about you. She had to tell him that Stephen Longworth was Frank Bly. Gesell was annoyed. Mother had to tell him everything then. He thinks either you or Mother killed Father."

Strawn rose heavily. "I'd better see Gesell and tell

him all the things I didn't tell him last night. I can't stand by and see an innocent man suspected."

Denise looked quizzical. "What you really mean, dear, is that you're afraid he'll suspect you *if* he finds out all these things before you volunteer them!"

When he had gone, she arched one silky, black brow. "Poor Dick! He thinks realism is cynicism. He lives in a world of illusion."

"Nan!" There was an urgent note in Bly's voice. "Do you think I killed your father?"

Time was suspended as she looked into his eyes. At last she whispered, "No."

"Then let me take you home."

He turned the car into a narrow track through the woods. He spoke quietly: "Nan, when are you going to tell me the truth?"

"About what?" She avoided his eyes.

He stopped the car and shut off the engine. He turned to look at her. "The money. You took it, didn't you?"

She kept her profile toward him, eyes veiled by thick, golden lashes. "How did you know?"

"It came to me in a flash of realization four years after I left Yarborough. When the money was stolen the others were all out on the river except you and me. That's why they were so sure I had taken it. But I hadn't, and there wasn't anybody else but you. They never even thought of you, did they?"

"No." Still, she avoided his eyes. "It was you who sent the money anonymously?"

"Yes.

"A few thousand didn't mean much to me at the time. I was making plenty and I was out in the Persian hinterland where there were few ways to spend it. Though

I hadn't taken the money I began to feel like an accessory, because I knew who had taken it and I wasn't telling. I couldn't write and tell them. That wouldn't have been fair to you. You were only nine then. I got to thinking about you and how you might have been struggling under a burden of secret guilt for the last four years, so I yielded to an impulse. I directed my New York bank to send the money in cash, anonymously to Strawn.

"I assumed he would tell your parents and you would hear about it and feel better. In the back of my mind there was a shadowy idea of letting four people in Yarborough know that Frank Bly had not forgotten them, including the one who had tried to kill him. I wanted that one to know that some day Frank Bly might come back. But I had to do it anonymously so no one would ask me who had taken the money."

"You must have been quite fond of me when I was a child?"

"I was. Now tell me why you took the money."

"It's so silly. I'm ashamed to tell you. Try to think back to your own childhood and remember what the mind of a child is like. Do you recall that you were going to make me a doll's house out of the packing-case the cabinet came in? And we were saving violet-and-silver wrapping paper from Mother's boxes of candied violets for the dollhouse wallpaper? That last afternoon you took the packing-case down to the boathouse and started work on it. And you said we needed just one more candy-box wrapper.

"I wandered into the locker-room and saw what looked like a new box of candied violets. I took it for the sake of the wrapping paper. I was going to give the candy box to Mother. I knew she wouldn't mind, because I had done that before. I had just got the package up to my room at the house when Agatha called me to my five o'clock supper. I ran downstairs, leaving it there, unopened, and then forgot all about it until that night.

"My room was over Father's study. I heard voices, yours and his and Dick's, so loud they woke me up. I crept downstairs barefoot in pajamas and listened at the door. I heard them accuse you of stealing money. Dick said it was wrapped in colored paper from a candy box and he'd left it in the locker-room. Then I knew what I had taken.

"Frank, I was scared to death. I could tell by your voice that you were frightened. And I was only five. I heard the word *police*. I thought that they would send me to prison for years. I slipped upstairs and unwrapped the package to make sure the money was inside. It was, and I remembered I had seen a fire when I passed the living-room door. I went downstairs again. Luck was with me. You were just crossing the lawn toward the boathouse, but Father was still in the study and Dick was in the dining-room. The living-room was empty. I put the money and the wrapping paper on the fire and waited until they were burned to ashes. Then I went back upstairs to bed and put my head under the covers and cried, without making any noise."

"And you never told your parents?"

"Never. There are so many things children cannot tell their parents. Next day it was pretty bad when I heard you had disappeared. Later, when I found that dead body face down in the water, my guilt made me sure that it was your body—that you had killed yourself because of what I had done to you. For my burning the money and keeping silent I had made it impossible for you to prove that you were not a thief."

"Poor little Nan!" He laid his hand over hers. "No wonder you were ill!"

"You forgive me? Now?"

"I would forgive you anything, anytime." He took her in his arms. "Now, Nan, at last I know why I came back to Yarborough."

Slowly tears welled under the tawny lashes. "Frank, I'm afraid. Who did it? Who killed Father? Of course I know it wasn't Mother or you, but who?"

He frowned, looking down the empty road, "It must be the same person who attacked me and killed that other man. When a murderer kills he does it to produce a definite result by eliminating the man he kills. For all practical purposes I was dead for at least four years, until I sent the money to Strawn suggesting that Frank Bly might be alive. What happened in those four years, when the murderer believed I was dead and eliminated forever, that would not have happened if I'd been here alive and active?"

"Mother and Father got a divorce. Dick and Denise got married. Mother and Father became poor. Dick and Denise became rich. I was ill; then I got better and was sent away to school and college. That's all that happened to any of us, really. Is there any one of those things that would not have happened if you had been here?"

"I don't know." Bly was still frowning thoughtfully. "It was the day the cabinet came that this began."

"You unpacked it yourself," Nan reminded him. "Was it empty or was there anything inside?"

"Only an old key." He switched on the ignition.

"Where are we going?" asked Nan.

"To your house, to take another look at that cabinet!"

The police had gone. The living-room was empty. Three tall windows framed the sky, three panels of a pure, cobalt blue. Nan crossed the room to the cabinet. Lovingly she put out a hand to touch the inlay. Wild hares peeked through the gillyflower stems. Birds flew here and there above the flowers.

Bly took the handle of hand-wrought iron and let down the drop leaf. There were two shelves inside, record albums on one, a pile of sheet music on the other. Behind the albums lay a flat parcel of old newspaper about eight inches long. Bly opened it. He was holding a great iron key, its bow star-shaped, its bit wrought in a pattern of lilies and roses. The paper fluttered to the floor, a newspaper fragment, old, brown, crumbling at the edges.

Nan picked it up. "French, dated May 2, 1926. I suppose the packers just used the newspapers of the day. What a pity they weren't saved. Think what interesting reading they'd make today!"

"I left them in the boathouse," said Bly. "They were probably burned when it caught fire."

Nan was still musing as she looked down at the fragment in her hand. "French columnists don't have to worry about libel laws."

"Not laws like ours. What have you there?"

"The end of a column signed Pierre Bourrelle. All about a murder trial. Some woman was acquitted of murdering her husband. He says the evidence proved her guilty. He blames the verdict on the traditional gallantry of a French jury."

Bly nodded. "They acquit most women murderers, the guilty along with the innocent. Who was this one?"

"There's no name here." Nan turned the fragment over. "Oh, what luck! Here's the beginning of the column on the other side. This murderer's name was—" Suddenly her voice blanched, the way color drains from a face in shock. "—Denise de Beaupré."

"Did I hear my own name?"

Nan started as if she were the one trapped and guilty.

Denise stood just inside the farthest of the French windows, still as a woman painted on a backdrop of cobalt. Her smile was brightly enameled with fuchsia lipstick. Her dress was black, with emeralds at one wrist, and a dark fur cape hanging from her shoulders. The leather bag in one hand was emerald green. "I had a suspicion you two were up to something when you left me. That's why I came here."

Still smiling, she descended three shallow steps into the room.

Bly rose and stepped between the two women. Nan was no actress. Her face was almost as white as her blouse. Bly achieved a smile for Denise. "We were admiring the cabinet. I wonder you had the heart to part with it."

"In those days five thousand dollars meant a great deal to me." Denise was crossing the room, tottering on her tiny, high-heeled shoes. She subsided prettily into the wing chair beside the hearth.

Bly followed and stood before her, resting one hand on the mantelshelf as he had last night after dinner. "I suppose that was why you took the risk of having the cabinet brought to this country."

"Risk? It was insured."

"I wasn't thinking of insurable risk. It wasn't the inlaid cabinet itself that started this chain of events fifteen years ago. It was the old newspapers the cabinet was packed in—French newspapers of the month and year when you were tried for murder in Paris. Evidently you didn't know the packers had used them for wrapping until that morning when the packing-case arrived and I broke it open on the terrace. I remember your gasp—like a cry of pain. I thought you were afraid I would hurt the cabinet with my penknife when I slashed the twine that held the padding in place.

"Your one hope was to get rid of those newspapers

before anyone who understood French looked at them. But you had no chance to do so. When I was alone on the terrace with Strawn I told him I could read French, and he said I could take the newspapers down to the boathouse. He must have mentioned that to you later when you were all out on the river in the cruiser. So you had to kill me and you had to burn down the boathouse where those papers were stored.

"With those papers burned unread there wasn't one chance in a thousand that anyone in a small American town like Yarborough would ever hear of anything that had happened so long ago and far away in an obscure murder trial in Paris in 1926. Ironically, you didn't know about the old key also wrapped in a newspaper. You were at the far end of the room when Vanbrugh and Tessie discovered that, and it's been hidden behind this pile of record albums ever since.

"Today I learned that the man buried under my name spoke as he lay dying. He said, *'I have pain at the head. . . . Your wife she is vicious, a murderess . . .'* The words are English, but the sentence structure is French. When I heard that, I knew he must have been French, and that you were the one most likely to have killed him. Vanbrugh, who heard him, thought the words, 'your wife,' referred to Tessie. But last night you said that your friends thought you were already married to Strawn when you sent for the cabinet. This Frenchman prowling around the Vanbrugh place where you were a guest saw and recognized you. The only man living in the same house was Vanbrugh. Believing you were married, the Frenchman mistook Vanbrugh for your husband, Strawn, whom he had never seen. 'Your wife' meant Denise de Beaupré, not Tessie Vanbrugh.

"Last night you claimed that you were alone in this

living-room at the time I was attacked. Now I know you lied. The living-room was empty then. Nan, a child of five, came in and found it empty at the very time you said you were here. Fortunately for her, she never mentioned that to anyone but me.

"Vanbrugh was less fortunate. He could see the path to the boathouse from his study window. Fifteen years ago he watched me go down that path. He must have seen you follow me, but your presence did not rouse his suspicion until last night, when he learned for the first time of the murderous attack on me just afterward. He didn't give you away when we were all together last night. He was too good a friend for that. He would wait for a private explanation. So you came back to his house a second time last night while your husband was drinking alone in his own living-room. You met Vanbrugh on the terrace, doubtless by prearrangement, and you induced him to go down to the pier with you, pretending you could only explain what had happened on the site of the attack. Once there safely away from the house, you killed him.

"All along I have realized that something must have happened to the Vanbrughs or Strawn or you in the last fifteen years that would not have happened if I had not been eliminated. Now I see what that thing was. Your marriage to Strawn. You were beautiful and I am sure that Strawn loved you. No ordinary obstacle would have kept him from marrying you—poverty, illness, scandal. But would he have married a woman who had murdered her first husband? A woman who was free only because she had been acquitted by an obviously susceptible jury? I think not. And evidently you thought the same way.

"Now, tell me one more thing. Who was the Frenchman, the stranger?"

Her face was still as a mask of white plaster with fuchsia-painted lips. Those lips scarcely moved as she whispered, "Pierre Bourrelle. A journalist. A friend of my husband's who hated me. He came here all the way from France when he heard of my second marriage. He prowled about looking for evidence against me. He had the presumption to say that my second husband should be warned. I was not married to Dick yet. I loved him. Of course I killed Bourrelle.

"I made two dreadful mistakes: Letting my father's lawyer know I was going to marry Dick when I wrote asking for the cabinet. But I was so proud of that! And then the other was using my true name in America, Denise de Beaupré. That was how Bourrelle traced me. But what could I do? The name was on my passport. I might want to leave the country at any time and I would have to have a passport. And I soon found that no one in America had ever heard of Denise de Beaupré for good or evil."

Bly felt a hard grip on his arm. Nan was standing close behind him. Anger blazed in her tawny eyes as she looked at Denise, sunk in self-pity. Nan spoke:

"I can understand your killing Bourrelle. He was like a blackmailer, only worse, because he was doing it for malice, not just for money. But I cannot understand your killing my father, your oldest and best friend here, just to save your own skin. And I can't understand your trying to kill Frank. Suppose he *had* read those newspapers? He would have seen you were acquitted."

"And he would also have seen in every editorial column that my acquittal meant nothing!" Fiercely Denise turned to Bly. "Would you have kept silent? After learning that I was going to marry Dick Strawn? Knowing that he didn't know the truth?"

"Even now you have no case against me," she went on more calmly. "I was acquitted of the murder of my first husband. There is no conclusive evidence that I killed Bourrelle or Geoff or that I tried to kill you. All you really have now is a motive for my trying to kill you."

"Then why did you admit all these things?" gasped Nan.

Denise was looking at Bly, desperately. "You understand, don't you? It's my way of asking for mercy. I'm telling you everything so you may see my side of it. I love Dick Strawn. That's the whole story in four words."

"Mercy? For you!" Nan's scorn was savage.

Bly spoke gravely. "I don't suppose I shall say anything to the police."

"Frank!"

Bly went on as if Nan had not spoken: "But I shall give this newspaper fragment to Dick Strawn."

The red mouth in the white face twisted, pulling muscles out of shape, plowing lines from lips to chin. There was something close to madness in the bright, dry glaze of the eyes. She whispered, "I don't believe you would do *that*? Would you?"

"I must do it." Bly's face was stony. "Strawn must know the truth now."

The catch of her green leather bag snapped open. The small, flat automatic seemed to leap into her hand with a motion of its own. Nan covered her eyes with her hands, but she could not shut out the loud report that shattered the stillness. Denise took two steps on her absurdly tight, high-heeled shoes, then lurched and sprawled heavily.

Only when he knew Denise was dead did Bly turn to look at Nan. She was sobbing as he took her in his arms. "That was dangerous. And brutal."

"Yes." He looked down at the head on his shoulder. "I've been told that I take too many risks. And that I have no mercy for my enemies. But a good hater makes a good lover."

He kissed her.

THORNAPPLE
by Ruth Rendell

Born in London in 1930, Ruth Rendell published her first mystery novel, From Doon With Death, *in 1964. It was an extremely clever debut that introduced her series detective, Chief Inspector Wexford. A wealth of novels and short stories followed causing Rendell to become one of the most honored of modern mystery writers. She is equally adept at the formal sleuthings of Wexford and the novels and stories of intense psychological suspense which are growing more numerous of late. Thus far her thirty novels and four collections of short stories have won her three Edgars from the Mystery Writers of America (one for best novel and two for best short story), two Gold Daggers and a Silver Dagger from the Crime Writers Association, and a National Book Award from the British Arts Council.*

This story, of crime and suspense rather than detection, shows Ruth Rendell at her best. James Alexander Fyfield, a boy who collects poisons, is a memorable character, like so many of Rendell's. It's a story you won't soon forget.

"Thornapple" was first published in the February 25, 1981, issue of Ellery Queen's Mystery Magazine *under the title "The Boy Who Collected Poisons." Under its present title it was collected in* The Fever Tree and Other Stories *(1982).*

The plant, which was growing up against the wall between the gooseberry bushes, stood about two feet high and had pointed, jaggedly toothed, oval leaves of a rich dark green. It bore, at the same time, a flower and a fruit. The trumpet-shaped flower had a fine, delicate texture and was of the purest white, while the green fruit, which rather resembled a chestnut though it was of a darker colour, had spines growing all over it that had a rather threatening or warning look.

According to *Indigenous British Flora,* which James held in his hand, the thornapple or Jimson's Weed or *datura stramonium* also had an unpleasant smell, but he did not find it so. What the book did not say was that *datura* was highly poisonous. James already knew that, for although this was the plant's first appearance in the Fyfields' garden, he had seen it in other parts of the village during the previous summer. And then he had only had to look at it for some adult to come rushing up and warn him of its dangers, as if he were likely at his age to eat a spiky object that looked more like a sea urchin than a seed head. Adults had not only warned him and the other children, but had fallen upon the unfortunate *datura* and tugged it out of the ground with exclamations of triumph as of a dangerous job well done.

James had discovered three specimens in the garden. The thornapple had a way of springing up in unexpected places and the book described it as "a casual in cultivated ground". His father would not behave in the way of those village people but he would certainly have it out as soon as he spotted it. James found this understandable. But it meant that if he was going to prepare an infusion or brew of *datura* he had better get on with it. He went back thoughtfully into the house, taking no notice of his sister Rosamund who was sitting at the kitchen table reading a foreign tourists' guide to London, and returned the book to his own room.

James's room was full of interesting things. A real glory-hole, his mother called it. He was a collector and an experimenter, was James, with an enquiring, analytical mind and more than his fair share of curiosity. He had a fish tank, its air pump bubbling away, a glass box containing hawk moth caterpillars, and mice in a cage. On the walls were crustacean charts and life cycle of the frog charts and a map of the heavens. There were several hundred books, shells and dried grasses, a snakeskin and a pair of antlers (both naturally shed) and on the top shelf of the bookcase his bottles of poison. James replaced the wild flower book and, climbing on to a stool, studied these bottles with some satisfaction.

He had prepared their contents himself by boiling leaves, flowers and berries and straining off the resulting liquor. This had mostly turned out to be a dark greenish brown or else a purplish red, which rather disappointed James who had hoped for bright green or saffron yellow, these colours being more readily associated with the sinister or the evil. The bottles were labelled *conium maculatum* and *hyoscyamus niger* rather than with their common English names, for James's mother, when she came in to dust the glory-hole, would know what hemlock and henbane were. Only the one containing his prize solution, that deadly nightshade, was left unlabelled. There would be no concealing, even from those ignorant of Latin, the significance of *atropa belladonna*.

Not that James had the least intention of putting these poisons of his to use. Nothing could have been further from his mind. Indeed, they stood up there on the high shelf precisely to be out of harm's way and, even so, whenever a small child visited the house, he took care to keep his bedroom door locked. He had made the poisons from the pure, scientific motive of *seeing if it could be done*. With caution and in a similar spirit of detachment, he had gone so far as to taste, first a few drops and then half a teaspoonful of the henbane. The result had been to make him very sick and give him painful stomach cramps which necessitated sending for the doctor who diagnosed gastritis. But James had been satisfied. It worked.

In preparing his poisons, he had had to maintain a close secrecy. That is, he made sure his mother was out of the house and Rosamund too. Rosamund would not have been interested, for one plant was much the same as another to her, she shrieked when she saw the hawk moth caterpillars and her pre-eminent wish was to go and live in London. But she was not above tale-bearing. And although neither of his parents would have been cross or have punished him or peremptorily have destroyed his preparations, for they were reasonable, level-headed people, they would certainly have prevailed upon him to throw the bottles away and have lectured him and appealed to his better nature and his common sense. So if he was going to add to his collection with a potion of *datura,* it might be wise to select Wednesday afternoon when his mother was at the meeting of the Women's Institute, and then commandeer the kitchen, the oven, a saucepan and a sieve.

His mind made up, James returned to the garden with a brown paper bag into which he dropped five specimens of thornapple fruits, all he could find, and for good measure two flowers and some leaves as well. He was sealing up the top of the bag with a strip of Scotch tape when Rosamund came up the path.

"I suppose you've forgotten we've got to take those raspberries to Aunt Julie?"

James had. But since the only thing he wanted to do at that moment was boil up the contents of the bag, and that he could not do till Wednesday, he gave Rosamund his absent-minded professor look, shrugged his shoulders and said it was impossible for *him* to forget anything *she* was capable of remembering.

"I'm going to put this upstairs," he said. "I'll catch you up."

The Fyfield family had lived for many years—centuries, some said—in the village of Great Sindon in Suffolk, occupying this cottage or that one, taking over small farmhouses, yeomen all, until in the early nineteen hundreds some of them had climbed up into the middle class. James's father, son of a schoolmaster, himself taught at the University of Essex at Wivenhoe, some twenty miles distant. James was already tipped for Oxford. But they were very much of the village too, were the Fyfields of Ewes Hall Farm, with ancestors lying in the churchyard and ancestors remembered on the war memorial on the village green.

The only other Fyfield at present living in Great Sindon was Aunt Julie who wasn't really an aunt but a connection by marriage, her husband having been a second cousin twice removed or something of that sort. James couldn't recall that he had ever been particularly nice to her or specially polite (as Rosamund was) but for all that Aunt Julie seemed to prefer him over pretty well everyone else. With the exception, perhaps, of Mirabel. And because she preferred him she expected him to pay her visits. Once a week these visits would have taken place if Aunt Julie had had her way, but James was not prepared to fall in with that and his parents had not encouraged it.

"I shouldn't like anyone to think James was after her money," his mother had said.

"Everyone knows that's to go to Mirabel," said his father.

"All the more reason. I should hate to have it said James was after Mirabel's rightful inheritance."

Rosamund was unashamedly after it or part of it, though that seemed to have occurred to no one. She had told James so. A few thousand from Aunt Julie would help enormously in her ambition to buy herself a flat in London, for which she had been saving up since she was seven. But flats were going up in price all the time (she faithfully read the estate agents' pages in the *Observer*), her £28.50 would go nowhere, and without a windfall her situation looked hopeless. She was very single-minded, was Rosamund, and she had a lot of determination. James supposed she had picked the raspberries herself and that her "we've got to take them" had its origins in her own wishes and was in no way a directive from their mother. But he didn't much mind going. There was a mulberry tree in Aunt Julie's garden and he would be glad of a chance to examine it. He was thinking of keeping silkworms.

It was a warm sultry day in high summer, a day of languid air and half-veiled sun, of bumble bees heavily laden and roses blown but still scented. The woods hung on the hillsides like blue smoky shadows, and the fields where they were beginning to cut the wheat were the same colour as Rosamund's hair. Very long and straight was the village street of Great Sindon, as is often the case in Suffolk. Aunt Julie lived at the very end of it in a plain, solidly built, grey brick, double-fronted house with a shallow slate roof and two tall chimneys. It would never, in the middle of the nineteenth century when it had been built, have been designated a "gentleman's house", for there were only four bedrooms and a single kitchen, while the ceilings were low and the stairs steep, but nowadays any gentleman might have been happy to live in it and village opinion held that it was worth a very large sum of money. Sindon Lodge stood in about two acres of land which included an apple orchard, a lily pond and a large lawn on which the mulberry tree was.

James and his sister walked along in almost total silence. They had little in common and it was hot, the air full of tiny insects that came off the harvest fields. James knew that he had only been invited to join her because if she had gone alone Aunt Julie would have wanted to know where he was and would have sulked and probably not been at all welcoming. He wondered if she knew that the basket in which she had put the raspberries, having first lined it with a white paper table napkin, was in fact of the kind that is intended for wine, being made with a loop of cane at one end to hold the neck of the bottle. She had changed, he noticed, from her jeans into her new cotton skirt, the Laura Ashley print, and had brushed her wheat-coloured hair and tied a black velvet ribbon round it. Much good it would do her, thought James, but he decided not to tell her the true function of the basket unless she did anything particular to irritate him.

But as they were passing the church Rosamund suddenly turned to face him and asked him if he knew Aunt Julie now had a lady living with her to look after her. A companion, this person was called, said Rosamund. James hadn't known—he had probably been absorbed in his own thoughts when it was discussed—and he was somewhat chagrined.

"So what?"

"So nothing. Only I expect she'll open the door to us. You didn't know, did you? It isn't true you know things I don't. I often know things you don't, I *often* do."

James did not deign to reply.

"She said that if ever she got so she *had* to have someone living with her, she'd get Mirabel to come. And Mirabel wanted to, she actually liked the idea of living in the country. But Aunt Julie didn't ask her, she got this lady instead, and I heard Mummy say Aunt Julie doesn't want Mirabel in the house any more. I don't know why. Mummy said maybe Mirabel won't get Aunt Julie's money now."

James whistled a few bars from the overture to the *Barber of Seville*. "I know why."

"Bet you don't."

"O.K., so I don't."

"Why, then?"

"You're not old enough to understand. And, incidentally, you may not know it but that thing you've got the raspberries in is a wine basket."

The front door of Sindon Lodge was opened to them by a fat woman in a cotton dress with a wrap-around overall on top of it. She seemed to know who they were and said she was Mrs Crowley but they could call her Auntie Elsie if they liked. James and Rosamund were in silent agreement that they did not like. They went down the long passage where it was rather cold even on the hottest day.

Aunt Julie was in the room with the french windows, sitting in a chair looking into the garden, the grey cat Palmerston on her lap. Her hair was exactly the same colour as Palmerston's fur and nearly as fluffy. She was a little wizened woman, very old, who always dressed in jumpers and trousers which, James thought privately, made her look a bit like a monkey. Arthritis twisted and half-crippled her, slowly growing worse, which was probably why she had engaged Mrs Crowley.

Having asked Rosamund why she had put the raspberries in a wine basket—she must be sure to take it straight back to Mummy—Aunt Julie turned her attention to James, demanding of him what he had been collecting lately, how were the hawk moth caterpillars and what sort of a school report had he had at the end of the summer term? A further ten minutes of this made James, though not unusually tender-hearted towards his sister, actually feel sorry for Rosamund, so he brought himself to tell Aunt Julie that she had passed her piano exam with distinction and, if he might be excused, he would like to go out and look at the mulberry tree.

The garden had a neglected look and in the orchard

tiny apples, fallen during the "June drop", lay rotting in the long grass. There were no fish in the pond and had not been for years. The mulberry tree was loaded with sticky-looking squashy red fruit, but James supposed that silkworms fed only on the leaves. Would he be allowed to help himself to mulberry leaves? Deciding that he had a lot to learn about the rearing of silkworms, he walked slowly round the tree, remembering now that it was Mirabel who had first identified the tree for him and had said how wonderful she thought it would be to make one's own silk.

It seemed to him rather dreadful that just because Mirabel had had a baby she might be deprived of all this. For "all this", the house, the gardens, the vaguely huge sum of money which Uncle Walter had made out of building houses and had left to his widow, was surely essential to poor Mirabel who made very little as a freelance designer and must have counted on it.

Had he been alone, he might have raised the subject with Aunt Julie who would take almost anything from him even though she called him an *enfant terrible*. She sometimes said he could twist her round his little finger, which augured well for getting the mulberry leaves. But he wasn't going to talk about Mirabel in front of Rosamund. Instead, he mentioned it tentatively to his mother immediately Rosamund, protesting, had been sent to bed.

"Well, darling, Mirabel did go and have a baby without being married. And when Aunt Julie was young that was a terrible thing to do. We can't imagine, things have changed so much. But Aunt Julie has very strict ideas and she must think of Mirabel as a bad woman."

"I see," said James, who didn't quite. "And when she dies Mirabel won't be in her will, is that right?"

"I don't think we ought to talk about things like that."

"Certainly we shouldn't," said James's father.

"No, but I want to know. You're always saying people shouldn't keep things secret from children. Has Aunt Julie made a new will, cutting Mirabel out?"

"She hasn't made a will at all, that's the trouble. According to the law, a great niece doesn't automatically inherit if a person dies intestate—er, that is, dies. . . ."

"I know what intestate means," said James.

"So I suppose Mirabel thought she could get her to make a will. It doesn't sound very nice put like that but, really, why shouldn't poor Mirabel have it? If she doesn't, I don't believe there's anyone else near enough and it will just go to the state."

"Shall we change the subject now?" said James's father.

"Yes, all right," said James. "Will you be going to the Women's Institute the same as usual on Wednesday?"

"Of course I will, darling. Why on earth do you ask?"

"I just wondered," said James.

James's father was on holiday while the university was down and on the following day he went out into the fruit garden with a basket and his weeder and uprooted the thornapple plant that was growing between the gooseberry bushes. James, sitting in his bedroom, reading *The Natural History of Selborne,* watched him from the window. His father put the thornapple on the compost heap and went hunting for its fellows, all of which he found in the space of five minutes. James sighed but took this destruction philosophically. He had enough in the brown paper bag for his needs.

As it happened, he had the house to himself for the making of his newest brew. His father announced at lunch that he would be taking the car into Bury

St Edmunds that afternoon and both children could come with him if they wanted to. Rosamund did. Bury, though not London, was at any rate a sizeable town with plenty of what she liked, shops and restaurants and cinemas and crowds. Once alone, James chose an enamel saucepan of the kind which looked as if all traces of *datura* could easily be removed from it afterwards, put into it about a pint of water and set this to boil. Meanwhile, he cut up the green spiny fruits to reveal the black seeds they contained. When the water boiled he dropped in the fruit pieces and the seeds and leaves and flowers and kept it all simmering for half an hour, occasionally stirring the mixture with a skewer. Very much as he had expected, the bright green colour hadn't been maintained, but the solid matter and the liquid had all turned a dark khaki brown. James didn't dare use a sieve to strain it in case he couldn't get it clean again, so he pressed all the liquor out with his hands until nothing remained but some soggy pulp.

This he got rid of down the waste disposal unit. He poured the liquid, reduced now to not much more than half a pint, into the medicine bottle he had ready for it, screwed on the cap and labelled it: *datura stramonium*. The pan he scoured thoroughly but a few days later, when he saw that his mother had used it for boiling the peas they were about to eat with their fish for supper, he half-expected the whole family to have griping pains and even tetanic convulsions. But nothing happened and no one suffered any ill effects.

By the time the new school term started James had produced a substance he hoped might be muscarine from boiling up the fly agaric fungus and some rather doubtful cyanide from apricot kernels. There were now ten bottles of poison on the top shelf of his bookcase. But no one was in the least danger from them, and even when the

Fyfield household was increased by two members there was no need for James to keep his bedroom door locked, for Mirabel's little boy was only six months old and naturally as yet unable to walk.

Mirabel's arrival had been entirely impulsive. A ridiculous way to behave, James's father said. The lease of her flat in Kensington was running out and instead of taking steps to find herself somewhere else to live, she had waited until the lease was within a week of expiry and had turned up in Great Sindon to throw herself on the mercy of Aunt Julie. She came by taxi from Ipswich station, lugging a suitcase and carrying the infant Oliver.

Mrs Crowley had opened the door to her and Mirabel had never got as far as seeing Aunt Julie. A message was brought back to say she was not welcome at Sindon Lodge as her aunt thought she had made clear enough by telephone and letter. Mirabel, who had believed that Aunt Julie would soften at the sight of her, had a choice between going back to London, finding a hotel in Ipswich or taking refuge with the Fyfields. She told the taxi to take her to Ewes Hall Farm.

"How could I turn her away?" James heard his mother say. Mirabel was upstairs putting Oliver to bed. "There she was on the doorstep with that great heavy case and the baby screaming his head off, poor mite. And she's such a little scrap of a thing."

James's father had been gloomy ever since he got home. "Mirabel is exactly the sort of person who would come for the weekend and stay ten years."

"No one would stay here for ten years if they could live in London," said Rosamund.

In the event, Mirabel didn't stay ten years, though she was still there after ten weeks. And on almost every day of those ten weeks she tried in vain to get her foot in the door of Sindon Lodge. Whoever happened to be

in the living room of Ewes Hall Farm in the evening—
and in the depths of winter that was usually everyone—
was daily regaled with Mirabel's grievances against life
and with denunciations of the people who had injured
her, notably Oliver's father and Aunt Julie. James's mother
sometimes said that it was sad for Oliver having to grow
up without a father, but since Mirabel never mentioned
him without saying how selfish he was, the most immature, heartless, mean, lazy and cruel man in London,
James thought Oliver would be better off without him.
As for Aunt Julie, she must be senile, Mirabel said, she
must have lost her wits.

"Can you imagine anyone taking such an attitude,
Elizabeth, in this day and age? She literally will not have
me in the house because I've got Oliver and I wasn't
married to Francis. Thank God I wasn't, that's all I can
say. But wouldn't you think that sort of thing went out
with the dark ages?"

"She'll come round in time," said James's mother.

"Yes, but how much time? I mean, she hasn't got
that much, has she? And here am I taking shameful advantage of your hospitality. You don't know how guilty
it makes me, only I literally have nowhere else to go.
And I simply cannot afford to take another flat like the
last, frankly, I couldn't raise the cash. I haven't been getting the contracts like I used to before Oliver was born
and of course I've never had a penny from that unspeak-
able, selfish, pig of a man."

James's mother and father would become very bored
with all this but they could hardly walk out of the room.
James and Rosamund could, though after a time Mirabel
took to following James up to the glory-hole where she
would sit on his bed and continue her long, detailed,
repetitive complaints just as if he were her own
contemporary.

It was a little disconcerting at first, though he got used to it. Mirabel was about thirty but to him and his sister she seemed the same age as their parents, middle-aged, old, much as anyone did who was over, say, twenty-two. And till he got accustomed to her manner he hardly knew what to make of the way she gazed intensely into his eyes or suddenly clutched him by the arm. She described herself (frequently) as passionate, nervous and highly strung.

She was a small woman and James was already taller than she. She had a small, rather pinched face with large prominent dark eyes and she wore her long hair hanging loose like Rosamund's. The Fyfields were big-boned, fair-headed people with ruddy skins but Mirabel was dark and very thin and her wrists and hands and ankles and feet were very slender and narrow. There was, of course, no blood relationship, Mirabel being Aunt Julie's own sister's granddaughter.

Mirabel was not her baptismal name. She had been christened Brenda Margaret but it had to be admitted that the name she had chosen for herself suited her better, suited her feyness, her intense smiles and brooding sadnesses, and the clinging clothes she wore, the muslins and the trailing shawls. She always wore a cloak or a cape to go into the village and James's mother said she couldn't remember Mirabel ever having possessed a coat.

James had always had rather a sneaking liking for her, he hadn't known why. But now that he was older and saw her daily, he understood something he had not known before. He liked Mirabel, he couldn't help himself, because she seemed to like him so much and because she flattered him. It was funny, he could listen to her flattery and distinguish it for what it was, but this knowledge did not detract a particle from the pleasure he felt in hearing it.

"You're absolutely brilliant for your age, aren't you, James?" Mirabel would say. "I suppose you'll be a professor one day. You'll probably win the Nobel prize."

She asked him to teach her things: how to apply Pythagoras' Theorem, how to convert Fahrenheit temperatures into Celsius, ounces into grammes, how to change the plug on her hair dryer.

"I'd like to think Oliver might have half your brains, James, and then I'd be quite content. Francis is clever, mind you, though he's so immature and lazy with it. I literally think *you're* more mature than he is."

Aunt Julie must have known for a long time that Mirabel was staying with the Fyfields, for nothing of that kind could be concealed in a village of the size of Great Sindon, but it was December before she mentioned the matter to James. They were sitting in front of the fire in the front sitting room at Sindon Lodge, eating crumpets toasted by Mrs Crowley and drinking Earl Grey tea, while Palmerston stretched out on the hearth rug. Outside a thin rain was driving against the window panes.

"I hope Elizabeth knows what she's doing, that's all. If you're not careful you'll all be stuck with that girl for life."

James said nothing.

"Of course you don't understand the ins and outs of it at your age, but in my opinion your parents should have thought twice before they let her come into their home and bring her illegitimate child with her." Aunt Julie looked at him darkly and perhaps spitefully. "That could have a very bad effect on Rosamund, you know. Rosamund will think immoral behaviour is quite all right when she sees people like Mirabel getting rewarded for it."

"She's not exactly *rewarded*," said James, starting on the tea cakes and the greengage jam. "We don't give her anything but her food and she has to sleep in the same room as Oliver." This seemed to him by far the worst aspect of Mirabel's situation.

Aunt Julie made no reply. After a while she said, looking into the fire, "How d'you think you'd feel if you knew people only came to see you for the sake of getting your money? That's all Madam Mirabel wants. She doesn't care for me, she couldn't care less. She comes here sweet talking to Mrs Crowley because she thinks once she's in here I'll take her back and make a will leaving everything I've got to her and that illegitimate child of hers. How d'you think you'd like it? Maybe you'll come to it yourself one day, your grandchildren sucking up to you for what they can get."

"You don't *know* people come for that," said James awkwardly, thinking of Rosamund.

Aunt Julie made a sound of disgust. "Aaah!" She struck out with her arthritic hand as if pushing something away. "I'm not green, am I? I'm not daft. I'd despise myself, I can tell you, if I pretended it wasn't as plain as the nose on my face what you all come for."

The fire crackled and Palmerston twitched in his sleep.

"Well, I don't," said James.

"Don't you now, Mr Pure-and-holy?"

James grinned. "There's a way you could find out. You could make a will and leave your money to other people and tell me I wasn't getting any—and then see if I'd still come."

"I could, could I? You're so sharp, James Fyfield, you'll cut yourself badly one of these fine days."

Her prophecy had a curious fulfilment that same evening. James, groping about on the top shelf of his bookcase, knocked over the bottle of muscarine and cut his hand on the broken glass. It wasn't much of a cut but the stuff that had been inside the bottle got onto it and gave him a very uncomfortable and anxious hour. Nothing happened, his arm didn't swell up or go black or anything of that sort, but it made him think seriously about the other nine bottles remaining. Wasn't it rather silly to keep them? That particular interest of his, no longer compelling, he was beginning to see as childish. Besides, with Oliver in the house, Oliver who was crawling now and would soon walk, to keep the poisons might be more than dangerous, it might be positively criminal.

His mind made up, he took the bottles down without further vacillation and one by one poured their contents away down his bedroom washbasin. Some of them smelt dreadful. The henbane smelt like the inside of his mouse cage when he hadn't cleaned it out for a day.

He poured them all away with one exception. He couldn't quite bring himself to part with the *datura*. It had always been his pride, better even than the nightshade. Sometimes he had sat there at his desk, doing his homework, and glanced up at the *datura* bottle and wondered what people would think if they had known he had the means in his bedroom to dispose of (probably) half the village. He looked at it now, recalling how he had picked the green spiny thornapples in the nick of time before his father had uprooted all the beautiful and sinister plants—he looked at it and replaced it on the top shelf. Then he sat down at the desk and did his Latin unseen.

Mirabel was still with them at Christmas. On Christmas Eve she carried up to Sindon Lodge the pale blue jumper, wrapped in holly-patterned paper, the two-pound box of chocolates and the poinsettia in a golden pot she had bought for Aunt Julie. And she took Rosamund with her. Rosamund wore her new scarlet coat with the white fur which was a Christmas present in advance, and the scarf with Buckingham Palace and the Tower of London printed on it which was another, and Mirabel wore her dark blue cloak and her angora hat and very high-heeled grey suede boots that skidded dangerously about on the ice. Oliver was left behind in the care of James's mother.

But if Mirabel had thought that the presence of Rosamund would provide her with an entrée to the house she was mistaken. Mrs Crowley, with a sorrowful expression, brought back the message that Aunt Julie could see no one. She had one of her gastric attacks, she was feeling very unwell, and she never accepted presents when she had nothing to give in return. Mirabel read a great deal, perhaps more than had been intended, into this valedictory shot.

"She means she'll never have anything to give me," she said, sitting on James's bed. "She means she's made up her mind not to leave me anything."

It was a bit—James sought for the word and found it—a bit *degrading* to keep hanging on like this for the sake of money you hadn't earned and had no real right to. But he knew better than to say something so unkind and moralistic. He suggested tentatively that Mirabel might feel happier if she went back to her designing of textiles and forgot about Aunt Julie and her will. She turned on him in anger.

"What do you know about it? You're only a child. You don't know what I've suffered with that selfish brute of a man. I was left all alone to have my baby, I might have been literally destitute for all he cared, left to bring Oliver up on my own and without a roof over my head. How can I work? What am I supposed to do with Oliver? Oh, it's so unfair. Why shouldn't I get her money? It's not as if I was depriving anyone else, it's not as if she'd left it to someone and I was trying to get her to change anything. If I don't get it, it'll just go to the government."

Mirabel was actually crying now. She wiped her eyes

and sniffed. "I'm sorry, James, I shouldn't take it out on you. I think I'm just getting to the end of my tether."

James's father had used those very words earlier in the day. He was getting to the end of his tether as far as Mirabel was concerned. Once get Christmas over and then, if James's mother wouldn't tell her she had outstayed her welcome, he would. Let her make things up with that chap of hers, Oliver's father, or get rooms somewhere or move in with one of those arty London friends. She wasn't even a relation, he didn't even like her, and she had now been with them for nearly three months.

"I know I can't go on staying here," said Mirabel to James when hints had been dropped, "but where am I to go?" She cast her eyes heavenwards or at least as far as the top shelf of the bookcase where they came to rest on the bottle of greenish-brown liquid labelled: *datura stramonium*.

"What on earth's that?" said Mirabel. "What's in that bottle? *Datura* whatever-it-is, I can't pronounce it. It isn't cough mixture, is it? It's such a horrible colour."

Six months before, faced with that question, James would have prevaricated or told a lie. But now he felt differently about those experiments of his, and he also had an obscure feeling that if he told Mirabel the truth and she told his mother, he would be forced to do something his own will refused to compel him to and throw the bottle away.

"Poison," he said laconically.

"Poison?"

"I made it out of something called Jimson's Weed or thornapple. It's quite concentrated. I think a dose of it might be lethal."

"Were you going to kill mice with it or something?"

James would not have dreamt of killing a mouse or,

indeed, any animal. It exasperated him that Mirabel who ought to have known him quite well, who had lived in the same house with him and talked to him every day, should have cared so little about him and been so uninterested in his true nature as not to be aware of this.

"I wasn't going to kill anything with it. It was just an experiment."

Mirabel gave a hollow ringing laugh. "Would it kill me? Maybe I'll come up here while you're at school and take that bottle and—and put an end to myself. It would be a merciful release, wouldn't it? Who'd care? Not a soul. Not Francis, not Aunt Julie. They'd be glad. There's not a soul in the world who'd miss me."

"Well, Oliver would," said James.

"Yes, my darling little boy would, my Oliver would care. People don't realize I only want Aunt Julie's money for Oliver. It's not for me. I just want it to give Oliver a chance in life." Mirabel looked at James, her eyes narrowing. "Sometimes I think you're the only person on earth Auth Julie cares for. I bet if you said to her to let bygones be bygones and have me back, she'd do it. I bet she would. She'd even make a will if you suggested it. I suppose it's because you're clever. She admires intellectuals."

"If I suggested she make a will in Oliver's favour, I reckon she just might," said James. "He's her great-great-nephew, isn't he? That's quite a good idea, she might do that."

He couldn't understand why Mirabel had suddenly become so angry, and with a shout of "Oh, you're impossible, you're as bad as the rest of them!" had banged out of his room. Had she thought he was being sarcastic? It was obvious she wanted him to work on Aunt Julie for her and he wondered if she had flattered him simply towards this end. Perhaps. But however that might be, he could see a kind of justice in her claim. She had been a good niece, or great-niece, to Aunt Julie, a frequent visitor to Sindon Lodge before the episode of Francis, a faithful sender of birthday and Christmas cards, or so his mother said, and attentive when Aunt Julie had been ill. On the practical or selfish side, getting Mirabel accepted at Sindon Lodge would take her away from Ewes Hall Farm where her presence frayed his father's temper, wore his mother out, made Rosamund sulk and was beginning to bore even him. So perhaps he would mention it to Aunt Julie on his next visit. And he began to plan a sort of strategy, how he would suggest a meeting with Oliver, for all old people seemed to like babies, and follow it up with persuasive stuff about Oliver needing a home and money and things to make up for not having had a father. But, in fact, he had to do nothing. For Mrs Crowley had been offered a better job in a more lively place and had suddenly departed, leaving Aunt Julie stiff with arthritis and in the middle of a gastric attack.

She crawled to the door to let James in, a grotesque figure in red corduroy trousers and green jumper, her witch's face framed in a woolly fuzz of grey hair, and behind her, picking his way delicately, Palmerston with tail erect.

"You can tell that girl she can come up here tonight if she likes. She'd better bring her illegitimate child with her, I don't suppose your mother wants him."

Aunt Julie's bark was worse than her bite. Perhaps, indeed, she had no real bite. When James next went to Sindon Lodge some three weeks later Mirabel was settled in as if she had lived there all her life, Oliver was on the hearthrug where he had usurped Palmerston's place and Aunt Julie was wearing Mirabel's Christmas present.

She hardly spoke to James while her great-niece was in the room. She lay back in her armchair with her eyes closed and though the young woman's clothes she wore gave to her appearance a kind of bizarre mockery of youth, you could see now that she was very old. Recent upheavals had aged her. Her face looked as if it were made of screwed-up brown paper. But when Mirabel went away—was compelled to leave them by Oliver's insistent demands for his tea—Aunt Julie seemed to revive. She opened her eyes and said to James in her sharpest and most offhand tone: "This is the last time you'll come here, I daresay."

"Why do you say that?"

"I've made my will, that's why, and you're not in it."

She cocked a distorted thumb in the direction of the door. "I've left the house and the furniture and all I've got to *her*. And a bit to someone else we both know."

"Who?" said James.

"Never you mind. It's not you and it's none of your business." A curious look came into Aunt Julie's eyes. "What I've done is leave my money to two people I can't stand and who don't like me. You think that's silly, don't you? They've both sucked up to me and danced attendance on me and told a lot of lies about caring for me. Well, I'm tired, I'm sick of it. They can have what they want and I'll never again have to see that look on their faces."

"What look?"

"A kind of greedy pleading. The kind of look no one ought to have unless she's starving. You don't know what I'm talking about, do you? You're as clever as they come but you don't know what life is, not yet you don't. How could you?"

The old woman closed her eyes and there was silence in which the topmost log crumpled and sank into the heart of the fire with a rush of sparks, and Palmerston strode out from where he had taken refuge from Oliver, rubbed himself against James's legs and settled down in the red glow to wash himself. Suddenly Aunt Julie spoke.

"I didn't want you corrupted, can you understand that? I didn't want to *spoil* the only one who means more than a row of pins to me. But I don't know. . . . If I wasn't too old to stand the fuss there'd be I'd go back on what I've done and leave the house to you. Or your mother, she's a nice woman."

"She's got a house."

"Houses can be sold, you silly boy. You don't suppose Madam Mirabel will *live* here, do you?" Mirabel must have heard that, James thought, as the door opened and the tea trolley appeared, but there was no warning Aunt Julie or catching her eye. "I could make another will yet, I could bring myself to it. They say it's a woman's privilege to change her mind."

Mirabel looked across and there was very little chance of conversation after that as Oliver, when he was being fed or bathed or played with, dominated everything. He was a big child with reddish hair, not in the least like Mirabel but resembling, presumably, the mean and heartless Francis. He was now ten months old and walking, "into everything", as James's mother put it, and it was obvious that he tired Aunt Julie whose expression became quite distressed when screams followed Mirabel's refusal to give him chocolate cake. Oliver's face and hands were wiped clean and he was put on the floor where he tried to eat pieces of coal out of the scuttle and, when prevented, set about tormenting the cat. James got up to go and Aunt Julie clutched his hand as he passed her, whispering with a meaning look that virtue was its own reward.

It was not long before he discovered who the "someone else we both know" was. Aunt Julie wrote a letter to James's parents in which she told them she was leaving a sum of money to Rosamund in her will. Elizabeth Fyfield said she thought there was something very unpleasant about this letter and that it seemed to imply Rosamund had gone to Sindon Lodge with "great expectations" in mind. She was upset by it but Rosamund was jubilant. Aunt Julie had not said what the sum was but Rosamund was sure it must be thousands and thousands of pounds—half a million was the highest figure she mentioned—and with her birthday money (she was eleven on 1 March) she bought herself a book of photographs of London architecture, mostly of streets in Mayfair, Belgravia and Knightsbridge, so that she could decide which one to have her flat in.

"I think we made a great mistake in telling her," said James's father.

For Rosamund had taken to paying weekly visits to Sindon Lodge. She seldom went without some small gift for Aunt Julie, a bunch of snowdrops, a lop-sided pot she had made at school, a packet of peppermints.

"Wills can be changed, you know," said James.

"That's not why I go. Don't you dare say that! I go because I love her. You're just jealous of me and you haven't been for weeks and weeks."

It was true. He saw that Rosamund had indeed been corrupted and he, put to the test, had failed it. Yet it was not entirely disillusionment or pique which kept him from Sindon Lodge but rather a feeling that it must be wrong to manipulate people in this way. He had sometimes heard his father use the expression "playing God" and now he understood what it meant. Aunt Julie had played God with him and with Rosamund and with Mirabel too. Probably she was still doing it, hinting at will-changing each time Mirabel displeased her. So he would go there to defy this manipulating, not to be a puppet moved by her strings, he would go on the following day on his way home from school.

But although he went as he had promised himself he would, to show her his visits were disinterested and that he could stick to his word, he never saw her alive again. The doctor's car was outside when he turned in at the gate. Mirabel let him in after he had rung the bell three times, a harassed, pale Mirabel with Oliver fretful in her arms. Aunt Julie had had one of her gastric attacks, a terrible attack which had gone on all night. Mirabel had not known what to do and Aunt Julie had refused to let her call an ambulance, she wouldn't go into hospital. The doctor had come first thing and had come back later and was with her now.

She had had to scrub out the room and actually *burn* the sheets, Mirabel said darkly. The mess had been frightful, worse than James could possibly imagine, but she couldn't have let the doctor see her like that. Mirabel said she hoped the worst was over but she didn't look very hopeful, she looked unhappy. James went no further inside than the hall. He said to tell Aunt Julie he had been, please not to forget to tell her, and Mirabel said she wouldn't forget. He walked away slowly. Spring was in the air and the neat, symmetrical front garden of Sindon Lodge was full of daffodils, their bent heads bouncing in the breeze. At the gate he met Palmerston coming in with the corpse of a fieldmouse dangling from his mouth. Without dropping his booty, Palmerston rubbed himself against James's legs and James stroked him, feeling rather depressed.

Two days later Aunt Julie had another attack and it killed her. Or the stroke which she had afterwards killed her, the doctor said. The cause of death on the certificate was "food poisoning and cerebral hemorrhage", according to Mrs Hodges who had been Aunt Julie's cleaner and who met James's mother in the village. Apparently on death certificates the doctor has to put down the main cause and the contributory cause, which was another piece of information for James to add to his increasing store.

James's parents went to the funeral and of course Mirabel went too. James did not want to go and it never crossed his mind that he would be allowed to on a school day, but Rosamund cried when they stopped her. She wanted to have her red and white coat dyed black and to carry a small bouquet of violets. The provisions of the will were made known during the following days, though there was no dramatic will-reading after the funeral as there is in books.

Sindon Lodge was to go to Mirabel and so was all Aunt Julie's money with the exception of Rosamund's "bit", and bit, relatively speaking, it turned out to be. Five hundred pounds. Rosamund cried (and said she was crying because she missed Aunt Julie) and then she sulked, but when the will was proved and she actually got the money, when she was shown the cheque and it was paid into her Post Office Savings account, she cheered up and became quite sensible. She even confided to James, without tears or flounces, that it would have been a terrible responsibility to have half a million and she would always have been worried that people were only being nice to her for the sake of the money.

James got Palmerston. It was set out in the will, the cat described and mentioned by name, and bequeathed "if the animal should survive me, to James Alexander Fyfield, of Ewes Hall Farm, Great Sindon, he being the only person I know I can trust . . ."

"What an awful thing to say," said Mirabel. "Imagine, literally to have a thing like that written down. I'm sure James is welcome to it. I should certainly have had it destroyed, you can't have a cat about the place with a baby."

Palmerston had lived so long at Sindon Lodge that he was always going back there, though he kept instinctively out of Mirabel's way. For Mirabel, contrary to what Aunt Julie had predicted, did not sell the house. Nor did she make any of those changes the village had speculated about when it knew she was not going to sell. Sindon Lodge was not painted white with a blue front door or recarpeted or its kitchen fitted out with the latest gadgets. Mirabel did nothing ostentatious, made no splash and bought herself nothing but a small and modest car. For a while it seemed as if she were lying low, keeping herself to herself, mourning in fact, and James's mother said perhaps they had all misjudged her and she had really loved Aunt Julie after all.

Things began to change with the appearance on the scene of Gilbert Coleridge. Where Mirabel had met him no one seemed to know, but one day his big yellow Volvo estate car was seen outside Sindon Lodge, on the next Mirabel was seen in the passenger seat of that car, and within hours it was all over the village that she had a man friend.

"He sounds a nice, suitable sort of person," said James's mother, whose bush telegraph system was always sound. "Two or three years older than she and never had a wife—well, you never know these days, do you?—and already a partner in his firm. It would be just the thing for Oliver. He needs a man about the house."

"Let's hope she has the sense to marry this one," said James's father.

But on the whole, apart from this, the Fyfield family had lost interest in Mirabel. It had been galling for them that Mirabel, having got what she wanted with their help, first the entrée to Sindon Lodge and then the possession of it, had lost interest in *them*. She was not to be met with in the village because she scarcely walked anywhere if she could help it, and although Rosamund called several times, Mirabel was either not at home or else far too busy to ask anyone in. James overheard his mother saying that it was almost as if Mirabel felt she had said too much while she stayed with them, had shown too openly her desires, and now these were gratified, wanted as little as possible to do with those who had listened to her confidences. But it suited the Fyfields equally, for the arrival of Mirabel was always followed by trouble and by demands.

The summer was hotter and dryer than the previous one had been, and the soft fruit harvest was exceptionally good. But this year there was no Aunt Julie to cast a cynical eye over baskets of raspberries. And Jimson's Weed, *datura,* the thornapple, did not show itself in the Fyfields' garden or, apparently, in any part of Great Sindon. A "casual", as the wild plant book described it, it had gone in its mysterious way to ground or else wandered to some distant place away over the meadows.

Had it appeared, it would have exercised no fascination over James. He had his thirteenth birthday in June and he felt immeasurably, not just a year, older than he had done the previous summer. For one thing, he was about six inches taller, he had "shot up" as his mother said, and sometimes the sight in a mirror of this new towering being could almost alarm him. He looked back with incredulous wonder on the child he had been, the child who had boiled noxious fruits and leaves in a pot, who had kept white mice in a cage and caterpillars in a box. He had entered his teens and was a child no more.

Perhaps it was his height that led directly to the drama—"the absolutely worst day of my life", Rosamund called it—or it might have been Mrs Hodge's operation or even the fact, that, for once in a way, the Women's Institute met on a Tuesday rather than a Wednesday. It might have been any of those factors, though most of all it happened because Mirabel was inevitably and unchangingly Mirabel.

The inhabitants of Ewes Hall Farm knew very little about her life since they hardly ever saw her. It came as a surprise to Elizabeth Fyfield to learn how much time Mrs Hodges had been spending sitting in with Oliver or minding him in her own home. It was Mrs Hodges's daughter who told her, at the same time as she told her that her mother would be three weeks in hospital having her hysterectomy and another goodness knows how many convalescing. Mirabel would have to look elsewhere for a babysitter.

She looked, as they might have know she would, to the Fyfields.

Presenting herself on their doorstep with Oliver on one arm and a heavy shopping basket on the other, she greeted James's mother with a winsome, nervous smile. It might have been last year all over again, except that Oliver was a little boy now and no longer a baby. James, home for the long summer holidays, heard her sigh with despair and break into a long apology for having "neglected" them for so long. The fact was she was engaged to be married. Did Elizabeth know that?

"I hope you'll be very happy, Mirabel."

"Gilbert will make a marvellous father," said Mirabel. "When I compare him with that stupid, immature oaf, that Francis, it just makes me—oh, well, that's all water under the bridge now. Anyway, Elizabeth dear, what I came to ask you was, do you think James or Rosamund would do some baby-sitting for me? I'd pay them the going rate, I'd pay them what I pay Mrs Hodges. Only it's so awful for me never being able to go out with my fiancé, and actually tomorrow I'm supposed to be meeting his parents for the first time. Well, I can't take a baby of Oliver's age to a dinner party, can I?"

"Rosamund's out of the question," said James's mother, and she didn't say it very warmly. "She's only eleven. I couldn't possibly let her have sole charge of Oliver."

"But James would be all right, wouldn't he? James has got so *tall*, he looks almost a grown man. And James is terribly mature, anyway."

His mother didn't answer that. She gave one of those sighs of hers that would have effectively prevented James asking further favours. It had no effect on Mirabel.

"Just this once. After tomorrow I'll stay at home like a good little mum and in a month Mrs Hodges will be back. Just from seven till—well, eleven would be the absolute latest."

"I'll sit with Oliver," said James's mother.

Mirabel's guarantee came to nothing, however, for far from staying home with Oliver, she turned up at Ewes Hall Farm three days later, this time to leave him with them while she went shopping with Gilbert's mother. She was gone for four hours. Oliver made himself sick from eating toffees he found in Rosamund's room and he had uprooted six houseplants and stripped off their leaves before James caught him at it.

Next time, James's mother said she would put her foot down. She had already promised to sit with Oliver on the coming Saturday night. That she would do and that must be the end of it. And this resolve was strengthened by Mirabel's failure to return home until half-past one on the Sunday morning. She would have told Mirabel so in no uncertain terms, Elizabeth Fyfield told her family at breakfast, but Gilbert Coleridge had been there and she had not wanted to embarrass Mirabel in front of him.

On the Tuesday, the day to which the Women's Institute meeting had been put forward, the fine weather broke with a storm which gave place by the afternoon to steady rain. James was spending the day turning out the glory-hole. He had been told to do it often enough and he had meant to do it, but who would be indoors in a stuffy bedroom when the sun is shining and the temperature in the eighties? That Tuesday was a very suitable sort of day for disposing of books one had outgrown, tanks and cages and jars that were no longer inhabited, for throwing away collections that had become just boxfuls of rubbish, for making a clean sweep on the path to adulthood.

Taking down the books from the top shelf, he came upon an object whose existence he had almost forgotten—the bottle labelled *datura stramonium*. That was something he need not hesitate to throw away. He looked at it curiously, at the clear greenish-brown fluid it contained and which seemed in the past months to have settled and clarified. Why had he made it and what for? In another age, he thought he might have been an alchemist or a warlock, and he shook his head ruefully at the juvenile James who was no more.

So many of these books held no interest for him any longer. They were kids' stuff. He began stacking them in a "wanted" and an "unwanted" pile on the floor. Palmerston sat on the window sill and watched him, unblinking golden eyes in a big round grey face. It was a good thing, James thought, that he had ceased keeping mice before Palmerston arrived. Perhaps the mouse cage could be sold. There was someone in his class at school who kept hamsters and had been talking of getting an extra cage. It wouldn't do any harm to give him a ring.

James went down to the living room and picked up the receiver to dial Timothy Gordon's number; the phone was dead. There was no dialling tone but a silence broken by occasional faint clicks and crepitations. He would have to go up the lane to the call box and phone the engineers, but not now, later. It was pouring with rain.

As he was crossing the hall and was almost at the foot of the stairs the doorbell rang. His mother had said something about the laundry coming. James opened the door absentmindedly, prepared to nod to the man and take in the laundry box, and saw instead Mirabel.

Her car was parked on the drive and staring out of its front window was Oliver, chewing something, his fingers plastering the glass with stickiness. Mirabel was dressed up to the nines, as Aunt Julie might have said, and dressed very unsuitably for the weather in a trailing, cream-coloured pleated affair with beads round her neck and two or three chiffon scarves and pale pink stockings and cream shoes that were all straps no thicker than bits of string.

"Oh, James, you are going to be an angel, aren't you, and have Oliver for me just for the afternoon? You won't be on your own, Rosamund's in, I saw her looking out of her bedroom window. I did try to ring you but your phone's out of order."

Mirabel said this in an accusing tone as if James had purposely broken the phone himself. She was rather breathless and seemed in a hurry.

"Why can't you take him with you?" said James.

"Because, if you must know, Gilbert is going to buy me something rather special and important and I can't take a baby along."

Rosamund, under the impression that excitement was afoot, appeared at the bend in the staircase.

"It's only Mirabel," said James.

But Mirabel took the opportunity, while his attention was distracted, of rushing to the car—her finery getting much spotted with rain in the process—and seizing the sticky Oliver.

"You'd like to stay with James and Rosamund, wouldn't you, sweetheart?"

"Do we have to?" said Rosamund, coming downstairs and bestowing on Oliver a look of such unmistakeable distaste that even Mirabel flinched. Flinched but didn't give up. Indeed, she thrust Oliver at James, keeping his sticky mouth well clear of her dress, and James had no choice but to grab hold of him. Oliver immediately started to whine and hold out his arms to his mother.

"No, darling, you'll see Mummy later. Now listen, James. Mrs Hodges's daughter is going to come for him at five-thirty. That's when she finishes work. She's going to take him back to her place and I'll pick him up when I get home. And now I must fly, I'm meeting Gilbert at three."

"Well!" exploded Rosamund as the car disappeared down the drive.

"Isn't she the end? Fancy getting lumbered with *him*. I was going to do my holiday art project."

"I was going to turn my room out, but it's no good moaning. We've got him and that's that."

Oliver, once the front door was closed, had begun to whimper.

"If it wasn't raining we could go in the garden. We could take him out for a walk."

"It *is* raining," said James. "And what would we take him in? Mum's basket on wheels? The wheelbarrow? In case you hadn't noticed, dear Mirabel didn't think to bring his push chair. Come on, let's take him in the kitchen. The best thing to do with him is to feed him. He shuts up when he's eating."

In the larder James found a packet of Penguin biscuits, the chocolate-covered kind, and gave one to Oliver. Oliver sat on the floor and ate it, throwing down little bits of red and gold wrapping paper. Then he opened the saucepan cupboard and began taking out all the pots and pans and the colander and the sieves, getting chocolate all over the white Melamine finish on the door. Rosamund wiped the door and then she wiped him which made him grizzle and hit out at her with his fists. When the saucepans were spread about the floor, Oliver opened all the drawers one after the other and took out cutlery and cheese graters and potato peelers and dishcloths and dusters.

James watched him gloomily. "I read somewhere that a child of two, even a child with a very high IQ, can't ever concentrate on one thing for more than nineteen minutes at a time."

"And Oliver isn't two yet and I don't think his IQ's all that amazing."

"Exactly," said James.

"Ink," said Oliver. He kicked the knives and forks out of his way and came to James, hitting out with a wooden spoon. "Ink."

"Imagine him with ink," said Rosamund.

"He's probably not saying ink. It's something else he means only we don't know what."

"Ink, ink, ink!"

"If we lived in London we could take him for a ride on a bus. We could take him to the zoo."

"If we lived in London," said James, "we wouldn't be looking after him. I tell you what, I reckon he'd like television. Mirabel hasn't got television."

He picked Oliver up and carried him into the living room. The furniture in there was dark brown leather and would not mark so it seemed sensible to give him another

Penguin. James switched the television on. At this time of day there wasn't much on of interest to anyone, let alone someone of Oliver's age, only a serial about people working at an airport. Oliver, however, seemed entranced by the colours and the movement, so James shoved him into the back of an armchair and with a considerable feeling of relief, left him.

There was a good deal of clearing up to be done in the kitchen. Oliver had got brown stains on two table-cloths and James had to wash the knives and forks. Rosamund (typically, he thought) had vanished. Back to her art project, presumably, making some sort of collage with dried flowers. He put all the saucepans back and tidied up the drawers so that they looked much as they had done before Oliver's onslaught. Then he thought he had better go back and see how Oliver was getting on.

The living room was empty. James could soon see why. The serial had came to an end and the bright moving figures and voices and music had been replaced by an old man with glasses talking about molecular physics. Oliver wasn't anywhere downstairs. James hadn't really imagined he could climb stairs, but of course he could. He was a big strong boy who had been walking for months and months now.

He went up, calling Oliver's name. It was only a quarter past three and his mother wouldn't be back from the village hall until four-thirty at the earliest. The rain was coming down harder now, making the house rather dark. James realized for the first time that he had left his bedroom door open. He had left it open—because Palmerston was inside—when he went downstairs to phone Timothy Gordon about the mouse cage, and then Mirabel had come. It all seemed hours ago but it was only about forty minutes.

Oliver was in James's bedroom. He was sitting on

the floor with the empty *datura* bottle clutched in his hands, and from the side of the mouth trickled a dribble of brown fluid.

James had read in books about people being rooted to the spot and that was exactly what happened at that moment. He seemed anchored where he stood. He stared at Oliver. In his inside there seemed to swell up and throb a large hard lump. It was his own heart beating so heavily that it hurt.

He forced himself to move. He took the bottle away from Oliver and automatically, he didn't know why, rinsed it out at the washbasin. Oliver looked at him in silence. James went down the passage and banged on Rosamund's door.

"Could you come, please? Oliver's drunk a bottle of poison. About half a pint."

"*What?*"

She came out. She looked at him, her mouth open. He explained to her swiftly, shortly, in two sentences.

"What are we going to do?"

"Phone for an ambulance."

She stood in the bedroom doorway, watching Oliver. He had put his fists in his eyes, he was rubbing his eyes and making fretful little sounds.

"D'you think we ought to try and make him sick?"

"No. I'll go and phone. It's my fault. I must have been out of my tree making the stuff, let alone keeping it. If he dies . . . Oh, God, Roz, we can't phone! The phone's out of order. I was trying to phone Tim Gordon but it was dead and I was going to go down to the call box and report it."

"You can go to the call box now."

"That means you'll have to stay with him."

Rosamund's lip quivered. She looked at the little boy

who was lying on the floor now, his eyes wide open, his thumb in his mouth. "I don't want to. Suppose he dies?"

"You go," said James. "I'll stay with him. Go to the call box and dial nine-nine-nine for an ambulance and then go into the village hall and fetch mum. OK?"

"OK," said Rosamund, and she went, the tears running down her face.

James picked Oliver up and laid him gently on the bed. There were beads of perspiration on the child's face but that might have been simply because he was hot. Mirabel had wrapped him very warmly for the time of year in a woolly cardigan as well as a jumper and a tee-shirt. He had been thirsty, of course. That was what "ink" had meant. "Ink" for "drink". Was there the slightest chance that during the year since he had made it the *datura* had lost its toxicity? He did not honestly think so. He could remember reading somewhere that the poison was resistant to drying and to heat, so probably it was also resistant to time.

Oliver's eyes were closed now and some of the bright red colour which had been in his face while he was watching television had faded. His fat cheeks looked waxen. At any rate, he didn't seem to be in pain, though the sweat stood in tiny glistening pinpoints on his forehead. James asked himself again why he had been such a fool as to keep the stuff. An hour before he had been on the point of throwing it away and yet he had not. It was useless to have regrets, to "job backwards", as his father put it.

But James was looking to the future, not to the past. Suddenly he knew that if Oliver died he would have murdered him as surely, or almost as surely, as if he had fired at him with his father's shotgun. And his whole life, his entire future, would be wrecked. For he would never forgive himself, never recover, never be anything but a broken person. He would have to hide away, live in a distant part of the country, go to a different school, and when he left that school get some obscure job and drag out a frightened, haunted existence. Gone would be his dreams of Oxford, of work in some research establishment, of happiness and fulfilment and success. He was not overdramatizing, he knew it would be so. And Mirabel . . . ? If his life would be in ruins, what of hers?

He heard the front door open and his mother come running up the stairs. He was sitting on the bed, watching Oliver, and he turned round slowly.

"Oh, James . . . !"

And James said like a mature man, like a man three times his age, "There's nothing you can say to me I haven't already said to myself."

She touched his shoulder. "I know that," she said. "I know you." Her face was white, the lips too, and with anger as much as fear. "How dare she bring him here and leave him with two *children?*"

James hadn't the spirit to feel offended. "Is he—is he *dying?*"

"He's asleep," said his mother and she put her hand on Oliver's head. It was quite cool, the sweat had dried. "At least, I suppose he is. He could be in a coma, for all I know."

"It will be the end of me if he dies."

"James, oh, James. . . ." She did something she had not done for a long time. She put her arms round him and held him close to her, though he was half a head taller than she.

"There's the ambulance," said James. "I can hear the bell."

Two men came up the stairs for Oliver. One of them wrapped him in a blanket and carried him downstairs in his arms. Rosamund was sitting in the hall with

Palmerston on her lap and she was crying silently into his fur. It seemed hard to leave her but someone had to wait in for Mrs Hodges's daughter. James and his mother got into the ambulance with Oliver and went with him to the hospital.

They had to sit in a waiting room while the doctors did things to Oliver—pumped his stomach, presumably. Then a young black doctor and an old white doctor came and asked James a whole string of questions. What exactly was the stuff Oliver had drunk? When was it made? How much of it had been in the bottle? And a host of others. They were not very pleasant to him and he wanted to prevaricate. It would be so easy to say he hadn't known what the stuff really was, that he had boiled the thornapples up to make a green dye, or something like that. But when it came to it he couldn't. He had to tell the bald truth, he had to say he had made poison, knowing it might kill.

After they had gone away there was a long wait in which nothing happened. Mrs Hodges's daughter would have come by now and James's father would be home from where he was teaching at a summer seminar. It got to five-thirty, to six, when a nurse brought them a cup of tea, and then there was another long wait. James thought that no matter what happened to him in years to come, nothing could actually be worse than those hours in the waiting room had been. Just before seven the young doctor came back. He seemed to think James's mother was Oliver's mother and when he realized she was not he just shrugged and said as if they couldn't be all that anxious, as if it wouldn't be a matter of great importance to them:

"He'll be O.K. No need for you to hang about any longer."

James's mother jumped to her feet with a little cry. "He's all right? He's really all right?"

"Perfectly, as far as we can tell. The stomach contents are being analysed. We'll keep him in for tonight, though, just to be on the safe side."

The Fyfield family all sat up to wait for Mirabel. They were going to wait up, no matter what time she came, even if she didn't come till two in the morning. A note, put into the letter box of Sindon Lodge, warned her what had happened and told her to phone the hospital.

James was bracing himself for a scene. On the way back from the hospital his mother had told him he must be prepared for Mirabel to say some very unpleasant things to him. Women who would foist their children on to anyone and often seemed indifferent to them were usually most likely to become hysterical when those children were in danger. It was guilt, she supposed. But James thought that if Mirabel raved she had a right to, for although Oliver had not died and would not, he might easily have done. He was only alive because they had been very quick about getting that deadly stuff out of him. Mirabel wouldn't be able to phone Ewes Hall Farm, for the phone was still out of order. They all had coffee at about ten and James's father, who had gone all over his room to make sure there were no more killing bottles and had given James a stern but just lecture on responsibility, poured himself a large whisky.

The yellow Volvo came up the drive at twenty to twelve. James sat tight and kept calm the way he had resolved to do while his father went to answer the door. He waited to hear a shriek or a sob. Rosamund had put her fingers in her ears.

The front door closed and there were footsteps. Mirabel walked in, smiling. She had a big diamond on the third finger of her left hand. James's mother got up and went to her, holding out her hands, looking into Mirabel's face.

"You found our note? Of course you must have. Mirabel, I hardly know what to say to you. . . ."

Before Mirabel could say anything James's father came in with the man she was going to marry, a big teddy bear of a man with a handlebar moustache. James found himself shaking hands. It was all very different from what he had expected. And Mirabel was all smiles, vague and happy, showing off her engagement ring on her thin little hand.

"What did they say when you phoned the hospital?"

"I didn't."

"You didn't phone? But surely you . . . ?"

"I knew he was all right, Elizabeth. I didn't want to make a fool of myself telling them he'd drunk half a pint of coloured water, did I?"

James stared at her. And suddenly her gaiety fell from her as she realized what she had said. Her hand went up to cover her mouth and a dark flush mottled her face. She stepped back and took Gilbert Coleridge's arm.

"I'm afraid you underrate my son's abilities as a toxicologist," said James's father, and Mirabel took her hand down and made a serious face and said that of course they must get back so that she could phone at once.

James knew then. He understood. The room seemed to move round him in a slow circle and to rock up and down. He knew what Mirabel had done, and although it would not be the end of him or ruin things for him or spoil his future, it would be with him all his life. And in Mirabel's eyes he saw that she knew he knew.

But they were moving back towards the hall now in a flurry of excuses and thank yous and good nights, and the room had settled back into its normal shape and equilibrium. James said to Mirabel, and his voice had a break in it for the first time: "Good night. I'm sorry I was so stupid."

She would understand what he meant.

THE FRIGHTENED MILLIONAIRE
by Craig Rice

During the late 1940s, Craig Rice (1908–1957) was one of the best-known mystery writers in America. She was the first one ever to appear on the cover of Time *magazine, and her books during this period were widely reviewed. Her writing career began with* 8 Faces at 3 *(1939), which introduced her lawyer sleuth John J. Malone. He was to appear in eleven novels and several shorter works, often teamed with a married couple, Jake and Helene Justus. When not writing her own books, Craig Rice found time to ghost-write two mystery novels for Gypsy Rose Lee and one for actor George Sanders. At the time of her death she was writing* The April Robin Murders *(1958) a humorous mystery about two other series characters, street photographers Bingo and Handsome. The book was completed by Ed McBain. A score of Craig Rice stories and one additional novel appeared during the ten years following her death, leading to the suspicion that other writers took over the name.*

"The Frightened Millionaire," features John J. Malone without the Justuses in a rare novella-length adventure. It's a good introduction for those who have not yet met the wisecracking Chicago lawyer.

"The Frightened Millionaire" first appeared in the April 1956 issue of The Saint Detective Magazine.

John J. Malone didn't like it. All things considered—he didn't like it at all.

Maggie had never been late for work before. Always when the little criminal lawyer arrived at his office—which might be any time, depending on where he'd been the night before—she'd be there at her desk, making excuses over the telephone for his absence.

But on this particular morning, there was no Maggie. Malone's watch told him it was twenty to ten—a fair average for his own appearance—and there was no Maggie. Nothing, in fact, to indicate that there ever had been a Maggie, or even that she might have come in and gone out again. The mail, which he kicked aside, had been shoved through the slot in the door.

Incredibly, and against all precedent, Mary Margaret O'Leary was late to work. Black-haired, blue-eyed, a judicious mixture of explosive petulance and almost divine patience, Maggie was alternately the bane of Malone's existence, and its mainstay. And on this particular morning he was counting on her to be the mainstay. At eleven Jake Charlotte, his best and most profitable client was coming in, and words of great pith and moment would have to be put on paper.

When a client is suing a multi-mullionaire for a cool million, he doesn't want a lawyer who doesn't have a secretary.

If he could only find *Maggie!*

Nothing to worry about, he told himself firmly. Maggie would never allow anything really disastrous to happen to him. He reached for the telephone and tried to decide whether to call the police, the hospitals or the morgue.

The telephone beat him to the punch.

"Malone!" It was Maggie's voice. "I've been calling and calling—"

"Maggie," Malone asked desperately, "Are you ill?"

"No," she gasped over the wire, "No, no, no. I feel fine. But Malone, grab a cab and come out to my house quick. There's six dollars in the emergency fund, and the key to it is behind the Winston Dictionary on the second shelf of the bookcase in the outer office."

Right away Malone knew it was a real emergency.

Never before had Maggie told him the location of the key.

"Don't get excited," the little lawyer said. "Keep calm. Don't worry about a thing. I'll be right there." Almost as an after-thought he added, "What happened?"

"Malone," Maggie said, "there's a dead sailor in Ronnie's bed." She hung up.

"I'll take care of the traffic tickets," Malone told a cab driver approximately sixty seconds later. He gave the Wrightwood Avenue address, and added, "Scoot!"

The cab moved out into the steam of traffic and quickly picked up speed. "What's the rush?" the driver growled.

"There's a dead sailor in my secretary's brother's bed, and shut up," Malone told him.

The O'Leary House didn't need a Welcome Door-mat to say, "Come in." Wide, wooden, and desperately in need of paint, it was sandwiched in between massive apartment buildings—a hold-over from the lavender decade. If there had ever been a key to the front door, it had been lost a generation before. More than once Malone had parked witnesses there, and he had lost count of the times he had gorged himself on Aunt Aggie's cooking.

Malone walked up the worn wooden steps with worry in his eyes, and tension in the set of his jaw.

Maggie opened the door and said with a gasp of relief, "Praise be, you're here!"

The rest of the family was in the big, slightly shabby living room. The four O'Leary brothers—appropriately named Matthew, Mark, Luke and John—were sprawled on the big, old-fashioned sofa. Ronnie sat self-consciously on a chair by himself. Katie, aged nine, reclined on her stomach on the floor, reading the *Herald-American* comics. Grand-father O'Leary sat in his wheel chair, as if ready to tell anybody at the drop of a hat about his extraordinary meeting with Big Jim Corbett in a Boston saloon. Aunt Aggie sat in her customary rocking chair with her usual bit of knitting.

The little lawyer managed an all-inclusive smile. "We can talk later," he said. "Maggie, where's the body?"

"In Ronnie's room," Maggie said in an amazingly small voice. "It's right off the kitchen. I'll show you—"

It was a dead sailor, all right.

"Anybody touched the body?" Malone asked.

She shook her head. "Malone, Ronnie works from twelve till eight. When he got home *it* was here. Or should I say, *this* was here? Or would *he* be better—"

"You shut up," Malone said, in a singularly gentle tone. "Shut up—and get out!"

A few minutes later he walked into the living room and said, "There's no identification on him. What is even more puzzling there are no visible marks of violence on his body. No bullet wounds, no stab wounds—"

Aunt Aggie looked up from her knitting with a severely disapproving frown. "Malone, *must* you use words like that? And in this house?"

"Why not?" Malone said imperturbably. "You've got a possibly murdered man in it."

He waited for the color to come back into her face. Stoical Irishwoman that she was, for a moment or two she'd been very close to shock.

He spoke quickly. "Suppose we start with the dead man. I just want to know whose friend he was, and how he got here. Somebody please talk, and let me do the worrying."

Everybody started talking at once, and Malone roared, "Hush!"

"Malone," Maggie said with pure desperation in her voice, "you'd better let me tell you. You know how it is in this house. People drift in and out. Some of them are friends of Matthew, Mark, Luke and John. Others know Ronnie. They come in at any hour of the day or night, raid the ice-box and spend the night. A few weeks ago I came home late—the night I helped you at the office getting out that Beeble contract—and found six ten-year-old girls sleeping on the living room rug."

Katie lifted her head from the comic section long enough to explain: "They were all members of my club, and their folks told them they could stay. So there!"

"Quiet," Malone said.

Katie gave him a mean look, walked out to the kitchen, and came back with an apple. Sullenly she resumed her reading.

"Malone," Maggie said, "this stranger—Malone, what shall we call him?"

"Just call him the corpse," Malone advised grimly.

"All right—Mr Corpse then. But he wasn't a corpse when he walked in here. He was walking, and talking. And he was alive—"

"Maggie," Malone said sternly, "if you become hysterical I'll get you a job in the police department. That's how mean I can be. *Calm down.*" He began to unwrap a cigar. "Now suppose we try to get the story straight."

"By virtue of age," Grandfather said, "I am the head of the house. Aggie, you be still. I was sitting right here in my chair, minding my own business and working on a crossword puzzle, when the sailor wandered in. He said he was looking for a friend."

"He found one," Malone commented dryly.

"I naturally thought he was a friend of one of my grandsons. I told him they were all out, but would be coming along presently. I told him there were four cans of beer in the icebox and to help himself."

"After one beer," Malone said, "he probably became a friend of yours too."

Mark got up—all six foot four of him—and said impatiently, "Maybe I can help. I came in a little after midnight. This sailor and Grandpop were sitting here guzzling beer—"

"*Drinking* beer," the old man interrupted, "and have more respect for your elders."

"All right, *Grandfather*. You and he were *drinking* beer, and you were telling him how you could have beaten Sullivan with your bare fists if you'd had the chance."

"Save your family fights till later," Malone admonished, chewing his cigar. "Who else saw him? Alive, that is."

Matthew, Luke and John had little of importance to contribute. They had each in turn seen the sailor alive. Matthew had assumed the silent visitor was waiting for Luke, and since Grandfather O'Leary had fallen asleep in his wheelchair he had, out of concern for his comfort, put him to bed.

Luke had come in a short while later, and found the visitor sitting by the window holding an empty beer can. He'd simply said he was waiting for somebody. John's story differed from the others in no important particular.

Everybody had assumed the reticent visitor was a friend of some other member of the family. Maggie and Katie? They'd both been asleep in bed at the time of the unfortunate man's arrival.

"I'd just like to know." Malone said vehemently, "who was the *last* person to see him alive."

"Malone," Aunt Aggie said, "it was myself. I should have told you before.

The little lawyer turned and looked at her admiringly. There were few people in the world he liked better. She was an old-maid aunt, and her aspect confirmed it.

But no one else could have done a better job of rearing a family of orphaned O'Learys.

"I came downstairs sometime past midnight and found him here," she said, "He was very weary, poor fellow. He told me he was waiting for a friend. I felt sure it had to be Ronnie, because everybody else was in. So I led him to Ronnie's room and advised him to rest himself on the bed."

Ronnie lifted his head and said, "I never saw the guy before in my life. But when I came home from work, there he was parked on my bed. I shook him to wake him up and make him move over. I just thought he was a friend of—"

"I know," Malone said hastily. "Go on."

"Well, he didn't move, and I thought maybe he was sick. Maggie was coming down the stairs and I called her. It didn't take us long to find out he was dead. Then Maggie started calling you."

"Maggie," Malone said, "call a cab. Make it an Ajax. There's a stand a block from here."

While she was busy telephoning Malone issued a warning. "I want you all to stick to that story. It should not be difficult because you have nothing to conceal. A few slight deviations, however, will do no harm when the police get here. Maggie left for work as usual. Ronnie—you didn't want to wake up a sleeping guest. You can discover the body, say, thirty minutes from now. If the police give you any trouble—and they will—call me."

"Cab's on the way," Maggie said, returning into the room.

Malone nodded. "We've got to move. Remember, we're taking a statement on the Charlotte-Forstman case. And we've still got to get those witnesses."

He shook hands with Matthew, Mark, Luke and John, gave Ronnie a pat on the shoulder, kissed Aunt

Aggie, promised Grandfather O'Leary tickets to the next fight, pulled Katie's pigtails, and wound up with: "You've got your story straight, now stick to it."

He shoved Maggie through the doorway just as a *beep-beep* sounded from the cab outside.

Halfway downtown the little lawyer said, "Maggie, I don't like this. I don't like it at all. He was wearing green socks."

Maggie said, *"What?"*

"Sailors don't ordinarily wear green socks," Malone told her. "And don't worry me with questions."

Back in the office, Malone threw his hat in the general direction of the couch, plumped down behind his desk, and began scanning a folder of papers he already knew by heart.

"Maggie," he said at last, "I don't like the Charlotte case either. But a million bucks is a million bucks."

"That," Maggie said, "you can say again and again and again. Even if you do get only forty per cent."

"What can you do with money," Malone said gloomily, "except maybe spend it. And possibly we won't even get it—not without those two witnesses."

"We've advertised for them," Maggie reminded him. Malone chewed savagely on his cigar, got up and began to pace restlessly up and down the room.

"One man was riding down the Outer Drive on a motorcycle. He didn't stop. But he must have seen the crash in every detail. The other witness, according to Jake Charlotte, was standing at a bus stop. Why did both of them have to vanish before the cops and the ambulance arrived?"

"The second witness," Maggie said gently, "could have been waiting for a bus."

Malone ground out his cigar. "Fine thing," he muttered. He started on another cigar and said, "Maggie!" He finally lit the cigar. "Five forty-seven in the morning and he was waiting for a bus!" He looked up. "Maggie, there wouldn't be any suit except that Arthur Forstman happens to have about half the money in this hemisphere. So at a very small hour of the morning he drives home drunk—"

Maggie interrupted him to say, "That will have to be proven in court, Malone."

The little lawyer shoved his half-smoked cigar viciously into an ashtray. "Don't worry, it will be. Drunk or sober, he runs head on into the car of a small-time fur dealer name Jake Charlotte—who, by the way, has promised you a nice bit of rabbit if we win. Question: What was Charlotte doing out at that hour? Deponent isn't saying. His wife's ankle was broken. His car was smashed. So he sues for a cool million."

"It's our case," Maggie said softly. "Don't let us talk ourselves out of it by finding for the opposition."

He smiled at her. "I always like to visualize the opposition's side. Here's my point. If Forstman hadn't long since lost count of his millions the entire affair would have been a simple little matter between insurance companies. Medical expenses, car repairs, et cetera. As it is—" He started on a new cigar. "Maggie, it must be hell to be rich!"

"I'd like to try it sometime," she said. "Malone—is everything going to be all right?"

"The sailor? Of course. All the O'Learys are in the clear—or soon will be." He hoped with all his heart that he was telling the truth. "Now go away and let me worry until Jake Charlotte comes in—or the cops come to tell me there's a dead sailor in your kid brother's bed."

Maggie managed a wan smile, went away, and came back fast.

"Malone," she said, "this was in the mail, along with a lot of bills you'd probably rather not see right at the moment. It might be important, and then again it might not be."

The little lawyer looked at the envelope. It was grimy, the stamp had been stuck on askew, and it was addressed in pencil. The name on the corner was HAROLD SPRUCE, and the return address was on North Clark Street. The note inside read as follows.

'Dear Sir, I saw your ad in the papers and I didn't go to the police account of I had a little trouble with the cops previous but I saw your ad and yes sir I was the man on the motorcycle.'

"Well, you've got one of the missing witnesses," Maggie said, elation in her voice.

John J. Malone mopped his brow and nodded. "I was pretty sure the ad would pay off," he said. "We'll contact him before he changes his mind and—"

The phone rang, and Maggie turned pale. Malone smiled at her with a reassurance he didn't feel and reached for the instrument himself. His eyes widened in swift surprise. Looking significantly at his secretary he said genially:

"Mr Featherstone? Good to hear from you! Just a minute while I transfer this call to my private office—"

He laid the receiver gently on the desk, and whispered to Maggie, "Plug in the extension phone and bring it in here—with your notebook. I want to have every word of this. It's Orlo O. Featherstone."

As she started for the extension phone she whispered back, "Isn't he the lawyer who saw Lincoln buried?"

"According to my information," Malone whispered in reply, "he saw Lincoln born." He smiled into the receiver and said, "Featherstone? Sorry about the delay. How about lunch at the Republican Club tomorrow? Or a date at the Chez? Oh, nonsense. How do you do it? I could have *sworn* you weren't a day over fifty. Now what can I do for you besides telling you the story of your life?"

Maggie managed not to choke over that. Malone leaned back and lit his cigar. He listened for a moment in attentive silence, nodding as the other talked.

"The Forstman case? Featherstone, you're backing the wrong Pullman train."

Featherstone immediately countered with a proposal for a settlement. All medical expenses and repairs to the car. After all, Arthur Forstman must have been driving with care, since he had been taking a girl home from a party. Malone made a gentle remark about the hour he'd taken the girl home. Featherstone pointedly suggested that Malone must have been young once himself, and Malone winced.

Malone pointed out that Jake Charlotte's wife might never be able to walk again, and that the car had been damaged beyond repair. Furthermore the car was important to Mr Charlotte's only means of livelihood, and there was such a thing as emotional shock—

Mr Featherstone said that his client would settle for all medical bills, a new car, and two thousand dollars in cash.

"Your client—"

Maggie caught Malone's eye just in time. Her lips said, "Watch yourself, my fine talkative friend!"

"Your client was driving through a red light," Malone went on. "Moreover, he was drunk. He had not had sufficient sleep. He struck Mr Charlotte's car—thereby putting Mr Charlotte out of business, and injuring Mrs Charlotte for life." Malone paused for breath. "We will settle," he said, "for one million dollars. Plus, of course, medical expenses and repairs to the car. Not to mention court costs and—this is most important—legal fees."

Orlo O. Featherstone pointed out that it might take five years for the case to come to court. Malone said cheerfully that he expected to live that long. He then asked Orlo O. Featherstone how he was feeling, in a very solicitous voice, and reminded him of the luncheon engagement at the Republican Club, and hung up with a smug smile on his face.

Maggie put down the notebook and said, "But Malone. How do you know?"

"I don't," Malone said. "I'm bluffing." He relit his cigar. "So far at least I'm holding only the joker. But once we get those witnesses—"

There was a little silence.

"Malone," she said at last. "Are you sure? About the sailor, I mean."

"A million buck lawsuit," Malone said, "and you worry me about dead sailors. I told you it would be all right. Switch all calls to my personal phone, and when Jake Charlotte turns up stall him in the office for a minute or two. Tell him I'm busy with an overseas call—and when I push the buzzer, send him in."

There was a sudden, quite alarmingly insistent pounding on the door. Maggie looked up, her face pale. "Malone, that's von Flanagan's knock! I'd recognize it through earmuffs."

"Keep your thoughts to yourself," Malone said. "Go on taking dictation and let me do the worrying."

The pounding grew louder. Malone yelled, "Why don't you just open it? Don't break it down."

Von Flanagan came in like a red-faced hurricane, with two uniformed cops behind him. He motioned the pair to be quiet, and slammed the door shut.

"Malone, one of these days you're going to push me too far!" he said.

Malone smile from behind his desk, and offered von Flanagan a cigar. "What's the beef?" he asked, his voice strangely gentle.

Von Flanagan sank down in the only easy chair in the office. He caught his breath, frowned at Malone, and refused the match Maggie offered him. "Thanks, I have a lighter." After a number of tries he accepted the match, and said, "Malone, we've been friends for a long time."

"Longer than that," Malone said. "You don't need to disrupt my morning's work to remind me, especially when I'm busy with an important lawsuit. Come on, what's the beef?"

"No beef," the big police officer said, breathing heavily. "I'm here to do a favor for Miss O'Leary, whom I have always looked upon as a friend." He nodded towards Maggie. "A guy turned up in her house dead. Dead as a doornail. Dead as a—"

"Never mind," Malone interrupted hastily. "Let's just say the man was dead."

"Just as you choose," von Flanagan said. "We were plenty thorough. We checked when he went in the house—and where he must have secured the poison."

Malone lifted a startled eyebrow.

"Chloral hydrate," von Flanagan said. "Chloral hydrate in a lethal dose. He seemed drunk when he strayed in, but actually he hadn't been drinking much. Maggie here is in the clear. Her whole clan is in the clear. That's according to the experts—and the time element."

He cleared his throat noisily. "But remember, Malone, I'm your friend. Once in a while I read newspapers too. We managed to identify the man."

Malone lifted the other eyebrow.

"His name," von Flanagan said, "was Harold Spruce."

Malone sat absolutely silent for what seemed to him like ten thousand years.

"Don't get up now," von Flanagan said gently. "Wait for the count of nine. What have you to lose?"

Malone considered a number of possibilities. One of them was jumping out the window. Another was shooting himself in front of the Tribune Tower, something he'd always wished someone would do. A third was to steal a small boat from Navy Pier and steer for South America.

He threw his cigar butt inaccurately at the corner wastebasket and said, "Green socks."

"Malone," von Flanagan said anxiously. "I know this has been a great shock to you, and if you'd like a drink to steady your nerves—"

The little lawyer shook his head. "No," he said. "I'd like forty percent of a million dollars, but I'm afraid it's slipping away from me. Be that as it may, my immediate concern is centered in the late Harold Spruce. I don't especially want to look at him. I want to look at his clothes."

"Malone," von Flanagan said, "are you sure you feel all right?"

"I never felt better in my life," Malone assured him.

"If you really want a drink don't let my being here stand in the way—"

"Nonsense!" Malone said. He found his hat with a little difficulty and muttered, "Green socks. Green light."

Von Flanagan said, "I hope you know what you're doing. Remember, I trust you as far as I can throw the City Hall into Lake Michigan." He turned to Maggie and said, "As far as you and your family are concerned we feel you're all in the clear."

She looked up at him and said earnestly. "This is the first time in my life I've ever *really* wanted to kiss a cop!"

"Don't!" von Flanagan said, and fled into the anteroom.

There was a slight rumpus going on there. Kluchetsky and Scanlon were standing by a furious little man who looked angrily at Malone and said, "Well, it's about time."

He was an ugly, unctuous little man, with very little that was commendable in his behavior and general aspect. His clothes had a conspicuously expensive look, but he wore them in such a way that they did nothing to enhance his dignity.

He gave Malone a smug smile and asked, "Well, how is our lawsuit coming?"

Malone gave him back the same smile and said, "Fine—just fine. I'm doing some important work on it now. I'll see you here in an hour, if you wish, and we can go over it in detail."

"Hold on, Mr Malone!" The little man was angry. "I just want to know—"

Malone swallowed his rage and said, "Mr Charlotte, if you want to transfer this case to another lawyer, you're entirely free to do so. I'll let you know when I need to talk to you."

He calmed down a little. After all, Jake Charlotte was his client, and a million dollars had a certain eloquence of its own.

He put a reluctant hand on his client's shoulder. "I'm on my way now to see one of your witnesses," he said. "Everything is proceeding satisfactorily. Go home, and don't worry."

Malone's voice had a soothing quality, and his expression carried conviction. Jake Charlotte relaxed and smiled.

"Then I'll hear from you, Mr Malone," he said, and took his departure.

After a minute's silence, von Flanagan growled, "You might at least have told him the witness you're going to see is dead."

On the way downtown Malone finally summoned enough composure to ask, "How did you identify him so quickly?" He had been on the point of adding "When there was no identification on him," but he caught himself just in time.

"Pure luck," von Flanagan said. "Plus, of course, some smart police work." He coughed modestly. "The guy had a girl friend who was waiting for him at home. He told her he had to go out on some important business, and promised to be back before midnight. Around ten o'clock this morning when her alarm reached the acute stage she started calling hospitals. Finally, she called the cops. By that time, of course, we had the dead sailor. She identified him, and so did his landlady."

Malone was beginning to feel that this was one of the days he should have spent sleeping.

The conviction grew on him even more after his second look within twenty-four hours at the dead sailor. He had died at a tragically early age but at least he'd died quietly and without pain. A handsome young man— with the daredevil smile of a motorcycle driver still on his face.

"According to the medical examiner," von Flanagan said, "he swallowed the poison about three hours before he died. It gave him time to move around a little. But why did he pick the O'Leary house?"

"Maybe he just picked the first house he came to," Malone said.

Von Flanagan shook his head. "Malone, it was the

only house on the street. The rest were all apartment buildings. I tell you, he was *aimed* at that house."

Malone said, "Let's get out of here." On the way out he demanded, "But who aimed him?"

The big policeman said nothing, in a nasty tone of silence.

"My missing witness," Malone mused out loud, "found dead in my secretary's house."

Von Flanagan's silence became almost profane.

"If you'll just let me take a look at those clothes," Malone said, "we'll remain friends."

This time von Flanagan gave him only a cold stare.

The expressive silence remained mutual all the way up to von Flanagan's office. The big police officer said a few terse words into the intercom and a moment later Scanlon came in with a bundle.

Malone looked over the contents, and made a swift inventory. A sailor suit. Underwear—not Navy issue. A pair of green socks. A crumpled handkerchief. Black shoes, newly polished.

He tossed the articles of clothing back on von Flanagan's desk. "Save these for me," he said.

The angry-faced police officer almost strangled on the single word, "Why?"

"Someday," Malone said, "I may want to give them to the Salvation Army. On the other hand, I might want to unravel them and knit them up into rugs. Or, crochet up a set of doilies . . . But how," he finished mildly, "did you know he was my missing witness?"

"Because," von Flanagan said, even more mildly, "he sent a little note to the police department mentioning you and saying that he'd decided to come forward. Now how about your other missing witness?"

"I hope the police find him," Malone said, "before the killer does."

The instant Malone left the elevator in his office building he knew that something was wrong. He went in through the door to his private office and buzzed for Maggie.

"Has anyone called?" he asked.

"Malone," she said in a very soft voice, "Mr Forstman is here to see you. Mr *Arthur Forstman*. The name should mean *something* to you."

Malone waited a full minute before coming to a decision. "Don't send him right in," he said. "Tell him I'm busy. I'll buzz you when I'm free."

"Malone," she whispered, "everything is all right, isn't it? About the—"

"It is," Malone said. "Now go away and don't worry."

He spent nearly ten minutes inaccurately working a crossword puzzle. Then he buzzed Maggie.

She ushered in Arthur Forstman. "Will you need me?" she asked and without waiting for Malone to shake his head, discreetly closed the door.

Malone rose from behind his desk, extended a cordial hand—it wasn't every day a multi-millionaire paid him a visit—and ushered his guest into the one comfortable chair.

"Sorry I had to keep you waiting," he said, "but I was on the long-distance phone. I was trying to get some information on this Harold Spruce person."

"Oh," Arthur Forstman said, fumbling for a cigarette.

The little lawyer gave him a close look. Forstman had the kind of face that should have been ruddy. Instead it was pale. His hands, that could so competently handle golf clubs, polo mallets, and racing cars should have been steady. But Malone had to leap around the desk and hold a match to a cigarette held between shaking fingers.

He didn't bother to ask if the wealthy sportsman would care for a drink. He rinsed out a glass, opened the file drawer labelled EMERGENCY and pulled out the bottle of brandy he'd been saving for a chance meeting with Grace Kelly, or Marilyn Monroe.

Arthur Forstman downed it straight without batting even one eyelash. "Malone, I've got to talk to you about something I can't discuss with anyone else."

Malone listened, very quietly.

"I'm here to make you an offer," the tall, slightly-graying man said. He slumped down in his chair.

Malone gave him sixty seconds, catfooted around the desk to refill his glass, and said, "Mr Featherstone has already made one, and I turned it down."

Arthur Forstman sat up very straight. "That isn't what I mean," he said. "Sure, I'd settle with that slimy little crook. It would be worth it to get him off my neck. But, Malone, this is something else. That man who was found murdered this morning—"

There was a little silence, and then Malone said, "Yes?"

"He was one of the witnesses. Obviously I'm going to be accused of having him done in. I'll pay you a five thousand dollar fee if you can prove I had nothing to do with it."

Malone got up, walked to the window and looked out. The customary Indian Summer heat wave was sending little light shivers across the tops of the buildings. Sooner or later there would be rain.

"And one thousand dollars down," the voice said behind him, "as a retainer."

Malone argued with the voice of temptation for about thirty seconds. The emergency fund was cleaned out, he might need money for Maggie, and he wasn't sure how Joe the Angel would react to a touch.

He turned around and said, "Put your money in

your pocket. Let's talk about more pleasant things. A cracked up car, and a badly injured woman—"

Forstman turned white and Malone reached for the brandy bottle again.

"We were driving home," Forstman said. "Sure it was late. We'd been to a party down on the south side to celebrate our engagement."

"Where?" Malone asked wearily.

"At William Turner's. The broker, you know. She's May Turner, his niece. It got to be late. I was driving her home. She went to sleep on the way." Forstman relit his cigarette with hands that shook only a little now.

"It all happened so suddenly. The street ahead was empty. I'd had a few drinks at the party, but I wasn't drunk. I may have been exceeding the speed limit, but I don't think so."

"Wait a minute," Malone said. "I'm the opposition lawyer, remember? Save your confession for the courtroom."

Forstman managed a thin smile. "I'm only trying to tell you the truth. Suddenly this car came out of a side-street and smashed into us. The rest was all pretty much confusion. I know I was completely stunned for a minute, and I guess the Charlottes were too." He crushed out the cigarette and started on another one.

"It's none of my business," Malone said, wishing he didn't like Arthur Forstman so much, "and I shouldn't be asking you this, being on the other side. But how did you know there were two witnesses?"

"I saw one," Forstman said. "It was just before the crash. He was standing on the bus stop corner. I remember hoping he wouldn't try to cross the street. And then, at the moment of the crash, this man on a motorcycle raced by. That's all I remember for a few minutes."

He closed his eyes for a moment. "I tried to get out

of the car. I wasn't hurt, but I was pinned in. I thanked God that May was all right. She'd waked up, a little frightened, but perfectly calm. We could hear Mrs Charlotte screaming. May could get out on her side of the car, and she ran out to see how badly Mrs. Charlotte had been hurt. Then she ran down the road until she could flag down a car to send a call for the police. The rest you know."

"May," Malone commented, "sounds like a level-headed girl in an emergency."

Arthur Forstman's eyes lighted up as though someone had struck a match to them. "May," he said simply, "is wonderful."

After a long moment he went on: "About this lawsuit. I'd be willing to settle on generous terms, but I'm damned if I'll have people going around saying I arranged for a witness to be murdered in order to avoid a lawsuit."

Malone tapped the ash from his cigar and said, "Obviously I can't take you as a client, since Charlotte has already engaged me. Neither can I take your money. I will do my best to ascertain whether you were or were not guilty of arranging for the murder of Harold Spruce. If you didn't, you have nothing to worry about. You don't need me. If you did—" he paused, coughed delicately and said, "We can talk about that another time. It would alter the entire picture."

He rose, walked around the desk, smiled reassuringly and said, "There's always the possibility that the murder of Harold Spruce had nothing to do with your little mishap."

Arthur Forstman said hoarsely, "In that case, why was his body found in your secretary's house?"

Malone reflected that he'd like to know that himself.

"It could be pure coincidence," he said. "Meantime, *don't worry!*"

Forstman's goodby handshake was a solid one.

Maggie came in—after he had left—with her notebook and said, "I got every word of it down. But I thought you always saved that 'don't worry' line for clients and prospective clients."

"For all I know," Malone said gloomily, "he *is* a prospective client."

"Malone," she said in a sad little voice, "what do we do now?"

He managed to smile at her. "We don't worry. I can say that to you because you're also a client, and I may be my own client before this is over. You do three things. First you check with your blessed family as to what time the sailor got there. Next, you call Doctor Flamm and ask him how long it would take for a fatal dose of chloral hydrate to take effect. Third, you bring me the classified phone directory. I've got to call up every costumer in town."

Malone looked at the directory wearily. So far it had been a busy day, and promised to be even busier.

Maggie stuck her head around the corner of the door. "Malone," she said, "try Campbell's first."

"Maggie," he said happily, "an inspiration! In fact, I think I'll try it in person!"

Naturally, it had to be Campbell's! Why hadn't he thought of it himself!

He caught himself on the verge of telling the elevator man to drive faster, and went back to thinking about Campbell's. There were other costumers in Chicago, and good ones. But the renting of the sailor suit was the job of someone who didn't ordinarily rent costumes.

With such a job in prospect Campbell's would naturally be the first place that came to mind. Almost everyone knew that Campbell's, highly listed in the Classified Directory, would rent anything—including, probably, a second-hand space ship, and certainly, a sailor suit.

And if he were wrong, he reminded himself, he could still tackle the others.

That reminded him of something else. He felt in his pockets and found fifty-five cents left over from the emergency fund. It was no time to go back and talk to Maggie, with all the worries she had on her mind.

With a heavy sigh, he walked down the street to Joe the Angel's City Hall Bar.

Joe greeted him with all the heavy cordiality he would have given to the main exhibit at a wake. He slid a drink across the bar without being asked. "Malone," he said mournfully, "I *am* sorry."

"Don't worry," Malone said, "you know you'll get it back."

Joe the Angel's eyes widened. "You mean you need *money*? Why did you not say so? How much you need?"

The little lawyer caught his breath and said, "Just cab fare."

"Cab fare to where?" Joe the Angel demanded. "State and Madison, or Gary, Indiana?"

"I don't know yet," Malone said, wishing he were asleep.

After a brief discussion, they settled for ten, and Joe the Angel marked it up on Malone's bill.

"And Malone," he said sadly, "I am sorry that you lose the witness. I read it in the papers."

"Oh," Malone said quickly, "*that!* Nothing important." He relit his cigar. "I have another one. And besides, I had an offer of a settlement. Maggie has it all down on paper." He puffed at the cigar. "For a million dollars."

Joe the Angel turned pale. He broke a rule of the house and poured himself a drink, gulped it down, coughed and said, "But, Malone! A million dollars—"

"— is a million dollars," Malone finished for him. He rose and started for the door.

"Wait, Malone," Joe the Angel gasped. He reached for the cash register. "Better you take another ten. And, one on the house, Malone!"

Campbell's in North State Street, was famous and fabulous. One window displayed sets of dueling pistols, another, a suit of armor. A sign read WE BUY, SELL, OR RENT ANYTHING.

Malone made his way through the semi-darkness of the elderly building, ducked away from a cigar store Indian who had a mean look, glanced briefly at a display of a fortune's worth of antique jewelry, bypassed a table loaded with second-hand kitchen utensils labelled ANYTHING YOU SEE, FIVE CENTS, and finally, a shaken man, wound up at the costume rental department.

"I'd like to see a man about a sailor suit," he said.

The pleasant-faced young man said, "I doubt if we have anything to fit you, sir, but—"

"No," the little lawyer said. "*No!* I don't want to rent a sailor suit. I just want to *ask* about one."

The young man, not looking quite as pleasant, said, "Yes, sir. Now if you will give me his size—"

"I don't know his size," Malone said explosively. "That's what I came to ask you!"

"Perhaps you'd like to talk to the manager?" the young man said anxiously.

"Perhaps I'd like to talk to you," Malone said. He lit a cigar and began to relax.

"If there's any complaint—" the young man said.

"I won't make it," Malone said warmly. "I'm just

asking about the rental of a sailor suit, sometime yesterday, or maybe the day before. Who rented it and when.'

"I'll check the books, sir," the young man said. "And
you are—?"

"Malone," the lawyer said grimly. "John J. Malone."

"*That* Malone!" A light came in the young man's
eyes. "I'll check for you, right away."

He came back in an amazingly short time, with the
records. The suit had been rented the day before, at
6:00 p.m., just before closing time. A deposit had been
left. The renter had signed for it as Jack Johnson, address
3145 East Huron Street.

Malone reflected unhappily that not only did the
name Jack Johnson show a shocking lack of originality,
but that 3145 East Huron Street would be halfway across
Lake Michigan. He said gently, "And what did he look
like?"

"I don't know, sir, *Mister* Malone, I mean. I didn't
see him, because I wasn't here. You see, I'm a substitute.
Usually, I'm in stuffed birds. The regular man here left
on his two weeks' vacation early this morning."

Malone said a very bad word under his breath, and
asked, "Where was he going?"

The young man looked even more unhappy, shook
his head and said, "Maybe the assistant manager would
know."

The assistant manager looked at Malone as though
he suspected him of attempting to shop-lift a suit of
antique armor.

"This gentleman," the young man said breathlessly,
"is trying to locate Walter—"

"I'm a lawyer," Malone said quickly. He handed out
one of the business cards Maggie had insisted on having
printed. "Walter may be the key man in a million dollar
lawsuit. If I can locate him—"

The assistant manager's eyes softened. "I wish I could help you. A million dollars is a lot of money, isn't it? But Walter left this morning on a fishing trip. He himself didn't know where he was going. He'll be back in two weeks." He accepted the cigar Malone offered him. "Tell you what I'll do. He's bound to send postcards or souvenirs. The minute we hear from him, I'll telephone you."

"More than fair enough," Malone said.

"Sir," the young man said, after the assistant manager had gone, "there's a chance someone in the store might have noticed him. Would you like me to ask around?"

"I would," Malone said. He leaned on the counter, and concentrated his gaze on a glass-encased bull-fighter's costume. He had about decided he would look well in it when the young man came back.

"I'm sorry, sir," he said. "Nobody noticed anything or anybody. That's a busy time of day. People are always coming in and out."

"It's all right," Malone said. "You did the best you could." He fumbled through his pockets. "Do you and your girl-friend like the fights?"

The young eyes brightened. "How did you know I had a girl friend?"

"You looked as though you would," Malone said. He handed over the fight tickets he'd planned to give to von Flanagan. "Thanks for everything, and have fun," he said and again fought his way through the maze.

In a state of utter despondency, he ignored an available cab, and rode the streetcar to his office.

So far, everything had gone wrong, and what would happen next he didn't know and didn't want to guess.

He snarled at the elevator man, a friend of many years standing, strode into his private office, slammed his door, threw his hat in the general direction of the couch, glared through the window at a sky that was already beginning to cloud, and finally slumped down in the chair behind his desk and yelled for Maggie.

She arrived as though she'd been jet-propelled.

He lit a cigar and glared at it. "Nothing," he said hoarsely. "Absolutely nothing." He added the details. "The chances are that if this clerk does turn up—it'll turn out that the man who rented the sailor suit was Harold Spruce himself."

"Malone," Maggie said, "don't be discouraged."

"I'll be discouraged if I want to," Malone said.

"There are a couple of women waiting to see you," Maggie said. "One, blonde."

"I don't care," the little lawyer growled, "if the whole Chez Paree chorus is waiting in the outer office. What did *you* find out?" He looked at her hopefully.

Her face clouded. "Malone," she said gravely, "a little less than nothing. I checked with Dr. Flamm. The sailor must have gotten the drink less than a few minutes—say, ten—before he got to our house. I checked with the family as to when he came in. And I called Matthew about bars. There isn't one within half an hour's walking distance. And since he had no car, he must have walked. Malone,"—her face whitened—"does that mean he got it after he came in our house?"

"No," Malone said, "no, no, no, no." He got up, kicked the wastebasket savagely and began pacing the floor. "Somebody drove him to, or near your door. The same somebody probably offered him a drink from a loaded bottle. *Why?* I don't know. *Who?*" He paused in his pacing. "I don't know that yet either."

Malone looked through his window at the Chicago rooftops. The dreary gray rain was beginning. Why was it, he wondered, that important crimes always happen during a record-breaking heat-wave, a blizzard, or the rainy season!

"Maggie," he said quietly, "I begin to feel as though I were hitting my head with a brick wall."

"You mean—" she began.

"I know exactly what I mean," he said.

"The word for it," Maggie said acidly, "is frustrated. And you have two people waiting—mother and child."

Malone managed a wan smile and said, "Bring on the dancing girls."

The girl was very young, very blonde, very pretty, and right now, very tearful. Her mother looked as though her face should be carved into the side of a mountain.

"It's about Harold," the girl said. "Harold Spruce."

Malone bounded to his feet and ushered them into the best chairs as though they were visiting royalty. He caught himself on the verge of offering cigars.

He excused himself, whipped into the outer office, and said to Maggie, "Phone the drug store and have them send up a quart of ice cream—strawberry—and rush. With dishes and spoons. And, you take down every word of what they say."

He slowed down at the door. "Sorry for the interruption," he apologized. "And very sorry I kept you waiting so long." He gave the girl his most reassuring smile and said, "Now, my dear—?"

She gave back a very small smile. "Mr Malone, my name is Dawn O'Day—"

"Emmaline," her mother said, in a voice as cold as an Eskimo's icebox, "tell the man the truth."

Her blue eyes freshened with a promise of new tears. "All right, Mr Malone, my name is Emmaline Biggers. But I'm studying to be a model, and you can't get far with a name like that. And Ma—"

Ma said, "My name is Mrs Emma Biggers, and I've gotten alone fine with it for years."

Malone smiled impartially at them both. "Never mind the names," he said. "How about Harold Spruce?"

"Ma said I should talk to you. Harold wouldn't want me to tell you this. I mean, he wouldn't *have* wanted to tell you this. But now he can't be hurt—"

The tears started again. Malone grabbed for his handkerchief, but Ma Emma beat him to it with a wad of Kleenex.

Providentially, the ice cream arrived at that moment.

"Don't cry into it," Malone ordered. "It doesn't taste good with salt."

The tears began to dry. Ma Emma looked as though a smile might appear on the great stone face.

"I really wanted to be a stenographer," Emmaline said, "like Ma wanted me to, and I went to a business school. But seemed like I couldn't learn to type, and my spelling isn't so good. Seems like I'm dumb." She gulped down another spoonful of ice cream.

Malone looked at her, at the face, the hair, and the figure, and decided she could afford to be dumb. He said gently, "Now that I've heard the story of your life, tell me about Harold Spruce. And *don't cry!*"

"Emmaline," Ma Emma said, for the third time, "tell the truth."

"Come on, Dawn," Malone said warmly. "He'd want you to tell me." He gave her the best smile he had at the moment. "You know he should have stopped at the scene of an accident."

She took another gulp of ice cream. "He couldn't stop," she said, "because of the motorcycle."

"You mean, the motorcycle wouldn't stop?"

"No, But he couldn't stop because it wasn't *his* motorcycle."

Malone counted to ten, slowly. "You mean he stole it?"

"He borrowed it," Emmaline said miserably. "It belonged to the owner of the gas station where he worked. He'd borrowed it a lot of times. But if the owner found out, Harold would have lost his job. He saw the wreck, but of course he couldn't stop. Maybe he should have stopped. He might have lost his job but he wouldn't have lost his *life!*"

"Now, Emmaline!" Ma Emma said. She reached for more Kleenex, just in case.

"Finish your ice cream before it melts, Dawn," Malone said gently.

"Well, then there was the lawsuit. It was in the papers. He said he was going to make so much from it that he wouldn't care about the job. He called up those people—I mean both of them—and told them he would be available as a witness."

"Tell the truth," Ma Emma said.

"Well, I mean he said he could—well, he could, for a price—" She gulped, wiped her eyes, finished the ice cream and licked the spoon. "He was offered five thousand dollars. Then he was offered a cut of the take."

"Emmaline!" Ma Emma said.

"Well, that's exactly the way he said it. And then one of the gentlemen got to be very friendly. He gave Harold a little money from time to time. And then yesterday Harold stopped by on his way from work."

She paused, blew her nose, and said, *"Ma!"*

Ma Emma passed over the rest of the ice cream.

The little blonde took a spoonful, looked at Malone and said, "He was very happy. His new friend had asked him to play a practical joke on someone. It was some kind of a birthday joke, Harold said. And Harold loved jokes. He was going to be paid for it."

Ma Emma said, "Tell the truth. Harold loved money even more than he loved jokes."

"Ma, please!"

"Don't bleat at me," Ma Emma said grimly. "Harold was a boy of no character. He loved money. He had a good job, but he came to the house almost every night. Not to see Emmaline, like she thought, but because he'd get a free meal."

"Ma!"

"Shut up," Ma Emma said. "I'm telling the truth. The only other thing he cared about was moving fast. That's why he borrowed his boss's motorcycle. He was saving his money to buy a racing car. That's why he was willing to take a bribe. And besides," she added disapprovingly, "he drank."

Malone thanked his lucky stars he hadn't offered Ma Emma gin instead of ice cream. "Now, Dawn, don't cry any more," he said soothingly. "Just tell me the rest of the joke."

"Well," she said miserably, "he was supposed to rent some kind of costume, and meet his friend and go to this house, and pretend to be a friend of the family."

"One thing more," Malone said. "Harold did see the accident, that we know. He must have described it to you." He wished for luck and said, "Did he tell you if the stop-light was green or red?"

"He didn't tell me," she said. "I guess because I didn't ask him."

The little lawyer counted to ten silently.

"That's all I know," she said. "That's all. Except that he's dead." She grabbed at the Kleenex again.

"Now, Emmaline," Ma Emma said, in a voice that was actually gentle. "Mr Malone, we'll be going now. And thank you for the ice cream."

Malone bowed them to the door as though they'd

been a pair of visiting Hollywood stars, and turned to Maggie. "How many of your brothers were in the Navy?"

"All of them," she said in an unhappy voice. Her face was pale. "Ronnie only two years."

"Therefore," Malone growled, lighting a fresh cigar, "your whole family would have been definitely receptive to a young man who turned up dressed as a sailor, looking for a friend. That explains the rented suit, and the green socks." He sighed deeply. "But we will seem to get right back to where we started."

"Find the other witness," Maggie said acidly.

"According to the latest census," Malone said just as acidly, "there are three and a half million people in Chicago. And no one, including Jack Charlotte, can give us a description of him. Just a shadowy figure at a bus stop, in the gray pre-dawn mist."

"Malone," Maggie said, "you'll never be a poet. Have any of you geniuses in this case thought of talking to the bus driver?" As Malone stared at her, she went on. "Your missing witness was waiting at a bus stop. Obviously, he was waiting for a bus. Obviously a bus must have come along. Obviously, there must have been a bus driver. There's less than a three-and-a-half-millionth chance you'll learn anything, but it's worth a try."

"Maggie," Malone said happily, "*You* are the genius in this case! Get me the address of the bus company!"

She grinned at him. "And incidentally, the exact census figure is three million, six hundred and twenty thousand, nine hundred and sixty-two."

"Now minus one," Malone said. "Hurry up, genius, get me that address."

For the first time that day Malone began to feel that life could be made worth living. The taxi he took to the bus office seemed to be a jet-propelled cloud.

The Head Dispatcher turned out to be a long-faced man with a definitely pessimistic disposition and, Malone suspected, ulcers. He looked even gloomier as Malone explained the situation.

"I'll look it up in the records," he said in a voice like a radio announcer advertising cut-rate funerals. He came back in a few minutes. "It was Melrose," he said. "Bill Melrose. But he can't help you, Mr Malone. He didn't see the accident. By his schedule, he must have gone by the corner just before it happened."

The little lawyer scowled. "Are you sure?" he said.

The Head Dispatcher looked at Malone as though he were an unwanted idiot child. He said patiently, "Because if he'd seen the accident, he would have stopped to see if he could offer emergency assistance. Then he would have reported it to the police, and put it in his own daily report here. Those are strict rules, and we enforce them."

Malone thought about the still unknown witness who had been waiting for a chance. If the bus had just gone by, he wouldn't have been waiting there.

"Just the same," he said stubbornly, "I'd like to talk with him."

The Head Dispatcher sighed again. "I'll see if I can find him for you. He's just gone off duty, but he may still be around."

He went away again and came back with a man with a friendly grin and built along the general lines of a top league basketball star. "Just luck he was still here," he said gloomily, "but he can't do you no good."

"That's right," Bill Melrose said. "I'm sorry, but I must have gone through that crossing about one minute before it happened. The papers say it happened at 5:47 a.m. because that's what both the dashboard clocks stopped at when the crash came. So according to my schedule, I must've gone past about 5:45 or 5:46."

Malone shook his head sadly. "Well, I had to check everything. Too bad you weren't a few minutes late that morning."

He turned on one of his best smiles and said to the Head Dispatcher, "Thanks for all your trouble. May I buy you a beer?"

"I'm still on duty!" the Dispatcher said, as though he were prophesying the end of the world.

Malone turned the same smile on Bill Melrose. "Why, yes, and thanks very much," he said.

There was, as always, a little place across the street, which, though not the best in the world, was at least, the nearest. Comfortably settled in a secluded booth, Malone suggested that his guest might like something better than beer.

Bill Melrose again said, "Thank you very much," and ordered gin and coke.

Malone winced, ordered rye with a beer chaser, and then quoted Ma Emma by saying, "Tell the truth, Bill," in his best courtroom manner.

Bill Melrose turned pale and started to say, "I am—" as Malone had expected he would, turned even more pale and said, "Well, you see—" as Malone had also expected he would. He'd intimidated far tougher witnesses than Bill Melrose.

"I've got a wife and kids." They always had, the little lawyer reflected. "I've also got an accident record. I know I should have stopped. But I see this pileup ahead of me and I lose my head. Maybe they figure I'm somehow involved. And I've been warned, one more and I lose my job. The bus is empty, so it's just a matter of driving by fast."

He took a big gulp of his drink. "But I see this guy

on the corner. He's one of my regulars. I think fast. I stop quick, open the door, grab him in. He seemed dazed. We was eight blocks up the street before he really comes to. I explain my situation. He understands it. He's been riding with me a long time. There aren't many passengers that early in the run, and we talk about this and that, and get to be good friends. So he agrees to keep his trap shut."

Malone waved for another round.

"Now," Bill Melrose said wretchedly, "I suppose I got us both in trouble and I suppose I'll lose my job." He took half his drink in one gulp, and said automatically, "Thanks very much." Then he added, "And me with a wife and five kids."

"Bless you, Bill Melrose," Malone said, downing his own drink, "and bless the wife and the five kids, too. You are not going to lose your job. Neither you nor your friend are going to get into any trouble. Just tell me where I can find this guy."

The grin and the color began to come back to the bus driver's face. "Why sure," he said. "His name's Don Cass. I don't know where he lives, but I know where he works." He looked almost cheerful. "The fact is, my car's right here, and I'll drive you there."

This time it was Malone who said, "Thanks very much." Joe the Angel's investment was dwindling rapidly. He was halfway in the car before he remembered his new friend's accident record.

His worst suspicions were immediately verified. Bill Melrose drove like an inspired madman in a hurry. Malone tried to keep his eyes closed and hoped that in time he would be able to forget.

They came to a squealing stop in front of a very small novelty store, one of the many selling cigars, cigarettes, candy and a few comic magazines. Malone had talked to the owners of enough of them to know that total sales from merchandise would probably not be sufficient to pay the light bill.

The fat faced woman behind the counter informed Malone that Don Cass had gone for the day. She looked at him suspiciously and added, "You can see him tomorrow. He's here any time after six-thirty."

Just in time, Malone thought, to get the early dope from the eastern tracks.

"I'm sorry," he said smoothly, "but it's urgent. I've got to see him today." He tried turning on a little charm and realized right away it wouldn't work.

Her hard eyes narrowed and she said sharply. "He isn't in any trouble, is he?"

"No," Malone said. "No, no, no, *no!*" He handed one of his cards. "He's wanted as a witness in a lawsuit. A million dollar lawsuit." He saw her eyes widen, and added quickly. "He'll probably make a good thing of it himself." It was amazing, he told himself, and sometimes heartbreaking—the effect that the magic words "a million dollars" had on practically everyone.

"That's a lot of money," she said dreamily. She was silent for a moment, and Malone could almost hear what was going on in her mind. Finally she said, a little warily, "I'll give you his address. But mind you don't get him into no trouble."

She pulled out a notepad, wrote quickly, and came up with a smile that cracked her pancake makeup almost from ear to ear. "And since you're here, I've got a very good thing for tomorrow. Mr Bat, in the fifth."

It was well worth the two dollars, Malone decided, as he walked out the door after a very cordial goodbye. And besides, Mr Bat might win.

Bill Melrose opened the car door and automatically Malone got in.

"She gave me his address," Malone said, and handed over the paper.

"Fine," Bill Melrose said, "Fine, fine." He reached over and slammed the door. "I'll drive you there," he said.

The little lawyer shuddered. Then he remembered that the way to stay young was to live dangerously, and hoped for the best.

The rain had turned to an unpleasant nasty drizzle. It had also turned the streets into something resembling a newly waxed floor.

"Y'know, Malone," Bill Melrose said, "I was a race track driver for a coupla years when I was a kid." Suddenly he scooted around a delivery truck, narrowly missing a car coming in the opposite direction. He said cheerfully, "Better to go around 'em than hit 'em. It saves time.

"As I was saying, Malone, I worked six years in New York, cabbing. One year, ambulance driving. Then I got married. Her folks live in Chicago so we came out here. Being a married man, I figured I'd get into something safe."

Passing a streetcar on the left, causing a momentary traffic tangle from which he emerged miraculously unscathed, he went right on, "So now I pilot a bus."

Malone said weakly, "Do you ever ride a bicycle? Or a horse?"

Bill Melrose took his hands off the wheel for a split second, glanced at Malone at the same time. *"Me?"* he said. "You think I'm crazy? Those things are dangerous!"

There was an immediate tangle with the driver of an opposition car, and an exchange of dialogue which included nouns, verbs and adjectives that even Malone had never heard before.

"See?" Bill Melrose said, still indignant. "Guys like that never heard of no safe driving." He muttered a few more words under his breath, and Malone hoped he could remember them. "Well, hang on, Malone. We're here."

He managed a completely illegal but successful U-turn, disregarding a symphony of indignantly honking horns, and stopped in front of a No-Parking sign in front of one of Chicago's better remodeled old mansions on the near north side. This time, the car didn't squeal to a stop. It only shivered. There was an echo from Malone.

"I'll go up with you," Bill Melrose said cheerfully, "and acquaint you with him, so he'll know you're all right. Then, on account of you might like to talk private, I'll exit. I gotta check these brakes anyway, on account of they don't work right. I've been putting it off too long."

For one of the few times in his life, Malone was close to fainting.

In the glassed-in vestibule at the top of the weathered brownstone steps was the usual list of tenants, and apartment numbers, some typed, some clipped from business cards, and some lettered in ink. Bill Melrose pushed the button opposite *Cass*.

It was almost a matter of seconds before a buzz sounded, and Bill Melrose shoved open the door.

The first door on the right opened, and a small figure appeared in the doorway. In the half dusk of the hallway Malone suddenly remembered the prophetic description he'd given Maggie. "A shadowy figure . . . in the gray pre-dawn mist."

The figure was shadowy, all right, the more so in the

dim-lighted hallway. Gray suit, light gray shirt, dark gray tie, gray hair. Gray eyes, too.

"This is a good friend of mine, Don," Bill Melrose said. "You can trust him. He's going to tell you how to make a lot of money, fast, Name's Malone. John J. Malone." He caught his breath and added, "I'll go fix them brakes, Malone." And vanished.

Don Cass said, in what might have passed for cordiality in an ice-cube tray, "Pleased to meet you." Then, fixing Malone with eyes that might have been those of an alligator left overnight in a deep freeze, he demanded, "What's the pitch?"

Malone said, "It's just a little piece of business for a client. There might be some money in it for you."

The alligator eyes thawed out just a trifle, and by the time Malone had explained the purpose of his visit they were, if not friendly, at least candid.

"It was early in the morning. I was a bit sleepy, I guess. Anyway, when my pal Melrose came along I hopped into the bus. Sure, I saw the accident, but Melrose asked me to keep my mouth shut. He didn't want to lose his job. I guess anybody'd do that much for a pal."

Malone said, "Did you notice whether the traffic light was green or red?"

"I didn't notice nothin'," Don Cass told him. "I told you, it was early in the morning. I was sleepy. I just hopped in and we was off before anyone could say—"

"Jackie Robinson," Malone prompted.

"Jackie who?"

"Never mind," Malone said. He had a hunch Don Cass was telling the truth about the lights, and decided to try another tack. "Okay, forget the lights. There was an accident. You're a material witness. Of course you could be subpoenaed—"

The eyes froze up again. "I ain't tanglin' with the law. Not me. Not for nobody."

"You don't have to," Malone told him. "Not if you follow my advice." He assumed his best cell-side manner. "I'm your friend, Mr Cass. I promise you that neither you nor Mr Melrose will be in any trouble. All you need to do is call up Mr Jake Charlotte and tell him you're the missing witness. Tell him you're ready to talk—at a price, of course."

He scribbled a telephone number and handed it to Cass. "Tell him to meet you here at eight o'clock tonight."

Don Cass looked down at the piece of paper Malone had handed him. "Are you sure it's—" he began, and dropped the question. "Is that all I got to do?" he asked instead.

"Just one more thing," Malone said. He scribbled another telephone number and handed it to Cass, saying, "When you've finished calling Mr Charlotte call this number and ask for Mr Arthur Forstman. Tell him you're the missing witness and you're willing to talk—at a price, of course."

Just the faintest crinkle of a smile played around the corners of Don Cass's steel gray eyes. "I see," he said. "Both ends against the middle. Pretty smart."

"Let's just say, playing it fair," Malone said. "Tell Mr Forstman to meet you here tonight at eight o' clock sharp."

"Wait a minute! What are you trying to do, get me surrounded?"

Malone reassured him. "There will be protection. I'll see to it myself. And there'll be money in it for you— cash money. If you play your cards right, understand?"

"I don't know nothin' about cards," Cass said. "Cards ain't my racket." He rose and followed Malone to the door. "But I can tip you off to a good one in the fifth at Hialeah. Black Jet."

Malone parted reluctantly with two of the three dollars he had left and took the streetcar back to the office.

"I drew a blank," Malone told Maggie as he tossed his hat on the rack and sank into his swivel chair. "Cass doesn't remember if the traffic light was red or green. I think he's telling the truth."

"The light was red," Maggie said.

Malone unwrapped a cigar in a slow double take, reached for the desk lighter and froze in shocking fashion just as he was about to light up. "What did you say?"

"The light was red," Maggie repeated, perfectly dead pan.

Malone just gaped at her, waiting for her to go on.

"Don't look at me as if *I* was the missing witness," Maggie continued. "It just occurred to me to ask them, that's all."

"Ask who?"

"Ask *whom*," Maggie corrected him. "Why, the traffic department, of course. I called them up and asked them to check on it. Those lights are clocked, timed to the split second. At five forty-seven a.m. the light was red. Forstman was driving through a red light. That means Jake Charlotte was driving through a green light. It's as simple as that."

Malone said, "Remind me to raise your salary five dollars. No, make it ten. Which reminds me—you couldn't spare a couple of bucks cash, could you? And get me von Flanagan."

Maggie produced two tired, crumpled dollar bills from her purse. Then she dialed police headquarters and got the chief of homicide on the phone.

"Meet me at one thousand and twelve Goethe Street at eight o'clock tonight." Malone told von Flanagan. "Be there with friends. We've got a date to meet the man who murdered the sailor." He hung up.

Maggie said, "I hope you know what you're doing."

"If I don't, you'll read about it in the obituary column in the morning paper," Malone said.

Early that evening at Joe the Angel's City Hall Bar the little lawyer, waiting for the appointed hour of the meeting at Don Cass's apartment, brooded over his drink while Joe nodded sympathetically, polishing glasses.

"A million dollars riding on the turn of a red or green traffic light, a dead sailor turns up in Maggie's apartment, and who is he? No friend of Maggie's, or of Matthew, Mark, Luke or John." Joe nodded, puzzled but pious at the mention of the apostles and went on polishing his glasses. "So what happens? It turns out he's wearing green socks."

"Sailors don't wear green socks," Joe said helpfully.

"Right," Malone said. "So it turns out he's Harold Spruce, the missing witness in the million dollar damage suit—dead."

Joe the Angel shook his head in genuine, if uncomprehending, sympathy.

"And so it goes," Malone said dolefully. "The guy saw the accident but he couldn't talk because he was driving a motorcycle that didn't belong to him and he had no business being out with. The bus driver saw the accident but he can't talk because he failed to stop. He had an accident record he concealed from the company when he got the job, so he was afraid of getting mixed up in the affair. Then there's the passenger who can't talk because he's afraid of getting his friend the bus driver in trouble. And everybody holding out till he sees how much there's in it for him."

Joe the Angel shrugged. "A million dollars is a million dollars," he said.

"So I've heard tell," Malone said sourly. He was beginning to wish he'd *never* heard it. He looked at his watch. It was time to be off for Don Cass's apartment. He looked across the bar at Joe.

"Speaking of a million dollars," Malone said, "you couldn't spare a five spot, could you? For cab fare. It costs money to make money, you know."

Joe the Angel rang up *No Sale* on the register and handed five singles across the bar to Malone.

"Thanks," Malone said, "you are one man in a million, Joe."

He went out to find a cab. It was beginning to rain, and before he succeeded in flagging down a vacant cab it was coming down in buckets and Malone was drenched.

"Pity poor sailors on a night like this," the driver sang out cheerfully as Malone stepped into the cab and gave him the address.

"This poor sailor's been busted for good," Malone came back.

"What for?" asked the driver.

Malone said, "For wearing green socks, I guess."

"Happens all the time," the cabby replied, and stepped on the gas.

Malone found von Flanagan waiting for him in the foyer. "Well," snapped the chief of homicide, "where is he? I've got the joint staked out. What's the set-up?"

Malone looked at his watch. "By now," he said, "either Jake Charlotte or Arthur Forstman should be showing up at Don Cass's apartment, whichever one is most anxious to buy off the missing witness. Whoever killed Harold Spruce because he was a witness to the accident will have just as much reason to try and buy off Don Cass."

"Or *bump* him off," von Flanagan put in.

"That's what you're here for," Malone replied. "To put the arm on him before he tries it. We'd better hide out now before he gets here."

"Wait a minute, Malone. I thought you said there were two, Jake Charlotte and this other guy—whom did you say it was? Forstman?" He paused and stared at Malone, the name ringing a bell in his mind for the first time. "Say, you don't mean Forstman! The millionaire, *Arthur* Forstman! Are you crazy, Malone? How does *he* figure in this?"

Malone gave von Flanagan a fast briefing on the case. "And now," he said, "we'd better get out of sight before they get here."

Kluchetsky and Scanlon were waiting in the chief's unofficial-looking car down the street. Malone piled in and they sat down to wait keeping an eye on the apartment house entrance for the arrival of Charlotte, Forstman—or both. Eight o'clock came, and passed. Eight five. Eight ten. Eight fifteen.

"Okay," Malone said, "maybe it didn't work. Let's go and have a look."

"Either you're pulling something," von Flanagan growled, "or Don Cass has run out on you."

"We'll see," Malone said.

They went back to the apartment house and rang Don Cass's doorbell. No answer. Malone punched at the bell till the landlady came out.

"Looking for Mr Cass?" she asked. She was as thin as a Saturday newspaper, and must have been born with a worried look, Malone reflected. "He must be in. I didn't hear him go out." She glanced at von Flanagan, who had never been able to shed his official look.

"No trouble at all," Mallone said. "Mr Cass may be

able to give us some important details in an accident case. I assure you, Mrs—?"

"Sheldon," the landlady said. She had relaxed a little. "Come on in. I'll show you his door."

Repeated knocking on the door brought no response. At a sign from von Flanagan Kluchetsky applied two hundred pounds of policeman to the door and it caved in. On the floor in a pool of blood they found Don Cass, his eyes vacantly staring.

Von Flanagan examined the body. "Dead as a doornail," he said. "Dead as a mackerel, dead as a—"

"Let's just say he's dead," Malone said. He turned to Mrs Sheldon who was wringing her hands and seemed on the point of hysterics. "Pull yourself together, Mrs Sheldon," he said, consolingly. "We know you didn't do it. Was anybody here to see Mr Cass today?"

"He—he made a couple of phone calls," she replied weakly, pointing to the phone out in the hall. "I heard him. Then a man came to see him—an hour ago, maybe a little more."

Further questioning brought out no more than the fact that she had heard a man going up but that when she had stepped out into the hall he was already up the stairs and around the landing. She hadn't seen him, but apparently he had knocked on Don Cass's door, for Mr Cass had let him in. She had heard Mr Cass saying hello to the visitor. And that was all. She didn't hear the man go and assumed he was still there.

By this time Kluchetsky had the place practically apart, looking for clues. Scanlon was peeping into closets and desk drawers as if he expected the killer to be hiding in one of them.

Von Flanagan, after a brief examination pronounced the victim dead for the second time, this time adding insult to injury by making the enlightening observation that the deceased had been killed with the traditional blunt instrument.

Malone said, "Okay, that makes it official. Now— who was it? Jake Charlotte or Arthur Forstman? Or somebody who lost two bucks on Black Jet in the fifth at Hialeah."

"Black Jet came in and paid nineteen dollars," von Flanagan told him. "He's got the book on him and if he wasn't a dead bookie now I'd have to take him in on a gambling charge. It wasn't a grudge killing and it wasn't a burglary." He held up the wallet he had taken from the victim's pocket, his lips set in tight lines.

Malone could see it was stuffed with bills to pay off the winning betters. Nineteen dollars of it would have gone to him, he reflected ruefully, and wondered if he could legally claim it, or just charge it up to expenses.

"One of them guys must have done it," von Flanagan went on. "Charlotte or Forstman. I'd better start checking on both of 'em right now."

An hour later, in von Flanagan's office, Malone heard the results of a police check-up. Arthur Forstman had been addressing a civic banquet at the time of Don Cass's murder. Three hundred alibis. So Forstman was in the clear. That left Jake Charlotte.

Malone rose and shook the cigar ashes off his vest.

"If you promise me you won't send your blundering flatfoot cops after him, and that you'll keep it out of the papers that Jake Charlotte is a suspect in the murder of Don Cass," he told von Flanagan, "I'll have the suspect in your hands by noon tomorrow." He made for the door without waiting for an answer.

A call to Jake Charlotte's home brought Mrs Charlotte hobbling to the telephone. She was still in a cast as a result of the accident. Mr Charlotte, she told him, had left the house directly after dinner and hadn't returned yet. Was it something important? A settlement of the lawsuit? And if so, how much?

"Mr Forstman hasn't named a figure yet," Malone told her, "but I've got a hunch the case is coming to a head and I've got to talk it over with Mr Charlotte right away—tonight. When he gets in tell him to wait up for me. I'm coming right over."

It took the last of Joe the Angel's five dollars to pay off the cab driver at Jake Charlotte's door. It was an old frame house with a "modernized" pink stucco front that was already beginning to crack and blister. In the light of the street lamp it looked like something out of Dali in one of his most nightmarish moods. The living room light was on. Malone rang the doorbell.

Mrs Charlotte's voice called out to him, "Come in, the door is open."

"I'm so worried about Jake," were the first words with which she greeted Malone. "It isn't like him to go off like this directly after dinner and not tell me what his plans are. And it's not like him to stay out so late. He is a homebody. Jake is. Besides, he missed his favorite television program."

She was a matronly woman with the harried but still hopeful look that one finds at the cosmetics counter at a drugstore *One Cent Sale*. Her injuries were evidently quite as extensive as the insurance investigators had reported. But she had managed to give her hair a few hurried touches and make up her face for the visitor with her one good arm.

I'm sure Jake will be along any minute now," she went on, to reassure Malone. "He *never* stays out this late. Can I offer you a cup of tea?"

Malone felt his gullet take a nose-dive into his solar

plexus. His throat was acutely parched—like a camel's after a non-stop journey across the Sahara.

"No, thank you," he said politely. "Tea aggravates my neuritis. I could stand a drop of rye, though—or anything else you might have in the house," he added quickly.

Mrs Charlotte looked over at him archly. "Well," she said, "if you promise not to tell Jake. He disapproves of liquor in the house. But I've got a bottle stashed away— if you don't mind getting it yourself. It's in the linen closet there, under the guest towels."

Malone made a beeline for the linen closet but before he was half way across the room there was a sound of the front door opening and he was barely back in his chair before Jake Charlotte entered the room.

Jake Charlotte looked, if anything, uglier and more unprepossessing than he had looked on his recent harried visit to Malone's office. If he was alarmed at finding John J. Malone in his living room he was trying not to show it.

He greeted the little lawyer with, "Well, well, it's nice seeing you again, Mr Malone. You have some news about our lawsuit, of course. How much is he willing to settle for?"

But before Malone could answer Jake Charlotte had turned to his wife. "You shouldn't have stayed up so late," he told her. "You know it isn't good for you to lose sleep like this. Come now, I'll help you to your room. Mr Malone will excuse you, won't you, Mr Malone?"

By sheer force but with an outward show of gentleness he got his wife out of the chair and limpingly into the bedroom—very much as one would half-drag and half-coax a reluctant but submissive child. Two minutes later he was back, closing the bedroom door carefully behind him and winking at Malone as if to say, "There, that's done. Now we can talk freely."

Meanwhile Malone had been doing some fast thinking. If Charlotte was guilty, and had given the sailor the lethal dose of chloral hydrate, and then had gone to Don Cass's house an hour before the appointment and murdered him with a blunt instrument to remove a second witness, then what would he not be prepared to do now? What would he not be prepared to do if he got wind of the fact that he was suspected of the crimes and that Malone had come at this late hour to deliver him over to the police for questioning?

Malone was beginning to wish he had told von Flanagan to let his cops make the arrest themselves. But after all, he reminded himself, there was still no direct evidence linking Jake Charlotte to either crime. Besides, the man was still his client and entitled to any legal protection he could give him.

Just the same he should have stopped off at Joe the Angel's City Hall Bar and borrowed Joe's gun, or at the very least fortified himself with a double shot of rye. His throat by this time was feeling like the last days of a California drought and a dangerous fire hazard.

"My wife is the worrying kind," Charlotte said. "And she hasn't got any kind of a head for business. You know how women are."

"The kind I've known have a good head for business, all right," Malone said. "And the only worrying they do is where the next mink is coming from. I just dropped in to talk over the case with you." He was sparring for time, trying to decide just what line of questioning to take with Charlotte in order to smoke out the facts.

"I thought it might help to make a better settlement with Mr Forstman if I could spring at least one good witness on him for our side," he went on quickly. "Do you think you could identify a witness if I produced one?"

Charlotte gave Malone a sly look, in which there was just the faintest trace of suspicion. "I guess I could identify a witness," he said, "if he was on our side. Who did you have in mind—and how much is it going to cost?"

"I don't know yet," Malone said. "I got a note in the mail a few days ago from somebody on North Clark Street, but I haven't been able to contact him. He left the house and hasn't been back since. I thought you might be able to give me a line on him. His name's Harold Spruce."

He saw Charlotte's face blanch and his hands flutter in a moment of panic. But only for a moment.

"The name don't mean a thing to me," Charlotte said, shaking his head. "I'd have to see the man. When you catch up with him let me know and I'll come over to the office—" He paused. "It's getting cold in here. I could stand a little nip or something."

He rose and went over to a desk in the corner of the room and unlocked one of the lower drawers. "I've got to take it on the q.t.," he said, lowering his voice to a conspiratorial whisper. "My wife disapproves of liquor." He disappeared into the kitchen where Malone heard him fiddling with ice cubes. "How will you have yours?" he asked, poking his head out of the kitchen door.

Malone's heart sank. "Thanks, but I don't ever touch the stuff," he said, remembering the sailor and the chloral hydrate. But when Charlotte returned he had a glass in his hand and another which he offered to Malone.

"You're kidding," he said. "Everybody knows John J. Malone never passed up a drink. Here, drink up."

Malone took the glass and set it down on the end table beside his chair. "Well, just a drop," he said, "when we've finished talking business. I've been tipped off that there's another witness—somebody who was waiting for a bus on the corner when the accident occurred." Malone was watching Charlotte narrowly as he spoke. "Somebody by the name of Cass—Don Cass."

The glass trembled in Charlotte's hand. He set it down and sank into a chair. There was a wary look in his eyes now. A hunted look. Malone decided to give it to him straight and braced himself for the next move.

"Don Cass is dead," he said. "And so is Harold Spruce. Somebody is bent on murdering all our witnesses. You wouldn't know who it is, would you, Mr Charlotte?"

The words were barely out of his mouth before Charlotte was out of his chair and making for him with a knife he had picked up in the kitchen and concealed in his breast pocket.

Knife fighting was not in Malone's line. He had dealt in his time with guns, blunt instruments, and broken whiskey bottles. But a knife was something else again. Instinctively he dived for Charlotte's weapon hand, dodging the blow as he did so. But he missed and both men came down in a heap on the floor. Malone managed to kick out at the knife hand and this time the weapon went clattering across the floor.

He was up and on top of Charlotte before the latter could recover the weapon. But a vicious blow to the jaw made his head reel and he found himself pinned down under a rain of blows from Charlotte, who was fighting like a madman now.

Mrs Charlotte had come hobbling out of the bedroom, and was screaming blue murder. Bells were ringing somewhere, but whether they were doorbells, telephone bells or bells in his belfry Malone couldn't tell at the moment.

He had a firm grip on his assailant now, probably on

the jugular, but he couldn't tell exactly. All he knew for certain was that he had to hold on because if he ever let go—Then there was a flash of fireworks in his head and suddenly everything went black.

When he came to again it was the face of Captain Daniel von Flanagan that swam into focus above him.

"Just take it easy," von Flanagan was saying. "all you need now is a stiff drink." He picked up the glass Malone had set down on the end table and held it out to the little lawyer.

Malone shook his head. "Take it away," he said, "and mark it exhibit A."

The Chief of Homicide turned to officer Kluchetsky. "You're a witness," he said. "This is the first time John J. Malone ever refused a drink. Remember that when the sanity hearing comes up."

The next day at the office, Maggie, between cold towels on his multiple swellings, bruises and contusions, plied the little lawyer with questions.

"Tell me this, Malone. If Harold Spruce was dickering with Arthur Forstman and Jack Charlotte, trying to sell his testimony as a witness to the highest bidder, why did he send a note to the police department offering to come forward and testify?"

"Harold Spruce was trying to bring pressure on both bidders," Malone said. "He figured that if they knew he had offered to talk they'd both get scared and up the ante. Jake Charlotte was up against it. He knew he couldn't compete with Forstman's millions, so he slipped Harold Spruce a lethal dose of chloral hydrate to get him out of the way. Which reminds me, is there anything in the emergency file?"

Maggie went to the filing cabinet and brought out a bottle of rye. "Joe the Angel sent this over when he heard you had met with—an accident," she said. "It's for internal use only."

"I can use it." Malone said, pouring himself a drink. "Have you heard from the police lab yet about that drink Jake Charlotte offered me last night?"

Maggie said, "Von Flanagan called up just before you got in. He said to tell you it was spiked with chloral hydrate. Enough to kill even a lawyer—and what he said about that I didn't wait to hear. I hung up. Anyway, it was a good thing he was having you shadowed and got there on time to save you from Charlotte, or—I don't even want to think what might have happened."

"I would have had him hogtied and ready for delivery," Malone said, "if his wife hadn't conked me on the head with the table lamp." He laid aside the cold towels and got up to go. "I've got some unfinished business to attend to," he said. "If von Flanagan calls up again tell him I'll be over later to confer with my client."

Maggie gave him a sharp look. "Your client?"

At the door Malone turned. "Mr. Jake Charlotte," he said. "He's still my client, isn't he? And remember, I never lost a client yet."

"No," Maggie said, "but this time your client nearly lost you."

At Joe the Angel's City Hall Bar, Malone sat staring glumly into his drink and turning the situation over in his mind. The million dollar suit had gone glimmering, of course. All the money he could expect for defending Jake Charlotte probably wouldn't pay for the drink in front of him, let alone what he already owed Joe the Angel. And the rent was due. And Maggie's back pay, to say nothing of what he owed her in cash loans. Things had never looked so black before.

Joe was morose, but sympathetic. "Why did the guy

have to go do things like that?" he said, shaking his head sadly. "And a mickey finn yet! It gives the saloon business a bad name."

"A million dollars," Malone brooded. "A cool million bucks—right out the window."

He was still brooding when he felt a tap on his shoulder and turned to find Arthur Forstman seating himself on the stool beside him.

"Your secretary told me I'd find you here." Forstman said. He took out his wallet, extracted five one thousand dollar bills, and laid them on the bar. "I promised to pay you five thousand to prove I was not the murderer," he said. "Here's your money. I'm sorry you got roughed up doing it."

Malone looked at the crisp thousand dollar bills. Joe the Angel was watching him, with a grin a mile wide, a grin that changed to a puzzled frown as Malone continued to stare at the bar. When Malone's hand went out to the money the grin returned to Joe's face, but only for an instant, for Malone was shoving the bills back at Forstman.

"I can't take it," he said. "I've already got a client, and I can't have two clients at one time."

Joe looked as if he was going to burst into tears.

"But I'll tell you what I *can* do," Malone said to Forstman. "I can steer you on to a hell of a good investment, and maybe we can both make some money. Just maybe."

"That would be just fine with me," Forstman said. "I'm always open to a good business proposition."

"Then wait for me out in the car," Malone said, "and I'll join you in a few minutes."

When Forstman had gone Malone said to Joe the Angel, "Joe, I'm cutting you in on the investment, too. All you need to invest is ten bucks."

"What kind investment," Joe asked suspiciously. But at the same time he handed over the money.

Malone said, "I'm taking Arthur Forstman out to a floating crap game on upper Wabash Avenue. You'll get your money back. Besides, it'll be good to be among honest men again."

MURDER GOES TO MARKET
by Mignon G. Eberhart

*Born in Nebraska in 1899, Mignon G. Eberhart is still
active as a mystery writer. Her long career dates from the
publication of* The Patient in Room 18 *in 1929, the first
of seven novels about Nurse Sarah Keate. Some fifty other
Eberhart novels, notably* Five Passengers from Lisbon
*(1946), lack series characters, but like some other mystery
novelists she has preferred series sleuths in her shorter
works. Mystery writer Susan Dare and banker Mr.
Wickwire have each appeared in several stories. The
former's adventures were collected as* The Cases of Susan
Dare *(1934).*

*One other Eberhart series character is all but unique
in mystery fiction. Bland, the butler-detective whom you
will meet here, appeared in three novellas during the
1940s. As Jon L. Breen has pointed out, the only other
butler-sleuth is probably P.G. Wodehouse's Jeeves, who is
occasionally called upon to solve a mystery. In this story
Eberhart uses the interesting background of a
supermarket in wartime Washington, during an era
when supermarkets were only beginning to blossom on the
American scene.*

*"Murder Goes to Market" was first published in the
July, 1943 issue of the* American Magazine, *and was
collected in Eberhart's* Five of My Best *(1949), a volume
published only in England.*

It was on Monday night that I returned to Washington after a six-weeks' absense; on Wednesday morning
I resumed the responsibilities of my small household—
comprising only Bland, the butler, his wife, and myself—by going to the market, early. The small wicker
market basket was on the hall table when I came downstairs. It looked like an ordinary, empty basket; in actual
fact it represented a feud between me and Bland.

He was hovering in the hall that morning as I picked up the basket, but pretended not to see me. The point was that both of us like to do the marketing; and since I could and did take a mean advantage of my position as employer to do the job, there was nothing Bland could do but register passive resistance. And while he has a gift for that sort of thing in the way of a lifted eyebrow and a chilly blue eye, I am used to Bland and pretend not to see either.

It was a late-summer day, the air languid and humid. Later, I knew, in spite of lowered shades, the small house would be hot. It was a gem of a house, really; one of the charming old houses in Alexandria, which had been perfectly decorated and furnished, by its owner. That's Frieda Merly, from whom I leased it when I was sent to Washington to do some writing in connection with the war.

Another attraction was the existence of a huge and altogether amazing Supermarket within walking distance of the house. I happened to know the owner, Sam Boomer; white-haired, handsome, urbane, he could talk the price of potatoes with the air of a distinguished diplomat. He might not have been so cordially accepted in the inner circle, however, if he hadn't been a beau of Frieda Merly's. She was that type of rich, charming, and social widow which national capitals seem to develop.

Sam Boomer's Bel-Air Supermarket was not only an enchanting spot; it practically amounted to a neighborhood club. It was really astonishing, the stray items of information one was likely to pick up along with one's cabbages and sweetbreads during a morning's tour of the place. I don't say that Bland liked gossip. But both of us liked the market.

So Bland was very austere when I took up the basket that morning in late August. The opening and closing of the door was almost violently unassisted by him. Once out on the small, clean doorstep I felt the heat fall upon me like a blanket.

Washington is one of the most beautiful and gracious cities in the world, but I had forgotten, during my short absence, how hot it, and its suburbs, can be. Petunias bloomed from the window boxes of the lovely, narrow brick houses, with their beautiful old doors and bright brass knockers. Neat iron fences marked occasional green pocket handkerchiefs for lawns. The ivy here and there looked cool, and so did the Venetian blinds, slanted low over dark interiors. But nothing was cool.

I turned another corner and came upon the Supermarket. Or, more accurately, the Super-super-market. It was colossal, it was Gargantuan. I had learned to make my forays upon the place at the earliest possible hour before it was crowded. On this occasion the doors were just being opened for trade as I rounded the corner.

I was not the first customer. A girl all in white, with a long, blue-black bob that cupped her little head smoothly and made her face look rather white in spite of her crimson mouth, came from the other direction. She was running quickly and lightly, her white, neat pumps making staccato taps along the sidewalk. I caught a flash of blue eyes under soft black lashes. She was very pretty, and she looked frightened, which was odd, and I knew her.

She was Cynthy Farish. She gave me a flashing blue glance and didn't see me at all, but whirled into the store.

The door closed behind her just as I cried, "Cynthy!" She didn't hear me, and by the time I had followed her into the store she was going rapidly along one of the aisles. She was literally empty-handed, for she carried no handbag. But then the white dress she was wearing must have had pockets, and anyway it was nothing to me how she carried money for the shopping she was obviously about to do.

Probably there is not a woman in America who is not thoroughly familiar with the Supermarket. Its plan is simplicity itself. Everything is made easy for the customer.

You enter a huge room which is railed off into aisles, along which the stocks of groceries, vegetables, fruits, and canned goods are arranged. At the starting point of your circuit you supply yourself with a cart which looks like a perambulator, and push it along ahead of you. You are at liberty to make your own choice, within the limits of the ration rules, to pause and take as much time as you wish to consider the relative merits of Camembert or Bel Paese, green beans or peas. Nobody hurries you. Nobody seems even to watch you. There are attendants, of course, if you want something raked down from the highest shelf along the wall.

But you can also venture a surreptitious pinch along the alligator pear bin, without being detected, or weigh in your hand every melon on display. That year there was a particularly good selection of melons, because Sam Boomer had made a specialty and hobby of melons. It was always something with him; the previous year it had been smoked turkey, and the year before that different kinds of bread. One could scarcely say "Good morning" to Sam Boomer without being obliged to listen to some fresh item about his current enthusiasm.

You put your selections in the perambulator, wheel it along ahead of you, and eventually emerge at a gate and a row of checkers. These sum up your purchases and send you on to the banks of cash registers, where clerks take your money and whisk you on through the gate. Here you may carry your loot away in a paper bag or in your market basket, or let a boy carry it for you. It is simplicity itself.

I selected my perambulator and dropped my bag inside it.

The attendants were as busy as bees about the chores that made the place ready for the day's onslaught of customers; it was all fresh and clean, and the air smelled deliciously of coffee, hot buns, and spice. I sniffed with pleasure and trundled over to the melons.

Shopping for fruit is a rite with me. I chose a long Cranshaw melon, mellow, heavy, and perfect. One that Bland himself would have approved.

And then I saw Cynthy. She was just entering the little brown door.

This was at the back of the great room, behind a long aisle stacked with rice and flour and sugar, and set into the wall, which was brightly lined with canned goods. It stood a litle ajar.

A moment or two may have passed before it occurred to me that there might be some special sort of delicacy stored beyond the little brown door. And if Cynthy Farish had opened it, I decided, why shouldn't I? So I dropped a carrot I'd been pretending to examine, went to the door, and had my hand on the door knob just as she came out, abruptly.

We met full tilt. There ensued one of those confused and ridiculous moments of grasping for balance and exclaiming; the melon she was carrying in her arm fell into my basket. I clutched the door casing, steadied us both, and cried, "Cynthy! Hello!"

It was only then, actually, that she saw me. She stood there momentarily frozen, pushing back her hair with one hand and looking at me with eyes that were direct and blue and—again I had to use the word—frightened.

She didn't say anything, and I said involuntarily, *"What's wrong, Cynthy?"*

She caught her breath and spoke, then, quickly: "Nothing. That is I—oh, I'm afraid I've dropped my melon." She scooped the melon out of my basket.

"But, Cynthy, I just got home! I want to see you."

"Yes, I know." Her blue eyes were almost desperate. "I'll telephone. I'll—I've got to go now. I'm sorry." And to my astonishment she flashed around the aisle and disappeared toward the front of the store, leaving me worried and a little heartsick.

For the fear in her eyes was unmistakable. And I liked Cynthy Farish. I had known her and her mother for years. When the mother died and the annuity they lived on too disappeared, I had made Cynthy come to me. I would have liked her to live in my home permanently. Even Bland was austerely devoted to her. But Cynthy was not only independent; she had a clear integrity of character which I liked too much to try to conquer; she refused my offer, and when I saw she was determined to leave I helped her to find a job. For nearly a year she had been secretary-companion to Frieda Merly.

Frieda liked her, too, and saw that she went places and enjoyed Washington. Frieda always had protegees of one kind or another; indeed, Frieda's jeweled fingers were poked gracefully into more Washington pies than I could count.

I stood there for a moment or two, thinking of Cynthy, and then my curiosity returned. What was beyond that little brown door to interest her? My hand was on the knob. I pushed the door open a little more and went into the room beyond.

At first sight it was not at all an interesting room. It was lighted brightly by large, high windows which let in floods of sunlight, and it was stacked with neat rows of cases, arranged with aisles between, to utilize the floor space. I went further into the room, and saw on the stenciled cases the names of all sorts of well-known brands of such things as canned tomatoes, ginger ale, and crocks of Vermont maple syrup.

I couldn't help noting with a housewifely eye that the Supermarket was as clean behind the scenes as it was in the great salesroom. But its very orderliness defeated me. I didn't think Cynthy had hurried into the stockroom to fasten her garter, and obviously she hadn't tucked a packing case under her arm. There'd been only the melon in her hands when we met at the door. I was a little shocked, thinking how carelessly she must have selected it in her hasty journey, the length of the big store.

I went still farther into the room, absorbed in discovery. I rounded a stack that held cases (*cases!*) of caviar, and went on, scanning the rows until I reached the wall. It was a housewife's paradise in these days of rationed goods. I made a dash for the shelves and saw, beyond the next stack of packing cases, some little earthenware jars that had a nostalgic look of familiarity. They held paté de foie gras with truffles, something that had assumed a collector's value and price. What a triumph to bring a jar home to Bland!

I reached up gloatingly, and then, with the precious jar in my hand, I looked down. Down and around the end of the stack of packing cases on my right. I don't know why I looked down. For the thing that lay there looking at me really didn't see me. Its eyes were open and full of reflected light, but perfectly still and glassy. Its mouth was open, too. Shockingly.

Then I was screaming, and I couldn't stop, because the man who lay there was not only dead—a knife was sticking out of his throat. A plain, long knife with a black handle. I shrank back against the packing cases and could not look away from the dreadful thing at my feet.

There was not really very much blood, I suppose because the knife was still in the wound. He was a man of about fifty; short and stocky, with vigorous black hair, and thick features, and black eyebrows. A ray of sunlight fell across the ring on the hand nearest me, an old-fashioned signet ring with the initials "A.B." scrawled upon it, so worn that I could scarcely read them. I stared at it, I remember, taking a queer kind of refuge in deciphering those faint and ornate initials. He wore a gray seersucker suit and heavy black oxfords. And I told myself to stop screaming, just as the door burst open and people ran into the room.

The first one to find us was an attendant in a white smock, carrying, of all things, a basket of tomatoes. He dropped the tomatoes, turned green, and after one pop-eyed look sagged over against the packing cases in a dead faint.

This was not a help. Tomatoes were bumping and thudding everywhere. But almost immediately more white-smocked figures rushed into the room and around the packing cases, and pandemonium began.

It was, however, rather controlled. Attendants in a market of that size are schooled sternly in dealing with crises; not murder, naturally, but crises of the deep and fundamental kind that arise when two women simultaneously select the same watermelon. Gradually I became aware of a kind of Greek chorus from all of them:

"Call the manager!"

"Call Mr Hibling!"

"Hurry—"

A clerk was running for the door, when it opened, and Sam Boomer himself came in, followed by policemen. Two of them.

"Mr Boomer!"

"Mr Boomer, there's an accident!"

"Now, then," said one of the policemen. "What's all this?"

Nine people told him; and everybody pointed.

There hadn't, of course, been time for anyone from the store to call the police. So someone else, obviously, had known of the murder and reported it. Cynthy? Was that why she had fled from the room? *Was that, by any fantastic chance, why she had come there?* I rejected the thought; I had to, but it lay there anyway, under the surface of my consciousness, while I listened and looked. Yet, if Cynthy had not reported the murder, then who had?

Suddenly no one was speaking. And both policemen were kneeling there beside the body and looking at it. One of them put his hand over the forever quiet heart.

Sam Boomer finally broke the silence. He knelt, too, tall and solid and neatly tailored in his thin gray suit, the sunlight making a silver cap of his white, thick hair. His usually rather rosy face was pale. He stared at the body and then at the policemen and said in a hushed voice, "My God, in my store! Who is he? 'A.B.' on his ring. Who do you suppose he is? That knife's from the cheese counter; I'll swear it's from the cheese counter." He looked up sharply towards the white-smocked clerks hovering around. "Get Hibling," he said.

"You don't know him, Mr Boomer?" said one of the policemen.

Sam Boomer shook his head. "Where's his wallet? He must have a wallet. Or some papers in his pockets."

With that, really, the investigation began. Investigation into the murder of a stout, swarthy man in a seersucker suit, with a knife in his throat. For the first baffling development was that there was no wallet in his pocket and, so far as they could discover, no papers and no identifying cards. Nothing except that signet ring, so old and so long worn that it was deeply imbedded into the flesh of his thick finger. There were no fingerprints on the knife.

It was a long time before the police, once launched, let any of us leave. The customers then in the store were asked to remain while their names and addresses were taken, and they were questioned concerning anything they had seen that morning. It was, however, evident that the death had taken place some hours before the store had opened. I was still there when the medical examiner arrived.

"It's murder," said the doctor. "No man ever drove a knife into his own throat at that angle. He's been dead at least twelve hours; can't say more definitely. Any idea who he is?"

No one had. By that time fingerprint men were arriving and another man was taking pictures of the body from all angles. It was about then, I believe, that I was asked to remain, pending the arrival of a lieutenant of police who would want to question me. I was politely escorted up a little stairway to what proved to be Mr Hibling's office. Sam Boomer went with me, and Mr Hibling himself, who came in just after the arrival of the man with the camera.

The manager was a brisk, efficient-looking man in spectacles, and more agitated by his tardy arrival, it seemed to me, than by the news of the murder. He apologized to Sam Boomer, who brushed his apologies aside, but who nevertheless had a certain measuring look in his blue eyes which made me feel that Mr Hibling's dereliction would not be forgotten.

"Go on downstairs, Hibling," said Sam Boomer, "and see to things. Anything the police say, goes. Say a soothing word or two to the customers. Don't let the clerks get out of hand. Put 'em to work."

"Yes, sir. Yes, Mr Boomer. Yes, sir," said Mr Hibling eagerly, and bobbed away.

Sam Boomer let his tall figure down into the swivel chair before Mr Hibling's desk, twirling it around to face me, got out a white handkerchief and mopped his glistening forehead, and said, "Gosh!"

I leaned back in my own chair and took off my hat to fan myself with it. We eyed each other for a moment, and he said again, "Gosh. I can't believe it. How'd you happen to be there? Did anybody tell you? Here—there ought to be a fan somewhere."

He twirled around again, found a fan on top of a steel filing cabinet, and turned it on; the little steady whir covered the sounds of the voices and heavy footsteps below. And I was brought squarely against what I had already realised was the problem of Cynthy Farish. With a swift sense of horror I saw that I could avoid it no longer.

The child had been running when I first saw her enter the store; she had gone swiftly and purposefully to the stockroom; she had fled from it with scarcely a word to me. And I didn't think that the time elapsing between our encounter at the stockroom door and the arrival of Sam Boomer with the police was enough to permit her to go to a telephone outside the store and report the murder.

No, someone else had reported it.

So what of Cynthy? True, she might not have seen the body. Because of the arrangement of the packing cases it would have been perfectly possible for anyone to enter the room and spend some time there, really, without chancing to go into the corner where the dead man lay.

But why had she gone into the room at all? And why was she so intent, so hurried, so frightened?

Boomer, of course, knew her. I hesitated, debating whether or not to tell him of her visit; and he said, sitting in the swivel chair and watching me, "This is going to be a nasty affair. But I don't think it'll hurt the store. It was you who found him just now, wasn't it? Somebody said—"

"Oh, yes," I said. "I found him."

"Tell me about it. What were you doing in the stockroom?"

Sam Boomer was nobody's fool; Frieda Merly, indeed, always spoke of his brilliance of mind, saying that with the right help he would go far. I rather surmised she meant with her help.

It was then I realized that if I told Boomer and the police of that visit, Cynthy Farish, with her youth and her sweetness, was going to be dragged into the sordid, long-drawn-out and horrible process of a police investigation into murder. I didn't for an instant think that she had had anything to do with the killing of the man who lay there in the stockroom. There was no real reason for her to become a suspect in a murder case. So I decided to trust my instinct.

This is not always a good plan. But I didn't have time to consider it further, for Sam Boomer was waiting for a reply.

"The stockroom," he reminded me, "is not open to the public. How did you get in?"

"It was open this morning," I said. "That is, the door was slightly open and I was curious. I thought there might be something—well, special, back there. I was merely prowling."

"Oh, I see," he said. "You didn't see Jim Allen, did you?"

"Jim Allen?" I seemed to remember the name only vaguely.

He said, "Yes. He's in my office. A nice kid, twenty-four or so. He actually found the dead man. Found him this morning, early, before the store opened. Came to tell me. I rounded up a couple of policemen and came along."

So that was how they had known. "Oh," I said slowly. "Then I wasn't the first one to—"

"No," he cut in. "That was Jim. Feel better now?" he asked with a sudden smile.

"Yes," I said, and meant it.

He swerved around, got out shell-rimmed glasses, put them on his good-looking nose, and looked not a day older. I could see why Frieda Merly liked him. He reached for the telephone, and as he dialed, said, "Jim, of course, came straight to me. Very properly, I think. He didn't seem to want to take the responsibility for reporting the murder to the police." There was a little pause while he listened into the telephone. Then he added, "He was thinking of me, and the store. But this won't hurt it. Jim's all right . . . Oh—hello, Rosita?"

Apparently someone said yes. He went on: "Rosita, Jim was right. The fellow's dead; seems to have been murdered . . . Yes, I thought Jim was having a brainstorm, too, but I guess he wasn't . . . No, I don't know who; the police are here now . . . Yes. Well, if the newspapers get hold of you, just keep quiet. Tell 'em you don't know anything. Williams will be back this afternoon. He'll take care of the newspaper end of it. And listen, Rosita—keep Jim there. It'd be better, I think. He's impulsive, you know. But tell him the police will want to question him. That's all. 'By, dear."

He hung up, and twirled around again. "My niece," he said. "I imagine I'd better get downstairs again. If you'll excuse me—" He got up, and at the door said, "I wonder if you'd phone Frieda for me? Tell her I'm with the police and I'll call her as soon as I can. Thanks."

He disappeared, and I telephoned to Frieda. Having leased her house, she was living in an apartment in Washington. It was still early, but her voice was, as always, alert and musical. It changed, however, when I told her what had happened.

"Good heavens!" she cried, shocked. "Who was murdered?"

"I don't know. Nobody knows yet."

There was a pause. "But somebody must know!" she said finally. "Did Sam see him?"

"Oh, yes. His wallet was removed. Probably by the murderer."

"His—" Frieda stopped again. And then said quickly, "Oh, yes, his wallet. I see, I suppose that makes it difficult. What does he look like?"

"Dark," I said. "Middle-aged. I'd rather not talk about him, just now."

"Oh, of course, darling. What a shock it must have been. Is Sam still there?"

"Yes. He asked me to phone you. He'll call you later."

"Oh." There was another little pause before she said, "Nice of Sam. Are reporters on hand yet?"

"No. That is, I don't think so."

"Oh," said Frieda, and again seemed to be thinking hard.

I said, "By the way, is Cynthy there?"

"Cynthy?" said Frieda, a note of surprise in her voice. "Why, I believe so. I don't know. I haven't seen her this morning. I'm still in bed, having breakfast. Do you want me to come over?"

"No. I think they'll let me go after a few questions."

Again she seemed to wait, as if reluctant to hang up.

Finally she said slowly, "You might let me know any— well, developments. It must have been horrible finding him like that. And nobody knows who he is?"

"Nobody," I repeated, and hung up.

I called Bland. His voice was still full of hauteur; when I did the marketing he always stayed mad until well past lunch, and only warmed up after tea or cocktail time.

"Yes, madam," he said now frostily.

"Bland, I may be late for lunch."

A late meal affects Bland strongly. After a pause he observed bitterly that we were having a souffle.

"I'm sorry, but I have to see the police. It may take time."

"The souffle will be ruined, madam," began Bland icily, and then he did an audible double take. "Police?" he interrupted himself to say.

"Yes. I ran into what looks like a murder over here."

"Murder, madam!" And this time there was an effect of yoicks and tally-ho in his voice.

"Yes, but you are not to come," I said. "That's all, Bland." And I hung up, with the result that twenty minutes later, just as the Lieutenant of police began to question me, Bland arrived. Big, pompous, toeing out discreetly, eyes blank and blue, he stood behind my chair with such an effect of remote and impersonal duty that not even the most astute policeman could have guessed that in reality Bland was practically bursting out of his neat alpaca coat to hear all, see all, and know all.

Perhaps an hour later we were allowed to depart.

Bland carried my basket as we walked home. The interview with the police had not been bad at all. I had been fingerprinted, it is true, but so had everyone else. I had told them several times everything I knew, which was little enough. And that was all, except that I still hadn't said a word about Cynthy Farish.

While the Lieutenant was questioning me, reports were brought to him constantly about the inquiry going on in another part of the store; of the customers, all of whom were allowed to leave very soon, and of the staff. The results were definitely on the negative side.

No one knew, or admitted knowing, the identity of the murdered man, nor was there any way of knowing how he had got into the stockroom. In fact, nothing in the way of clues or evidence had developed up to the time I was permitted to leave.

Although none of the clerks confessed to remembering the murdered man, he might very well have walked through the store and into the stockroom unnoticed in the late afternoon rush. Or of course he might have entered, or been admitted, after hours.

There was a back door to the stockroom, as well as the entrance through the store, and the matter of keys was gone into rather thoroughly. I knew that, for I had heard them talking of it. Mr Hibling had a key; but Mr Hibling also had an alibi: he was in the dentist's chair from four o'clock until closing time, and in bed with a hot-water bottle and aspirin tablets until shortly before his arrival at the market that morning.

Sam Boomer had a key, and he, too, had an alibi. He had been in his office in Washington until five; Jim Allen, he'd told them (and I heard the stenographer read a transcript of his exact words to the lieutenant), was with him. He and Jim Allen had gone to the Mayflower for a drink, after which Jim had gone to take Rosita to a cocktail party somewhere and Sam Boomer had sat around the Mayflower bar talking to several people he knew.

"Who?" said the lieutenant.

The stenographer read four or five names. A plainclothes man, who had turned up by then, stopped fanning himself with his white straw hat and said that he had already checked Boomer's story by telephone. "Seems to be right," he added gloomily. "All five men say they saw and talked to him after five, and one of them—Claussen, works on a newspaper—left him in time to keep a six-thirty appointment at the Carlton. That's five minutes' walk away."

"Did Boomer leave then?"

"About then," said the stenographer. "Here it is."

He read: "Mr Boomer replied, 'I was waiting for Bill Williams, a friend of mine. He'd been in New York and thought he might get an afternoon train back to Washington. I was to meet him at the Mayflower bar, but he didn't turn up, so I went home—to my house near Rock Creek Park—about six-thirty. I'm not sure of the time. My niece, Miss Rosita Boomer, was out. Allen was with her. They came home about seven-thirty and we all had dinner together. I didn't go out again. I stayed home and read. Rosita was at home, too; so was Jim Allen. He lives in my house. Works for me.'" The stenographer paused.

The plain-clothes man sighed. "Maid at the Boomer house says he came in before seven. She doesn't know the exact time, but she saw him. There isn't time between six-thirty and seven, at the outside limit, for him to drive to Alexandria, commit a murder in his store, and drive home again. So it looks like an alibi. But I'll keep working on it, if you think he's drunk enough to murder a guy here, and leave him to be found."

"Hm-m," said the lieutenant thoughtfully. His eyes fastened absently on the toe of my white slipper, and then sharpened and became alert, as if he had forgotten my presence and Bland's and only then remembered. He turned to the stenographer again: "Did Jim Allen have a key?"

"A key," said the plain-clothes man. "And an alibi. Drinks with Boomer, cocktail party with Boomer's niece. Complete. You can check him off."

"We can't check anybody off," snapped the lieutenant, "till we know when the fellow was murdered."

Certainly, according to Hibling, there were no more keys, which, however, did not limit the suspects at all. In the first place, anyone knows how easy it is to have a duplicate key made, provided you can get hold of the original for an hour. Also, there was no particular evidence tending to prove that the back door had been used at all.

Indeed, it began to look more and more as if the murdered man, and his murderer, had quietly entered the store late the previous afternoon, along with some hundreds, probably, of other people, that they had entered the stockroom unobserved, and then, later, the murderer had calmly walked out.

The cashiers were questioned about people coming in and out of the store late the previous afternoon, for if the murdered man had been dead about twelve hours, the conclusion was, naturally, that he could have been murdered some time shortly before or after the store had closed; at five-thirty, that was. But none of them remembered anything.

It was just then, however, that I had rather a bad moment, for one of them said, as a kind of afterthought, that there were not many customers in the store in the morning at the time the murder was discovered, and that only one had left the store, for he had rung up only one charge—for a Cranshaw melon—just before the scream began in the stockroom.

The lieutenant had visibly pricked up his ears. "Do you remember the customer?" he asked.

"A young woman," said the cashier. "Pretty. Black hair and a white dress."

I held my breath, but the cashier proved to be a laconic man, not given to fine descriptions.

The lieutenant muttered rather fretfully that there were probably a thousand young women in Washington, black-haired, and wearing white dresses. And since, obviously, the murder had not been committed within the hour of my own grisly discovery he let the inquiry about Cynthy drop.

However, I knew that the investigation had barely begun. Eventually they would identify the dead man; eventually all the business of photographs and fingerprints and detailed and tireless inquiry would bring to light a few solid facts which, in turn, would lead to others. I had too much faith in the efficency of our modern police system not to be worried about Cynthy's part in this ghastly mystery.

That was, in general, how things stood when Bland and I walked home. Bland carrying the wicker basket with my melon in it. The heat made the old, worn bricks waver before my eyes, but Bland was unaffected by the heat or by the murder.

By more or less adroit and exceedingly detailed questioning, he made me go over the whole story of my discovery—except that I didn't mention Cynthy even to him. He had, however, to admit himself baffled. " 'A.B.' on his ring," he muttered, shaking his head. "Not very helpful. Do you mind telling me again, madam, exactly what you, and everyone else said and did? Before I arrived, that is," he added, with an effect of modesty.

I didn't mind, and told him again in great detail, but there was little to tell, and Bland looked discouraged.

When we reached home, however, he had cheered up enough to make a long, cool drink and bring it to me as I lay in a deck chair on the tiny, enclosed lawn.

But he had scarcely padded away, when he padded back again. "Madam," he said, and pushed a silver waiter at me, on which reposed the melon I had bought and hardily clung to through murder, police investigation, and heat.

Except it wasn't.

My melon—a long, large Cranshaw melon—was whole and sound; the melon on the waiter, likewise a Cranshaw, had a large brown spot on it.

I cried, wounded by Bland's accusing look, "I didn't buy that melon! Bland, you know I wouldn't have bought a bad melon. Take it back at once."

Bland drew a long hissing, breath. "Madam, may I venture to inquire," he said, venturing right ahead, "exactly why madam has secreted this—object within the melon?"

With which, and with an air of great drama, he pulled out of the melon a long, thin piece of metal. It wasn't a poniard but it was like one. There was no handle; it was only a vicious, sharpened piece of steel, with one end horribly pointed.

It had thoroughly and neatly slit its way into the melon, which was easily long enough to conceal it. It was so small and thin that the slit it made in the outer rind of the melon was barely perceptible and easily overlooked, as we had overlooked it. It was, also, so firmly imbedded in the melon that Bland practically had to dig it out with his finger tips, even though he had cut into the melon with a knife.

"Where did it come from?"

"It was as you see, inside the melon."

You brought the melon home," I said, remembering. "I didn't. It's *your* melon,"

"Certainly. I'll turn it over to the police at once."

Police. And Cynthy hurrying out of the stockroom, bumping into me and my basket, dropping her melon, snatching it up again, and dashing away. Only, it was my melon she had mistakenly snatched up; not the melon she had dropped.

I sat up and reached for the poniardlike piece of steel. Bland drew it quickly away from me, his light blue eyes suddenly showing very bright and black pupils. "I beg your pardon," he said. "One must take a shive by the end. The square end."

"Square?" I said. And then: *"Shive?"*

Bland looked a little swollen around the chops. "I meant to say, madam," he said, "knife."

"You said *shive*."

"Why, I—Perhaps I did, madam. The term escaped me, inadvertently."

"Go on, Bland; come clean."

He contrived to look pained. "Very good, madam. I—er—as you may know, have not had an uneventful life." He took a long breath, fixed his blank blue eyes upon a goldfish in the pool. "At one time I was acquainted with a gentleman whose past was not only eventful, but dramatic. He told me a shive is a file, sharpened down into a dagger. A very efficacious dagger, as a matter of fact. This one, I would say, was sharpened to its present state in a cell block at one of our larger prisons."

"Bland! You mean it's a file that has been smuggled into a penitentiary and sharpened by a prisoner until he can use it to—kill somebody? A guard or—"

"Possibly, madam; very possibly."

He looked broodingly at the dagger. I looked, too,

naturally. This put another ingredient in our drama of the morning. A prison. And someone who had been in prison; someone whose tireless, deadly patient hands had ground down that file to be the lethal and horrible thing it now was.

Shock coursed through me as it suddenly occurred to me: Cynthy Farish almost certainly had inserted that dagger—shive—in the melon. It was an ideal receptacle and hiding place for the shining, deadly sliver of steel that Bland was holding. Cunningly, knowingly, she had concealed that awful weapon of death.

Or was it? For the dead man had been killed with another knife. A cheese knife.

Bland said, "Shall I telephone the police, madam?"

Police! This was evidence. They would make me explain the thing; they would go straight for Cynthy Farish.

"No, Bland, I want to think about it. I want to wait."

There was an instant of silence. Then Bland said very softly, "Madam, might I venture to inquire how you got this melon?"

"I—" My hands made airy and futile gestures. "I just picked it up, Bland. I didn't know there was a knife in it. I mean a shive, of course. Such an interesting—"

"The exact nomenclature doesn't really matter, madam," said Bland. "Am I mistaken, or did you inform me of the fact that this was not the melon you chose? I believe you told me you wouldn't choose this one, because it had a brown spot."

"I must have done so, of course, without seeing the brown spot."

"Madam"—Bland's voice was solemn—"If you are trying to protect anyone it is a mistake. Murder is a dangerous business."

"Bland!" I sat up. "That will do!"

"Very well, madam."

"I'll have lunch now, please. Leave the knife here. On the table."

"Very good, madam. Very good." The sudden but suppressed fury in his voice was like a seething volcano. "I'll leave it here, madam. But perhaps madam had better know that to conceal evidence is to make oneself an accessory after the fact."

I was sure he was right. But I said, "Does it really, Bland?"

After that, lunch was a rather strained meal; and by five o'clock I still didn't know what to do. I had placed the shive in one of the two Victorian vases on the mantel in the little library, first making sure that Bland was not watching when I did it. But further than that I was at a loss. Clearly, my duty was to go to the police, and I simply couldn't do it. Not then, at least; not until I had talked to Cynthy.

At five o'clock Frieda Merly called up, ostensibly to remind me of the Simpsons' cocktail party, and really to say that according to the evening papers the identity of the murdered man had still not been established. She was brief and crisp, as she usually was; still, there was something worried in her voice. I hung up slowly, and rather horribly wondered whether she had been really surprised that morning when I telephoned her.

So I went to the cocktail party, and there I rather took the spotlight for a little from the visiting celebrity. But then Washington is full of celebrities; they are constantly underfoot, and a murder in a grocery store was a little unusual.

Ellie Wilde, an old school friend, asked me if there really were jars of paté, and such an acquisitive and earnest look came into her face when I said there were, that I took the first opportunity to detach myself from the others in the warm, scented garden and go into the house and find a telephone.

The butler directed me to a little, mirrored telephone-room, and after I'd got Bland on the telephone and told him to go straight out to the Supermarket and purchase the paté, he informed me loftily that he had already done so. This annoyed me naturally, no end, so I hung up, and it was then that I saw Cynthy.

Rather, I saw a slice of her; her profile and a smooth shiny pompadour—she'd put up her black hair—and part of a yellow dress. She was standing in the hall outside the little telephone room talking to someone beyond my range of vision.

The talk held plenty of feeling on both sides, for a man's voice said, "But I saw you, dammit! I saw you. Cynthy, what were you doing there?" And she said in clipped and cold accents, "Exactly what do you think I was doing?"

A kind of hollow groan came to my ears. The person out of sight said, "All right. If you don't want to tell me you don't have to."

"Certainly I don't have to," said Cynthy.

There was a little silence, and I considered venturing into the hall.

But just then the man said, with an effect of patience held hard, "Listen, Cynthy, I only asked you what you were doing in Boomer's study this morning. I started down the stairs just as you came out of it and I saw you go out the front door. I only asked you why you went there, and you turn on me like a tiger."

"I didn't," said Cynthy. "I didn't say anything. I—" Suddenly her voice changed. "Oh, Jim, I do believe in you! Why won't you tell me the truth?" she cried, and instead of anger there was something in her voice that suggested tears.

Jim. Was this the Jim Allen whom Sam Boomer had mentioned? If so, it was he who had actually found the murdered man that morning, and told Sam Boomer instead of the police; who had been kept at home by Rosita Boomer, the niece.

He said, in a stunned way, "Why, Cynthy. What do you mean? You're not making sense. I don't under— *Why, Cynthy! You look as if you're going to cry!*"

And at that point a door banged, and a new voice, a girl's voice, cried, "Oh, there you are Jimmy dear! I've been looking for you . . . Oh, hello, Cynthy. I believe Mrs Merly wants you."

I could see Cynthy move forward, looking so stately with her black hair high on her head, and yet very young. She said, "Hello, Rosita. Thanks. Where is Mrs Merly?"

"On the terrace," the new voice said.

Cynthy said coolly, "Thanks." There were quick footsteps, and a door slammed.

Jim said, "For God's sake—"

"What's the matter, darling?" said the girl's voice.

Rosita, Cynthy had called her. So it must be Sam Boomer's niece. Rosita went on smoothly, "Jim dear, what's wrong? What were you talking to Cynthy Farish about?"

"I just asked her why she didn't stop and say hello this morning at the house."

"Cynthy! Was she at the house this morning?"

"Yes," he said. "But—Did you say you were looking for me? Has Mr Boomer come?"

"Yes, he was held up. The police talked to him again this morning, and then a reporter asked for a statement."

"Oh," said Jim. His voice was all at once extremely alert. It even struck me as being rather anxious. "Did he give them one?"

"He did. Williams got in on an afternoon train. He said to give a statement at once, and prepared it himself."

"Then that's all right," said Jim. "He's a good press agent. He knows his job."

There was a little silence. "Jim," said Rosita, "You really didn't know him—the murdered man, I mean. Did you?"

"Good Lord, no. I told you that this morning when I got back to the house and told Mr Boomer. You heard everything."

"Well, not quite everything," said Rosita. "I came downstairs just as you and Uncle were talking about it. I never heard how it was that you happened to—to find him."

"It was just as I told Mr Boomer. I'd gone to take a look around the market, as I usually do in the mornings before the staff gets there. I'd gone into the stockroom to look at some windows that the manager, Hibling, has been wanting bars for. Then I saw the body."

"How horrible," said Rosita.

He ignored that. "I started to phone to get the police. Then I thought I'd better tell Mr Boomer first and let him handle it. So I locked up again and got to the house as soon as I could. That's all."

Then the girl said, "But, Jim, it was murder, wasn't it?"

Jim said briefly, "Yes, couldn't have been anything else. That knife—"

"What knife?" said the girl. "What kind of knife was it?"

"It came from the cheese counter."

"Cheese!" The girl gave a kind of giggle.

"It's not funny," said Jim. "I tell you it was horrible. The police had me come over to the station and took my fingerprints."

"Oh. They suspect you?"

"Suspect—My God, Rosita, I didn't kill him! I told you I never saw him before."

"I didn't say that you did, Jim darling. Come on; let's get a cocktail."

"I don't want a cocktail," said Jim.

"Nonsense. Come along."

"No. I've got to—to telephone."

"I'll wait."

"Don't. It'll take a long time."

But I knew that it wouldn't take him long to locate the telephone, so I emerged. Quietly, really, but they both jerked around and stared as if I'd been a jack-in-the-box. Rosita was a very blond young woman, handsome in a somewhat buxom fashion.

Jim Allen was young, tall, red-headed, and very angry. As I started toward the terrace door trying to look nonchalant, he got his breath, strode to the door of the little telephone-room, and flung it open. He realized then, that I was not passing through the hall but must have been in the little room for some time, and thus had heard everything that had been said. He whirled toward me. "Who are you, anyway?" he demanded rudely.

And Rosita cried, "Why, it's—Jim, *she* found the body! I mean, after you did. This morning."

I had reached the terrace door. "Sorry," I said. "But if you want to shout you can't expect people not to hear you."

The screen door made a sharp period. Behind it I heard Jim say, "You mean *she* was at the store?"

More people had arrived and the cocktail party was in full sway. I had reached the end of the terrace, when Frieda Merly saw me from a distance and came over at once.

"Well, you look very handsome," she said. "No one would think you'd fallen upon a murder this morning.

What a terrible experience! But then you weren't the first to find him, were you? I'm told Jim Allen did that."

"Yes. Who is he, really, Frieda? I mean, beyond the fact that Sam Boomer employs him."

"Jim? Oh, he's another of Sam's proteges. A young lawyer who worked himself through school; he began, I think, as a page boy. Then, about five or six years ago—just after Sam came to the capital—Sam saw him somewhere and got interested in him, and loaned him money for law school. He always gave him work during vacations, and Jim graduated last spring. I think Sam had some idea of employing him permanently, but of course the war changed all that. I believe Jim expects to get in the air force and leave soon for training. Why?"

"I only wondered."

She eyed me. "You don't have an idea that Jim had anything to do with the murder of that man in Sam's market, do you?"

She took off her large, brimmed hat as she spoke; we had drawn away from the others and were standing under a tree, and the light drifting through the leaves fell strongly upon her fine-featured, nervously alert, rather lovely face. She held her broad-brimmed hat in one slim white hand and looked at me, and I felt again that Frieda was worried.

I said, replying to her question, "Heavens, no. Just because Jim Allen found him, that doesn't mean he murdered him. I was there, too, and I certainly didn't. I suppose you know Sam's niece, Rosita?"

"Yes, of course." She spoke abstractedly, her eyes roving uneasily over the groups of people. "She came to play hostess for him this summer. She's rather taken with young Allen. And he with her."

"I thought he liked Cynthy," I said tentatively.

"Cynthy?" She was still looking over her shoulder.

"Oh, I don't think so. They've only known each other a few weeks. I remember they met at my house; Jim came in with Sam one night and I introduced them."

It was then that her eyes found their target and became fixed. Not only fixed but so intent that she seemed to be trying to hear with them. I turned to follow the direction of Frieda's gaze. And there across the green lawn, standing a little apart from the other clusters of people, were Sam Boomer, Cynthy, and another man whose back was turned toward us.

The three standing there, silhouetted against the laurels, were deeply intent upon their conversation. Sam Boomer was apparently questioning Cynthy, who replied; and then I saw Sam's eyes go to the man facing them, as if he had spoken. It wasn't Jim Allen. This man's hair was not red, but an indeterminate gray-brown; and he wore a suit of some thin, light material. There was nothing particularly identifiable about him.

Frieda murmured something that I didn't hear. I glanced at her, and when I looked back toward the three they were looking at Frieda.

No. It gave me an odd startled sensation to observe that they were looking very intently at me. Cynthy and Sam, that is. The other man's back was still turned.

Then abruptly Sam bowed to us across the width of close-cropped green lawn. He said something to the second man, who moved away as Sam and Cynthy came toward us. We watched their approach; Sam debonair and handsome, with his white hair and smile; the girl slim and pretty and unsmiling.

It was an opportunity to ask her about the melon; and I had to do it. It ought to be fairly easy to draw her away from Frieda and Sam, who were such close friends.

It was not, however, as easy as I had thought it would be. Frieda put her arm through mine, and when

I made a motion or two to draw away, the light pressure of her arm became curiously tenacious.

"It does seem queer," said Frieda, "that no one knows who the man was. There should be a hundred ways of identifying him."

Sam shrugged. "Oh, they will, eventually. But with people pouring in and out of Washington these days, it may take a long time. Nobody has reported this fellow missing. I understand the police have tried to check the hotels, but it would take weeks to do it that way. In any city, I suppose, it's possible for a man's identity to be lost, but now, in Washington, nothing could be easier."

"Do the police believe the murderer removed his wallet to make it hard to identify him?" asked Frieda, her voice light and pleasant, her eyes worried.

"Of course. At least it seems logical enough," said Sam.

"Then—if they could identify him they would know who the murderer is?"

"Looks that way," said Sam. "Still, you never know. Maybe it was merely a ruse to hold up the police and give the murderer more time to escape. I'm no Sherlock, Frieda."

Cynthy, who had said nothing rather conspicuously, lifted her blue eyes to give Boomer a long look. And I resolutely disengaged my arm from Frieda. "Let's snare some of the food and drink, Cynthy," I said, and slid my arm through hers, much as Frieda had done to me.

Sam said, "See you and Jim tonight, Cynthy," as we moved away. And then quite distinctly, although in a lowered voice, he said to Frieda, "Don't worry. I'm all right."

I heard Frieda's reply; it was quite cool and self-possessed. She said, "I'm not worrying about *you* darling."

Cynthy heard, too; she couldn't have helped hearing,

for there were no other groups near enough to submerge with talk our own little island of quiet, on the tranquil lawn.

Not as tranquil as it seemed, however. It was late; the sun had gone. The sky was a soft and opaque gray, and the lawn and the shrubs looked suddenly very green and very still.

"It's going to storm," I said to Cynthy.

"Yes."

It was only a word, polite and brief, but I could feel the child steeling herself against me. There was no question in my mind but that she knew why I had drawn her away from the others. That meant that she knew I had the wrong melon. And that meant—well, what?

I glanced at her; she was walking slowly beside me, chin up and her lovely red mouth set. I cast about for an opening, didn't find any, and said rather desperately, "Cynthy, I saw you this morning."

There was a little pause. Clearly she wasn't going to be trapped into any quick and impulsive statement. Then she said, looking straight ahead, "Yes, of course. In the market."

I stopped, so she had to stop, too. "Cynthy, look at me."

She met my eyes then, but her own were blue and dark and unfathomable. I said, "Cynthy, that knife. That dagger. I've got to give it to the police. I wanted to tell you."

Her face was white and miserable, for she liked me and I knew it; but her eyes didn't waver and she wouldn't speak.

I said finally, "I don't want to. I don't want them to drag you into a murder investigation. It's an ugly thing, Cynthy dear. No matter how little you know of it, or how innocent you are—and of course, I'm sure you're innocent—I mean—" I was floundering and distressed.

She just got whiter and straighter, while her eyes kept staring into mine.

I put out my hand instinctively, as one does to draw a person back from danger. "Cynthy," I said, "Please tell me."

She said, after a moment, stiffly, "Tell you what?"

There was no use beating against the barrier she had put up. Somewhere near us a bird twittered in sharp alarm, as if it, too, had been suddenly made aware of storm portents. I said, "Listen, Cynthy. Think of what I've said. I want to help you. I don't believe you had anything to do with the murder. It's preposterous, even to think of it. But—"

Unexpectedly she put out her brown, slim hand and touched my arm. "Thank you," she said. "I've got to think. There's something—I don't know what to do. I've got to decide something. May I telephone you? Tonight?"

Of course I said yes. I left her then. But as I walked slowly toward the long, beautiful house, I felt exactly as if I'd been run over by a power mower. It was strange that the short and altogether unsuccessful interview could leave me feeling so flat and exhausted. Or was it, already, the queer pressure in the air induced by the coming storm?

I was going home. I started to hunt for Ellie Wilde, who lived near me and I had suggested we walk home together, but I became involved with one group and another, and was finally dragged to meet a Chinese dignitary. I couldn't, of course, get away again without due, if brief, politenesses exchanged through a smiling member of his entourage who acted as interpreter.

By the time I was disengaged, the sky was faintly darker. I was about to start on alone when Ellie turned up. She was ready to go, and she had seem Sam and Frieda.

"They left a few minutes ago," she added. "Together. Do you suppose there's a marriage in the offing? It would be queer, after all these years, if Frieda were married again, and to Sam Boomer. Of course, he's rich, they say. But I always thought Frieda was—well, ambitious. You know. She likes power and position and I don't think she'd marry again without getting it."

I murmured some remark, but I wasn't really interested. I was too busy trying to explain to myself my rather odd sense of exhilaration. The sky was gray and close, and the heat was terribly oppressive. Nothing certainly was any different, except that I had left the cocktail party behind and was out on a busy street, with a normal and natural world around me. Natural and without evil.

Suddenly and rather shatteringly I realized that the word "evil" was like a chink of light thrown upon a dark and nebulous experience. That was it; there had been evil at that cocktail party, unseen but threatening. It was not a nice thought. It was extremely fanciful and unreasonable. I heaped adjectives up in my mind and still felt exactly the same.

I said good-by to Ellie at her corner some distance from my own, and walked on alone through hushed and quiet streets. It was growing darker, quickly, on account of the storm, so it seemed later than it really was. When I reached home and saw that the lights had not been turned on, the blank windows surprised me. Bland was usually very prompt and watchful about lights.

The gate clanged behind me. I had my key, but I rang anyway, thinking the exercise of coming to open the door was good for Bland, who had lately been developing a decided thickness through the middle. He didn't come to the door, however, and after waiting a moment I let myself in.

It was very quiet in the house, too. Almost as if no one was there, which of course was absurd, for it was not the Blands' day out. But the tension of the storm, the forebodings of my thoughts about the cocktail party, my uneasiness about Cynthy—everything made me nervous and irritable. I put my thumb squarely on the bell and kept it there.

And no one answered.

I put down my bag and hat and gloves and went quickly to the dining-room bell and rang that. Still no one answered. I went into the pantry, and it was dark. The kitchen was even darker, so the shapes of tables and cupboards and stove loomed up dimly and somehow threateningly. I made myself turn on the kitchen light, and the gleaming porcelain and glass and white paint leaped into visibility, all perfectly orderly and natural— except it wasn't. What would have been natural would have been Mrs Bland preparing dinner and puttering around in the pantry; the homely smell of cooking; and all the light and sounds of activity of seven o'clock in anybody's kitchen.

There were no Blands, and no note anywhere telling me where they'd gone.

By the time I got back to the front of the house again and turned on more lights, it was so dark that the windows reflected the lights and me in a rather unnerving and sentient way, as if they or someone out in the gathering night were watching me. Obviously the thing to do was get myself some kind of dinner; there must be food in the refrigerator. Settle myself with a book and wait for the Blands to return and explain themselves.

Yes, that was the thing to do. But first I would see that the doors and windows were locked.

Nerves, of course. I was getting a delayed shock from my ugly experience of the morning. But nevertheless—

I made the whole circuit of the house, upstairs and down. It didn't take long for it is a small house, and I hurried. I didn't go into the cellar; I didn't even open the cellar door, which Bland had apparently left unlocked, and resolved to speak to him sharply about it. Then I ran upstairs and saw no more windows. There was still no wind, no lightning, no rain. One thing was certain, I remember thinking as I came downstairs again: *Nobody is in the house.*

But I was going to call the police.

I was going to call the police, and I knew why. The house was empty. Nobody but me was in it. The doors were locked, the windows bolted. But there was fear in the house. And I was in danger.

All I could do was stare at emptiness and lights, and swallow hard, and listen. Listen with all my ears, listen with every nerve and every drop of blood in my body, so that I felt paralyzed and frozen.

Don't be a dolt. Go to the telephone. Call the police, call the police, call the police!

I don't think I knew what I was going to tell them. It didn't matter. The thing that mattered was to move, to walk into the little library, to take up the telephone and—what was the number for the police? Where was there a telephone book? In my bedroom, of course; on a shelf on the bedside table. But Bland had a book in the pantry, too.

Well, then, don't go upstairs. Walk through the dining-room and use the pantry telephone. That's quicker.

Besides, you'll be nearer the front door; nearer other people; nearer a way to escape.

Again I had very briefly that horrible feeling of

nightmare helplessness. I struggled within its grip, knowing all the time that I must hurry. There was some reason, some strong and terribly urgent reason for me to call the police. No matter how much my mind questioned that impulse, all my instinct was for it. And somehow I managed to force myself into motion.

I went through the dining-room, where a mirror gave me a glancing reflection, and pushed open the pantry door, which squeaked loudly. I all but ran to the telephone, on the table by the window. A telephone book was there. I must hurry, I had to hurry. I—

Someone was breathing. Someone was in that empty house. Someone was standing in the doorway to the kitchen. Someone was watching me. I could see a reflection of that figure in the dark windowpane in front of me.

I turned around like a doll, stiff and without feeling. A policeman stood there, watching me quietly.

He was rather slender, with sharp features in a dark face, grayish dark hair, and extremely quiet and narrow dark eyes which did not move from me. It seemed extraordinary; it seemed miraculous, indeed. I had only looked up the number, and there he was, materialized out of space, in that silent and empty house.

My knees were shaking; my hand was shaking, too. I realized dimly that I was still holding the telephone, and I put it down clumsily in the cradle, so that it clattered and slid off and I had to retrieve it.

The quiet figure in the doorway said, "I'm afraid I startled you."

I tried to answer. I tried to tell him that something was wrong in the house, that I'd started to call the police, that I wanted him to—Well, to do what? Look over the house. Find out what was wrong. Protect me from—Well, from what?

I said none of those things. My hands were gripping the little table behind me, holding to it as if it were a raft on a dark and dreadful sea.

He said, "I'm sorry. I only came to get the melon."

I did speak then. I said numbly, "Melon." Just like that; neither question nor statement.

He said, "I *am* sorry. You are very frightened. There's nothing to be afraid of. What were you doing with the telephone?"

"I was going to call the police."

"The police? Why?"

I didn't answer. There was still something wrong in the house. A policeman was there talking to me, yet something in the house was wrong.

He said, "Were you going to tell them anything? Something you omitted telling them this morning? Were you going to tell them about the girl you met at the door of the stockroom? And the melon she dropped in your basket?"

So they knew.

Probably at the moment they were taking Cynthy to the station for questioning; I suddenly knew that I must say nothing.

He came a step nearer, and absurdly I pushed harder against the table behind me.

He said, "Don't be frightened. It's all right. We know about the girl and the melon. It's evidence. You don't need to tell us about it now. The girl admitted it. Forget the whole thing. Promise me."

"Promise—"

"Promise you'll forget it . . . What frightened you so? Is there anything else you know besides the fact the girl was there?"

"No—no, of course not. Only, she didn't do it."

"Didn't she? How do you know?"

"Why, I know her. She wouldn't—"

"Any other reason?"

"No. But—"

"Sure?"

"Yes, I'm sure. That is, I don't know who did murder the man, if that's what you mean."

"You don't know who murdered him?"

"No. Certainly not. I'd tell you if I did. I'd have told the police this morning."

"I see. That's all. I'll go along now. I'm taking the melon. I got it out of the refrigerator." He smiled then and said, "Good night," and turned around. As he did so there was something briefly familiar about him; then he disappeared into the kitchen.

I didn't move and I heard his footsteps, a soft click, and then the opening and quiet closing of the door that led from the kitchen to the step outside.

I knew he had gone but I couldn't move for a long moment or two. My thoughts were whirling around Cynthy, the melon, the police, murder, the empty house, but there was something in the center of it all; something that was a pivot, a small hub. Something I couldn't discover because the wheel was going too fast.

There'd been something; a small sound—a click.

Why, that was it!

The click was the sound of the back door being unlocked. *I had locked it.* So that meant that the policeman had been in the house while I went over it, locking doors and windows. And that meant two things: first, that he'd hidden somewhere in the house—in the tiny vegetable pantry, or in the cellar, or in some closet—and, second, that while I was upstairs closing the windows, he could easily have left without seeing me, or being seen. Yet he hadn't done so. Why?

The conclusion was only too clear: He'd wanted to

question me, in order to find out how much I knew of the murder. And he'd wanted to keep me from going to the police about Cynthy.

Why should a policeman act like that?

And then suddenly I knew the answer. But the answer was no longer important in itself, because it meant just one thing:

Cynthy was in danger. Terrible danger.

I was as sure of it as if someone had told me. As, in effect, someone had.

There was a distant roll of thunder, soft and sure of itself, as if it were aware of the power it could unleash whenever it chose. I went to the kitchen and looked in the refrigerator. The melon was gone. But the policeman hadn't known that Bland had taken the dagger from the melon and that I had hidden it in the vase in the library.

I went into the library and standing on tip toe, tilted the vase and explored within it, cautiously. But the dagger—shive, as Bland had called it—wasn't there.

Well, it didn't matter. Cynthy was the important thing.

I called Frieda's house, and was told by the maid that Miss Cynthy was gone and so was Madam. The maid knew only that Cynthy had gone out to dinner, and that Madam was not expected back till late.

I remember going to the hall closet and getting out a raincoat and tying a red scarf around my head, peasant fashion. Sam Boomer had said he would see Jim Allen and Cynthy that night, so it was possible that Jim had taken her to the Boomer house for dinner. It was worth a try, anyway, and there was no time to waste. After I had Cynthy in a safe place I could think and reason.

As I hurried through the hall I gave another thought to the Blands. Their absence fitted right into the pattern of ugly surmise that was forming in my mind. Lightning flashed across my eyes as I opened the door, and the gate and the trees loomed up eerily for an instant, looking yellow and strange. The trees were moving now, swaying and gathering motion mysteriously; yet I could feel the wind and there was as yet no rain. I ran back toward the garage, and as I fumbled for the door I discovered it had been left open.

My car was there, although Bland's smart coupé was gone. I slid into the seat and turned on the ignition and dashlight, so that I could see the gasoline gauge. There wasn't much gasoline, and I'd already used up my ration for that period. But I had to take the chance. I backed out, scraping a fender.

It was working up to a wild night. After I left the dimmed lights of Alexandria and took the road past the airport, with the terrible and fantastic bulk of the Pentagon Building away ahead of me, mine seemed to be almost the only car on the road. Lightning was clearer now and nearer, more nerve-shattering in its sudden brightness, particularly since my lights were dimmed.

I took the first bridge over the Potomac; the river was like ink except where it reflected bright flashes of lightning. I passed the Lincoln Memorial, and it suddenly occurred to me that I didn't know the exact address of Sam Boomer's house, only that it was near Rock Creek Park.

Winding curves of roadway and trees brought me eventually into a business street. I stopped at a drugstore and called Frieda's house again. The maid promptly gave me Sam Boomer's address.

"Is Miss Farish with Mrs Merly?" I'd known all the way from Alexandria that I ought to have asked that question when I first telephoned Frieda's house.

"Mrs Merly—" began the maid, and apparently fainted away, maybe died, for all I know. For there was a sudden and terrific crackle along the telephone wire, and the whole street outside lit up. The line buzzed a while and then went dead.

It was a long time before I found Boomer's house. There is a section near Rock Creek Park that is a maze of irregular turns and twists and unexpected small "Places" which now and then prove to be dead ends. Twice I got into someone's driveway and had to back out again.

And then almost unexpectedly, I found the address I was looking for. It was a large, substantial brick house, set well back of some thick shrubs. There was a small light turned on above a bronze number, so I knew I was right. I went past it, stopped, and turned off my engine and lights. Now for it.

I crawled out of the car, cowered under a brilliant flash of lightning, and then crossed the sidewalk into the shelter of a thick, high hedge.

Suddenly and disconcertingly I caught the quick shadow of another movement farther down the walk. Rather as if the hedge had momentarily bulged out toward the sidewalk and then flattened again. I crouched against the foliage beside me, stared into the darkness ahead, and listened. But another flash of lightning revealed only a straight line of hedge and white sidewalk, and a car standing at the entrance of a driveway some sixty feet ahead. Before I had seen anything, it was no longer there. Then the lightning was gone.

I was left wondering again, rather desperately, exactly what to do. Walk up to that house, all at once so forbidding in the gloom beyond the hedge, and demand Cynthy? And then what?

I took another step forward and, as if at a signal, the curtain rolled up, to the accompaniment of a lingering roll of thunder. Rather it shot up.

The big house beyond the hedge had been dark behind its carefully drawn blackout curtains.

Now, as the front door was flung open, a path of light shot startlingly across the porch. Two figures came hurrying out of the house, a woman and then a man. I crouched back close to the hedge as they came rapidly down the walk toward the street.

As the first figure reached the break in the hedge, the door was flung open again and closed with another bang. Footsteps came running down the steps and along the sidewalk, and a voice called hurriedly, "Go back. He wants you. Quick! Something's happened. I'll see to—" It was a man's voice but so hurried and blurred that I couldn't identify it. And just then a hot gust of wind shook the trees and shrubbery wildly, drowning all other sounds.

When it began to die away, footsteps again were pounding along the walk leading to the Boomer house. Then there was silence.

It was a curious silence, because only one person had gone back to the house; I was sure of that. Therefore two people must be standing on the other side of the hedge not far from me. Yet they neither moved nor spoke—No, I was wrong.

For the frantic sigh and murmur of the trees above us stopped altogether, as if the conductor of that stormy orchestra had made a motion with his baton. And I could hear voices, a man's and a woman's, muffled but jerky and vehement, as if in anger.

There was something terrifying about that muted quarrel, there in the deathly lull of the storm. It was impossible to distinguish words, but there was no mistaking the passionate urgency of the argument.

And then the man's voice came clear: "I tell you

you've got to go. She's waiting. It's the best for you and for everybody."

The conversation stopped then, and the curtain swept up on a second act. For a vivid flash of lightning came, and I saw two figures running toward the car that was parked in Boomer's driveway. The man I did not know: the girl was Cynthy.

The man had Cynthy by the arm, urging her in the direction of the waiting car. I had the impression that she was reluctant. Then everything was blotted out as the darkness swallowed up the blue-white glare of lightning. There was a long, long crash of thunder. I put my hands to my ears and held my breath. I didn't know that I had shut my eyes too, until whiteness beat upon my closed eyelids again. I opened them to another flash of lightning, and this time I saw a queer thing.

Cynthy was getting into that car. But she was alone; the man who had been with her was gone. And though she was moving hurriedly, there was no longer any suggestion of unwillingness on her part.

I saw only that; then it was dark again.

I knew then that I was really terrified. Not as I had been before, in my queerly empty house, afraid of the unknown, but wildly terrified of a menace I now knew to be real.

Scarcely knowing what I was doing, I started toward the car, running along the sidewalk in a blackness so dense that only the touch of the hedge brushing my arm and shoulder guided me. The engine of the car ahead started; I heard it just as I stumbled upon something very soft and still. I lost my balance and fell to my knees on the sidewalk. My flailing hands touched something horribly inert and quiet.

It was the body of a man.

I saw it only dimly, not clearly enough to discover

who it was. He was lying close within the black line of shadow made by the hedge.

I didn't know what had happened, but one thing was clear. He had been attacked, obviously, during that long roll of thunder; it had been a swift and merciless attack, devilishly spaced, so that it occurred during the darkness between the lightning flashes. Did Cynthy know?

I was just stumbling to my feet, when a man threw open the door to the Boomer house and came hurtling down the steps and along the walk. He stopped almost at my shoulder to stare at the moving lights of the car, which was already turning into the street, and began to swear. I knew who it was.

I told him, "Cynthy's in that car."

There was an instant's silence as a faint glow of lightning revealed us to each other. Jim Allen clutched my shoulder so tightly it hurt. "Cynthy is in that car? Who's with her?"

"I don't know. But there's a man here beside the hedge. He's dead."

He bent quickly and groped about. Then the car began to move down the street, and at the sound he shot up again. He started to run after the car, and I ran after him.

"Wait—wait! I've got a car."

He slid to a stop. "Car? Where?"

"It's back this way. Hurry."

We left that dark huddle in the shadow of the hedge as if it had never been a man. It now seems inhuman; it wasn't then. I only thought of Cynthy. We had to find her.

When we reached my car, Jim Allen got into the driver's seat with a decision that gave me no chance to argue about it. Then I began to see that I could very easily have jumped from the frying pan into the fire.

Obviously, he was pursuing Cynthy, and I had leaped to the conclusion that his motive was the same as mine. Yet it might be something quite different.

We reached the corner, turned, and saw no car anywhere along the street. We reached another cross street in what seemed a split second, and hesitated there while Jim Allen peered one way and then another and then swerved. "Here we go," he said. "Into the park it is."

We turned into a narrow, steeply sloped road. At that moment the storm broke.

There followed something out of a nightmare. If we could have talked, even, there might have been some sort of order and direction to the thing, but the sudden lashing of rain, the constant crackle of lightning and frantic rolling of thunder, the slippery, glistening road visible only in wavering patches through the streaming rain, made talk impossible. What we did say had to be shouted; we were lost in a world of bedlam, both straining our eyes and every nerve to see ahead.

Suddenly Jim stopped the car. "It's no good," he shouted. "It's like looking for a needle in a haystack. We could have missed them at twenty different curves. Three, anyway." He turned, and in the glow from the dashlight, I could see his face. "What are you doing in this?" he demanded. "You're the woman who found Benkham, aren't you? And you were at the party this afternoon. Why are you after Cynthy?"

"I'm one of Cynthy's friends." I told him my name.

He recognized it instantly. "Oh, of course. Cynthy has talked of you. I'm sorry."

It was only then that something struck me as queer about what he had said. Something out of the picture, something sharply new. *"Benkham!"*

Jim Allen was getting into gear again and leaning

forward to peer through the rain. I said it again, "*Benk-ham!* Is that the name of the murdered man?"

We shot forward. "Yes."

I shouted, "But no one knew him! *You knew his name*. Who is he? How do you know?"

He didn't bother to answer. He swerved around the curve. "I'll get the police! I've got to find Cynthy. If she's gone voluntarily—But she knows. She knows something. I've got to find her.

It didn't answer my spoken questions, but it answered a big unspoken question. If he was willing to get the police to help him find Cynthy he didn't intend to murder her.

It was just then that he said slowly and with a kind of horror, "What the hell!" For at exactly that moment the gasoline gave out.

Jim tried over and over to start the engine, and got nowhere. Finally he said despairingly, "Lost in Rock Creek Park. No gas, and Cynthy—oh, my God." He gave another push on the starter, then reached for the door.

"What are you going to do?" I asked.

"Walk back to a phone and call the police. Nothing else to do. I was a fool to try to follow her in the first place." He opened the door.

"I'm going, too."

"You can't."

"I can't stay here. Don't try to stop me. I'll follow you. You may as well let me come along."

I got out, and the rain drenched me through in a couple of seconds. I gasped at the coldness and fury of the onslaught. Jim Allen was drenched, too; I caught a glimpse of his face, glistening from the rain, and his red hair already dark and wet. He seemed to decide that he didn't care what I did, gave a shrug, and started along the road. I went with him. Rain and darkness and wind and more rain. I hoped he knew where he was going; I didn't. The lightning and thunder had worked away toward the north, but the rain seemed never-ending.

All at once Jim said, "Why are you after Cynthy? What's your part in this?"

"Cynthy never killed that man, and I think she's in danger."

"She didn't kill him. But she's mixed up in it, and she's worried and scared."

It was queer walking there in the rain, with the tumult of the storm dying away, speaking what we knew of the truth.

"You said his name was Benkham?"

"Yes. Alfred Benkham. Williams knew him."

"But who *was* Benkham?"

"I don't know." We trudged on in silence. At last he said, "I don't know why, but I think you're all right. I mean—well, you're on Cynthy's side. There's something going on, and I don't understand it. But his name was Alfred Benkham, all right. Williams knew it, and said so to Frieda Merly. She was there for dinner tonight. So was Cynthy. So was I. Williams came in later. I kept trying to get Cynthy alone; I'd got to thinking, and I had to talk to her. It was a short dinner. Boomer was a little tight, and Mrs Merly didn't like it. She's been boosting him, you know. The idea is to marry him if things go well and he gets launched into his political career."

"Political career! Boomer?"

"Of course. He's ambitious; wants to run for office in his native state. She has advised him from the beginning. She's ambitious, too. He's got the money and Mrs Merly's got the brains and political acumen. But she gets furious if he drinks a spot too much. He's a swell guy and only gets a little exuberant, but she likes him better suave and dignified. So it was an unpleasant and a short dinner. Rosita got Boomer upstairs, and I got hold of Cynthy and started to take her away to talk; but just as we got out of the house, Boomer sent for me. I went back, but Rosita said he hadn't sent for me at all. By the time I got out of the house again, there you were, and Cynthy—" He gave another groan and said, "Can't you walk any faster?"

"But that's not all," I said. "Why did Williams tell Frieda Merly the name of the murdered man? How did you know he was talking about the murdered man?"

"Oh, he said so. They spoke of the murder, in the library just after Boomer went upstairs. She wanted to know if the murder could affect Boomer's career, and she asked Williams because he's Boomer's press agent, you know. That and general adviser. Boomer depends on him for everything. Doesn't say a word or move a finger unless Williams approves."

"What did Williams say?"

"He said the murder of a man like Alfred Benkham couldn't hurt anybody's political career. She picked him up, of course. Her face got very queer and sharp, and she said, '*Alfred Benkham!* So that was his name!' It was just then that I had a chance to grab Cynthy and get her out of the house, and I did."

"Did Frieda know Benkham?"

"Did—? Why, what makes you think so?"

"The way you quoted her. You said, she said, 'So that was his name!' As if she knew it."

"Oh. Well, yes; that's the way she said it. But all I was thinking about was Cynthy."

"Didn't you ask Williams how he happened to know the man's name?"

"No." Again he seemed to brood heavily, while our steps squashed steadily and wetly along the road. Finally he said, "No, I didn't. Williams somehow always does get the low-down on things. If any of us would know who the murdered man was, it would be Williams. I mean he'd find out." He added thoughtfully, "Unless, of course, he already knew him."

"Whoever murdered that man knew him!"

He frowned down at me. "But Williams *couldn't* have. He was out of town."

"Are you sure?"

"Reasonably. Anyway, it could easily be established by the police. Why, it was Boomer's alibi that he was waiting to meet Williams at the Mayflower, and that Williams didn't turn up. They check all those things."

"How about Boomer?"

"I'm his alibi; he's mine, too, I guess. I left him in the Mayflower bar last night, as I said, waiting for Williams. I went back to the Boomer place, picked up Rosita, and we went on to the Drake cocktail party. Boomer came home a little later, when Williams didn't turn up. The maid let him in. She told Rosita he was a little tight even then. He went to his room, where he keeps a liquor cabinet, and that was the last she saw of him. But it's an alibi, in its way. And Hibling, the manager of the store, seems to have an alibi. Yet whoever murdered Benkham had to enter the store before closing hours, or else had to have a key."

"Had Williams a key?"

"Not that I know of; but it would have been easy enough to get one. I think the murder must have been done after the closing hour. It would have been too dangerous to try whilst there were people around."

"That means whoever did it had to have a key. If Cynthy doesn't have one—"

"I'm sure she hasn't. Besides, Cynthy wouldn't murder anybody!"

"Why are you so worried about Cynthy?"

"Because—well, the fact is, she knows something. I don't know what. She was at the house this morning. I was on the stairs as she went out, and she wouldn't even stop and speak to me. Then this afternoon—"

"Yes, yes, I know. I heard you. You've forgotten. What you don't know is—" I paused for another brief self-reassurance about Jim Allen; decided again that I could trust him, and hurriedly told him all. Or almost all. I told him about meeting Cynthy in the store; I told him why I had not mentioned her presence to the police; and I told him about the melon with the dagger in it.

He gave a sharp exclamation when I came to that, and when I went on to tell of what finally happened to the melon I brought home, he said, "For God's sake! Well, go on! What then?"

"That is all," I said, "except that Cynthy is in terrible danger. Because of the knife—"

"Shive," he interrupted. "It was mine."

I stopped literally in my tracks. *"Yours!"*

"Yes. And I"—He stopped, too. He reached out and clutched my arm, and then abruptly put his hand over my mouth. Which was just as well, for I looked then, and saw what he saw.

We had rounded a black blotch of trees and shrubbery. Behind it was a thin path of light streaming from the lights of an automobile which had been run up over the curb and onto the wet grass.

Directly in the path of the light a man, big and bulky, was stooping over something that lay like a log on the grass. I thought it was Cynthy, but it wasn't Cynthy, for all at once I saw her, too. She was sitting on a rock, at the very edge of the path of light, taking off her stockings.

We stood there as if paralyzed. She calmly removed one stocking and then the other, and thrust her slim white feet back into sodden pumps. She got up and went to the man stooping over, she gave him the stockings. He bent still farther and seemed to be very busy, while Cynthy, her hair wet and plastered away from her face, watched.

"My God!" said Jim Allen huskily. "He's tying something. He's—Who is he? I never saw him—Cynthy!"

He called that out loud and plunged toward the girl, who turned wildly to meet him as if she couldn't believe he was there. And the big man in the middle of the light finished whatever he was doing and straightened up and looked, too, toward Jim.

It was Bland.

He stood between me and the figure on the grass. But of course I knew who it must be.

I have never understood Bland, but I am fairly well conditioned to him, so that his activities gave me little or no surprise. This, however, was one of the times when the conditioning broke down. He didn't see me at first, for Jim was standing, with Cynthy, in the glow of the headlights and Bland just stood watching in majestic and somehow triumphant silence. I struggled on up the slippery little slope; then emerged into the lights, too.

Bland saw me and gave a fishlike gasp. "Madam," he said. "Dear me."

He moved chivalrously but unnecessarily to block my view of the thing at his feet, just as Cynthy remembered his presence.

"This is Jim," she cried, turning her face toward Bland. "This is the man—Jim Allen."

So she'd told Bland about him.

Bland said, "Good evening, sir. May I suggest that you take Madam and Miss Cynthy in that car to the Boomer house? If you'll kindly get in touch with the police then, and send them here, I'll join you at the house shortly. Thank you," he concluded with the finality and decision of a great conqueror. And wafted us toward the car.

As Jim backed hurriedly into the road, Bland was seen taking stately refuge under a pine tree. "They'll be here right away," shouted Jim back.

I held onto Cynthy around the curves, but she was crying softly and I couldn't talk to her.

We were unexpectedly close to the Boomer house; it couldn't have been more than three or four minutes before we turned into the street before it. But the house was different; it was a blaze of lights, and there were cars out in front, police cars. Three policemen fell upon us just as an ambulance swept around the corner and stopped behind our car. It had come for the man who still lay there on the sidewalk.

There were policemen everywhere. They moved us along, and presently we were inside an old-fashioned library with worn brown leather furniture. Frieda Merly was standing beside the massive table, her small head uplifted, her fine features set and determined.

It was Frieda who dominated the scene that followed. Frieda, that is, until Bland arrived. Jim must have sent police to him instantly, for very soon he appeared, genie-like, in the doorway, and quietly became, as only Bland can do, the scene's most vital figure.

But it was Frieda, at first. She saw Jim and me and Cynthy. Her small head went a little higher, and then she smiled defiantly. "Oh there you are, Cynthy," she said. "I'm glad."

Cynthy went to stand beside her.

Jim said, "It's all over, Mrs Merly."

Frieda said quietly, "Thank you, Jim. I think I understand." She turned to the police lieutenant, who had apparently been questioning her. "It's all right, then," she said. "This is the child I was worried about. As you see, she is safe."

The lieutenant nodded. "Now then, Mrs Merly, if you'll tell me the whole story—"

"Certainly," said Frieda. She looked very pale and put her small, jeweled hand upon Cynthy's. "You knew," she said. "Didn't you?"

"I heard the name tonight," said Cynthy. "Alfred Benkham. I remembered he had called to see you yesterday; the maid said 'Mr. Alfred Benkham.' I happened to see him leave. So this morning when I was sent to the market to get the dagger that belonged to Jim—" She closed her eyes as if to shut out the picture, and then met Frieda Merly's searching gaze. "I saw him. I recognized him. I'd been told that there was danger to Jim; I'd been told that Jim had been at the market early, that he'd come back here with a story of a murdered man, that police had to be called, and that a dagger that belonged to Jim and could be traced to him was in the storeroom."

"What else were you told, child?" asked Frieda gently.

"I was told that Jim was in danger from the police; that he'd got himself in a jam—I wasn't told what—but if I—liked Jim I could help by removing the dagger before the police arrived. I was told not to tell *anyone* that I knew of the dagger. It was all said very quickly and very convincingly. I was told to get the dagger, to have faith in Jim, to keep quiet. Explanations would came later; the main thing was to hurry. Jim had showed it to me."

Jim said quietly, "Everybody knew it; it was a kind of curiosity. I had a client, during a short time when I had a job in a law office, a client who had been in and out of penitentiaries most of his life. He was really innocent of the current charge and I got him off. In gratitude he gave me the shive."

"Made in one of the cell blocks of—" I named the prison Bland had named. It was almost my only contribution to the moment; but it elicited a somewhat speculative glance from the police lieutenant.

Jim nodded. He said. "I didn't know it was missing till this evening, when you told me."

I said, "Cynthy, who was Alfred Benkham? Why was he murdered?"

Frieda broke in: "Yes, Lieutenant. You wanted to know, too. When I telephoned for the police a few minutes ago I did so, first, because this child"—she pressed Cynthy's hand again—"had disappeared. I didn't know where she'd gone. I only knew she'd left the house before I could stop her. I had been talking to Williams; he told me it was Benkham. It gave me a—kind of shock. I came here, to this room, to be alone for a moment in order to think and arrange my course of action . . . After a little I realized the house was quiet, terribly quiet. Then I looked, and Cynthy was gone, and I was afraid. So I called the police. But I also did it because I—well, sooner or later I knew I'd have to tell the police the whole story."

She took a long breath. "I've got to be on the right side of this, Lieutenant. I hated the publicity, but the truth, or part of it, had to come out sooner or later. I won't be in a pretty position, either way, but I've got to be at least on the side of the law—"

"Go on, Mrs Merly," said the lieutenant. "Who was Alfred Benkham?"

She took another long breath; the jewels in her ears gleamed and flashed under the light. She said steadily, "He was a shyster lawyer. Many years ago he defended Sam on a charge of using the mails to defraud; it was some get-rich-quick scheme. The point was, he cleared

Sam, but he knew Sam was actually guilty. Benkham not only knew it, but he managed to get and keep the evidence that would ruin Sam." She paused, and said to Cynthy, "It's all in an envelope in my bedroom desk. The upper left-hand drawer."

"Oh," said Jim. "You paid for the evidence Benkham had?"

A little flush crept up into Freida's charming, well-bred face. "I needn't spare myself anything," she said. "I—bought Benkham, or thought I did, because I wanted to keep him quiet, yes. Sam's future was going to be my future. However—" She swallowed and went on, "I also thought it an excellent idea for me to have that particular—source of control in my own hands. It sounds—however, that was what I did. Our arrangement was fairly practical."

I liked Freida more at that moment than I had ever liked her before. It was not her courage in admitting the truth; it was the quality in her that made her see it, which is a quite different and rarer thing.

Cynthy put her arm around Freida's slender waist. Freida looked at her and said quietly, as if only she and Cynthy were in the room, "What happened? Just now, I mean."

Cynthy replied as quietly, "Williams came after Jim and me when we left the house. He stopped us and told Jim that Mr Boomer wanted him at once; he said it was urgent. Then, as soon as Jim was gone, he told me that the police had learned of my presence at the market. He said they were going to question me, and that the thing for me to do was to go with Rosita to a little town in Virginia. He said she'd meet me at the train and she'd bring some clothes for me; he said I had to go and stay away until the thing blew over.

"I didn't know what to believe or what to do. I

started toward the car, and then I don't know what happened. He let go my arm and seemed to hang back. I decided to go on and get in the car, and drive away alone if I could. But before I could find the starter, someone opened the door and told me to move over. He said he'd take me to meet Rosita, and we started out."

"And that was—?" began Frieda stiffly.

Bland, in the doorway, said, "That was Sam Boomer. He murdered Benkham. He murdered Williams." His light blue eyes shifted to me. "Let me get you a chair, madam."

He did so, and I sat down. "He also," said Bland, "was about to murder Miss Cynthy. This time I believe it was to appear to be suicide or accident."

Cynthy was looking very white. She said slowly, "When Mr Boomer phoned me early this morning he didn't tell me there was a murdered man in the stockroom; he just said Jim would be in trouble if the dagger was found. He said he would go and get it himself, or send Jim back, but that he had to call the police at once, and if I hurried I could get there and away before the police came. I didn't suspect Mr Boomer even when I saw the murdered man. He had sounded so natural when he talked to me, and it was so like him to help Jim. He— he was always so friendly and charming."

"It was what he was building his career upon," said Frieda.

"But then," said Cynthy, "I didn't know what to do. I recognized Benkham and I knew it was murder. I knew Jim always went to the market early in the mornings, and that he had a key. And Boomer had said he wanted to help Jim. And I knew Mrs Merly knew Benkham. If I went to the police—I didn't know what to do! So I did what Sam Boomer had told me to do. Then in the afternoon Williams came to the party, and he and Mr Boomer told me I hadn't brought the shive. I knew of course what had happened to it, and I told them. As soon as I had done it I was afraid. I don't know why—there was just something about the way they took the news."

She looked at me. "I was going to come to you," she said. "I was going to tell you everything I knew. But I wanted to talk to Jim first, and Mrs Merly." She stopped, and Frieda said, "Thank you, child," and smiled faintly.

It was like Cynthy, of course; caught by her loyalties, plunged into a horribly perplexing situation, fighting through as best she could alone. All of it complicated by the shock and horror of the morning.

Bland said suddenly to Frieda, "And you believed, madam, that Miss Cynthy was in danger?"

Frieda gave him a long look before replying. Then she said, "Not until after Williams had told me it was Benkham; and then I felt it only because Cynthy was gone and I knew something was wrong, and I knew— I knew Sam had already murdered once." She shivered, and said, as if it told the story, "The house was so terribly quiet."

The lieutenant said, "Mrs Merly, have you any idea what Williams thought he would gain by sending Miss Farish out of town?"

She thought for a moment, and said, "It would have been merely a temporary expedient, of course, but it was an *expedient*. It would keep Cynthy away from the police for a few days, and it might serve until Williams had time to make a better plan for ensuring Cynthy's silence. Also, he knew Sam. He knew that Sam's blind panic had already led him into murdering Benkham, and into the fatal mistake of sending Cynthy for the dagger. Sam must have realized later that Cynthy would get to thinking Jim was innocent, and that she'd better tell the police the story. Once he realized that, he might have lost his head again and tried to get rid of Cynthy. So Williams, to avoid another murder, tried to send Cynthy away, until he could evolve a better plan."

The lieutenant said suddenly, "And your theory about the murder, Mrs Merly?"

She looked at him wearily. "It's quite obvious, isn't it? Benkham got all he could out of me; then he went to Sam. Williams was gone. If he'd been here he'd have kept Sam on an even keel. But Sam alone . . ." She shrugged. "He lost his head completely."

The lieutenant said, "You don't believe, then, that murder was premeditated?"

Frieda frowned. "I don't know. Knowing Sam, I'm inclined to think that he did not admit to himself that he had determined to murder Benkham; perhaps he hadn't determined to do so. But I think it was in his mind, nevertheless, as a recourse if Benkham held his ground. That's why he took the shive, obviously; not only because it was a lethal weapon, but because it belonged to Jim. And it would have been easy for a man as important as Sam to frame an unknown assistant like Jim, a man with no close connections but himself."

With a little choked cry, Cynthy reached for Jim. He drew her down on the big sofa and sat close to her, with her trembling hands caught in his two big ones.

The lieutenant said quietly, "But he sent for the shive the next morning. He told Miss Farish to keep quiet about it, to protect Allen."

"Yes," said Frieda painfully, "but—don't you see?— it wasn't really to protect Jim, but to protect himself *from* Jim. I don't like to say this, because, after all, I meant to marry Sam, but I do know that he could be friendly, charming, even go out of his way to help a person, as long as that person did not interfere with his own aims. But he was a pusher. He'd come up the hard way, and he had never really matured; he'd never learned, the way most people do, the line where ambition stops and love of your fellow men becomes the most important thing in life. It's a hard thing to say, but Sam, with all his—yes, his lovable traits, simply had no moral sense." She turned to Jim. "I'm sorry. I had no idea how far he'd really go."

Jim said gruffly, "If he'd wanted to throw the blame on me, why didn't he leave the melon in the stockroom? It would have been found without his interfering. He could even have called the attention of the police to it. It would have been easy to pin a knife like that on me."

The lieutenant said, "I can answer that. From the point of view of the police, a knife, no matter how sinister, hidden in a melon, is not incriminating evidence. It's a crazy idea to stick a knife in a melon, but we couldn't put anyone in jail for it. Besides, we knew you hadn't committed the murder. Your alibis had been thoroughly checked; there was no evidence pointing that way. You couldn't have done it—"

"That's just why Sam couldn't let you find the knife," Frieda cut in excitedly. "Because, if you found the knife, Jim would know where it came from! Jim kept it on his desk, in Boomer's own house. Lots of people had seen it there. He had to get it back to Jim's desk before it was missed."

Jim said, "If he forgot the shive, why didn't he return it to the store during the night?"

The lieutenant said rather dryly, "Perhaps the concrete and imminent fact of police investigation threw him into a panic."

Frieda nodded. "Yes. That would be like Sam; he wasn't very clever about murder, was he?" she said in a queerly weary tone.

The lieutenant replied, "No, he wasn't clever. No

murderer is really very smart; if he were he wouldn't murder. No murderer is infallible, either, or he wouldn't be caught. It's their mistakes that make discovery and conviction possible."

Frieda said, "He made his first mistake in the way he hid the knife. A Cranshaw melon is an ideal place for inserting a sharp weapon of that shape. The very hiding place an impulsive man like Sam would choose, without considering how he could get it out. I believe what happened was this: He may have left an end sticking out of the melon, but when, in the course of his talk with Benkham, he realized the—murder must be done, he discovered the end had slipped inside the melon, out of reach. Either the other knife was at hand, or he may have left the room on some pretext and gone for it. Afterward, he left the place in a panic, forgetting the melon."

I asked, "But why would the knife ever have been found? After all, a melon has a right to be in a grocery store."

Jim said, "Not in the stockroom of our store. No perishable goods were ever placed there. Anyone noticing the melon would have examined it and found the slit where the knife went in. Boomer knew that."

"Yes, he saw that, too late," said Frieda, very white but somehow gallant. "But Sam's biggest mistake was sending Cynthy for it. He knew she would do it, because she loved Jim; I see that now. He didn't stop to think that her very love would make her believe in Jim's innocence and confide in him sooner or later. Sam simply acted, and then waited for Williams to put the whole thing in his hands. That's all," she said. "Except that he and Williams had different views about—" She stopped.

About Cynthy, of course. When Sam realized his mistake, he must have decided to save his own pink, well-cared-for skin at any cost—even Cynthy's life.

Eventually they pieced it all together, the lieutenant and Jim and Frieda. And Bland. But first they asked me why I had felt that Cynthy was in danger. My first inkling came, of course, I told them, when I recognized Williams, dressed as the policeman, when he turned to leave my pantry. I'd seen him talking to Boomer and Cynthy from just that angle scarcely more than an hour before, though he'd carefully kept his face hidden from he. He'd hurried away from the cocktail party and rented a policeman's uniform, and gone straight to my house. He wanted to get hold of the melon and shive, of course, but the uniform was a perfect disguise in which to confront me and question me as to how the situation stood.

It might have worked, too, if I hadn't caught that particular view of Williams. I realized then that he might have been sent by Boomer to recover the shive. That didn't necessarily mean that either of them had murdered Benkham; it did mean that they knew something about it, and they knew that Cynthy knew and had been sent to recover the knife.

That was what was important; for no matter why Cynthy had been sent, she was in danger, *for she knew who had told her to get the dagger.*

I felt proud of my detection of Williams's identity and wasn't quite prepared for the look of shame on Bland's face when I concluded. He coughed delicately. "Madam," he said, "you have forgotten to tell them the clue."

The lieutenant snatched on the word with joy. "Clue?" he said.

I said it, too: "Clue, Bland?"

"Yes, of course, madam. The initials on the ring. You described them most minutely to me."

"Yes. A.B. But—"

"And then, madam, Mr Boomer came into the stockroom, looked at the body, and said, if I remember accurately what you told me 'Who is he? A.B. on his ring. Wonder who he is.' "

"Yes. I—"

"But, madam, you told me that the initials were very worn and difficult to read, yet Mr Boomer was not wearing his glasses."

"Why, Bland!" I cried. "That's true. You asked me hundreds of questions. But to think you remembered that one little detail."

Bland interrupted, loftily, "Thank you, madam, I had occasion to confirm my impression this evening. I—er—had a chat with the cook here just before I took refuge in Williams's car, which he left in the driveway. She said that Mr Boomer could scarcely see his hand before him without spectacles. So—" Bland coughed lightly. "It appeared to suggest his implication in the crime; he must have known that ring, and what initials were on it, for he couldn't have deciphered the initials without glasses.

"Furthermore, while his alibi was apparently substantiated for the time between five o'clock and about six-thirty, there was no real alibi for him for the hours between six-thirty and seven-thirty. The housemaid let him into the house but was not sure of the time, only that it was about six-thirty and certainly not later than seven. But it developed when I had a few—er—quiet words concerning household routine, that she was busy laying the table for dinner and pressing a dress for Miss Boomer, and would not have seen or heard Mr Boomer leave the house. As I suggested he did, very quietly, at once. She would not have been likely to note his return, later, either. An hour gave him all the time he needed, to meet Benkham at his store, which would have seemed a natural rendezvous to the unhappy victim, yet would seem an unlikely place for murder, since suspicion would so obviously point to the owner."

The silence in the room seemed to catch him in full flight. He stopped; all of us were staring at him, but no one spoke for a moment. Then the lieutenant voiced what I believe we were all thinking. "Exactly what is your story?" he said.

Bland blinked; his glacial blue eyes were perfectly blank. "Oh, quite simple, sir. Not much, really. I simply sifted in my mind the evidence I had learned from madam, but I had no clues until this evening, when a policeman came to tell me and my wife that we were wanted at the police station in Washington. He said he would stay at the house in order to send you, madam"—he nodded austerely at me—"when you returned. I took my own car set out, but on the way I realized that he was not a policeman at all, so I left Mrs Bland at a movie in order to ensure her—er—safety and returned to the house. I was in time to see the policeman leave with the melon in his hands; and it was no trick to follow him. He came straight to the Boomer place, where I judge, he changed clothes again quickly.

"I didn't know just what course to follow, however. The cook, who let me in under the impression that I had an appointment for an interview concerning a job, was told by the housemaid that I had no such appointment. I believe she spoke to Miss Rosita. At any rate, I was obliged to tell them I had come to the wrong house and leave. In order to make sure that Williams and Boomer did not escape without my knowing it, I got into the back seat of Williams's car. The rest of it you know."

"But we don't know," said Jim rather savagely. "Did Boomer try to murder—?"

It's all right, dear," said Cynthy quickly.

Bland said, looking at the ceiling, "There was a steep bank and a ravine, a few feet beyond the spot where he stopped the car. He had dropped the heavy spanner—

with which he must have killed Williams, under cover of the storm—in the back of the car as he got in. Barely missing me," Bland added, with a look of haughty disapproval in his face. "However, he provided me with a weapon. When he stopped the car, in order to arrange what I imagine he thought would look like an accident, it was a simple matter to—er—eliminate him."

Jim hadn't looked at Bland during the whole speech, for he hadn't taken his eyes from Cynthy. But all at once, ignoring the other people in the room, he put both arms tight around her and drew her close to him. She said, into his shoulder, "I didn't know. I didn't know what had happened to Williams. I didn't know what Boomer— not until the last minute or two. Then I was—*I wanted you.*" Her voice wavered upward.

At that Jim gave a frenzied look around, and suddenly put Cynthy on the sofa and came over and wrung Bland's hand in an inarticulate way. The lieutenant coughed this time. And as he did so Rosita, in hat and coat, walked into the room.

"I got tired of waiting for Cynthy," she said simply. "Williams told me to take her to the place in Virginia and stay there. He said it was important and he'd explain later. But I came back. I've been listening. I went upstairs, and this was in Uncle—in his room. Under the mattress. It was pretty silly of him not to destroy it but—anyway, here it is. I only wanted to say I had nothing to do with all this, so you can't hold me." At which she put a black leather wallet on the table.

It was Benkham's wallet. It had various identifying cards in it and a few bills. It also had a check signed by Frieda Merly.

That, really, was all. The lieutenant said, in a worried way, "Of course, I'll have to check on all of this. I'll have statements drawn up."

"You'll want the shive, I presume," said Bland, in exactly the manner he gives a departing guest a hand with his topcoat.

"Oh, yes. The shive—"

"It's in a vase on the library mantel," began Bland.

I interrupted. "No, it isn't. That's where I put it, but it's gone."

"I beg your pardon, madam," said Bland, looking slightly ashamed of my obtuseness. "It is in the other vase. I thought it an excellent hiding place. I merely shifted it."

There was a silence. Cynthy seemed to move a little closer to Jim.

Then the lieutenant said suddenly, to Bland, "Look here, how did you know Williams was a fake policeman?"

Bland's eyebrows lifted coldly, but there was a dreamy look in the blue eyes below them. "I have had occasion in the past to observe policemen and their methods somewhat closely. Not for myself, I might say, but for—"

He left that point unelucidated and glided suavely on: "Therefore on the way to the station it suddenly struck me that Williams, presumably a Washington policeman, was wearing a New Orleans badge. I daresay it was on the costume he rented and he did not look closely; they are somewhat alike. The San Francisco badge, now, and the New York badge—" He stopped delicately again and said, "But I'm sure you aren't interested in these little technicalities. It's merely a hobby."

I think it was then that Cynthy got up from the sofa and went to Bland and kissed him.

He neither blushed nor froze with disapproval; he liked it. "Thank you, Miss Cynthy," he said, with what was practically a beam. "And may I be the first to wish you well."